MY LADY'S
SHADOW

Coirle Mooney

SAPERE
BOOKS

MY LADY'S SHADOW

Published by Sapere Books.

24 Trafalgar Road, Ilkley, LS29 8HH,
United Kingdom

saperebooks.com

ISBN: 978-1-80055-717-8

For my brother, Brecan, who was like a work of art. For Noel, the clear-sighted one.

ACKNOWLEDGEMENTS

I'd like to thank my discerning editor, Amy and the team at Sapere Books for their scrupulous dedication to the best storytelling. Special thanks always to my first readers, Nina and Susan, for their soft-pawed guidance. My inspiring parents, Noirin and Brian, my siblings, the Monaghan clan and my cherished friends for their support. Huge thanks to all you readers!

PART ONE

CHAPTER ONE

Château de Turenne, France, 1198

I wanted so badly to follow the count, Hugh La Marche, for I could see he was in pain and I wanted to ease it for him, whatever it took. My lady, Lady Maria of Turenne, did not deserve his love.

I could swear La Marche had been crying; I could see the red in his eyes from where I was hiding behind the pillar. He was facing outwards, towards the crowd, and sometimes he glanced upwards, to where he expected my lady to appear on the balcony. But when he turned in towards the pillars, to rest, when he thought nobody could see, I saw.

I saw that La Marche, for all his magnificence, was no different really from I. A creature seeking to sup deep and greedy from the cup of love. And from a secret inner chamber below my navel, a violent heat rushed out to him in sympathy and something more, which brought me pleasure. My lady was all sighs and appearing full of woe, but that was just a face to please the crowd. *They're fools, the lot of them, they think it's all a game.* And so it was before, but not so now.

The argument was this: that Lady Maria, daughter of the viscount of Turenne and known courtly-lover of the count of La Marche, claimed that she would always have suzerainty over the latter. For by the rules of this game of folly they'd been playing, she was his commanding mistress whilst he was her devoted knight. This was the way it had carried on between them for more years than I could say, but now he sought acceptance as her equal and demanded the rules be changed to this decree. And I knew why. I knew she had never given herself to him in bed, because I slept in the chamber adjoining hers.

It was at last light of this bluish-grey day when we gathered in the courtyard. Some people carried unlit torches. Many came, as was customary, in livery after the working day. Some children were also in attendance — scruffy-looking ones whose parents (if they had them) — couldn't care less. In my opinion, the court was no place for innocent children.

There were plenty of high-born lords and ladies too, dressed in fine and subtle attire; fat men and lean alike conducted themselves with an easy confidence most evident in the range of contrived pleasantries with which they greeted the ladies of their class. The latter were a fascinating bunch with opaque eyes of many colours set in varied faces. The younger ones looked fresh and unpainted as newly blossomed roses; the older were more puffed but powerful. It was the widowed ones amongst the latter bunch who received the most attention from the handsomest young men. What cared they for love as long as their purses were full? But blood was hot all the same, and I had sometimes watched these men leave stealthily by the back door of some houses looking shamefaced but satisfied.

But none of these fine women were as beautiful as Lady Maria. La Marche was her sworn, devoted knight. Oftentimes, the people hastened to witness the exchange between these two at just a few short hours' notice. As with this evening, the post went up just after noon advertising their meeting, and by six o'clock the place was swarming. But something was not right today and the people could sense it.

La Marche was pacing erratically, unsmiling, without utterance, without making any attempt to please the crowd. He was creased-looking with tiredness. The crowd was growing fidgety watching him. I was anxious for him and getting worse with every passing second.

It was expected that when Lady Maria came down to greet him, it would be like the sun appearing to disperse the rainclouds. He was to blame, the crowd felt, for the dour atmosphere. The light was failing but still nobody lit a torch. The scene was matt and foreboding. Even the red and orange-flaked *rosa mundi* which fringed the grass was tinged a sickly green, as if some distorted glass had been expertly placed to cast its illusory light over Nature herself. All was ugly, clouded, wasted, like the disappointed aftermath of unreturned love.

When Maria finally appeared, she was wearing an emerald dress. The people went mad with cheers. She brought with her a whirlwind of energy which fairly spun La Marche toward her. I flitted, unobserved, between two pillars.

I was stealthy and well-balanced, and I easily passed unnoticed in a crowd. But I believed that I was fair enough, and certainly my body was shapely. Sometimes I sensed that men were conscious of this, and I saw their eyes roaming over my curves and guessed their secret fancies with some pride. I had never had a lover in verse or in bed; the former was reserved for those of noble birth. Nor was I so lowborn that I could take a tumble with whomever I desired. I should, rather, wait my turn until I received a suitable offer of marriage from a man I did not abhor. In the meantime, I would continue to serve as attending-lady for Maria, whose cousin was married to my uncle — a court advisor.

I had long resided at court and was accustomed to the ritual they called 'courtly love', which we were witnessing this evening. I wished some knight at court would pen lyric verses which sang of my goodness and beauty but, sadly, it was not my birthright.

I would never forget the first time I saw this practice when I was a child of seven and newly arrived at court. I could not understand it then, and still the rules confounded me. It was fiddlesticks that the lady made her knight prove his worth as a lover in words, through lyric prowess, before a public audience. In private, he often attempted to prove his worth in deed as well and this, to me, made good sense.

If the lady was sympathetic, she would not be so cruel as to make him wait five years before she lay with him. In my opinion, this foretaste was also to the lady's advantage, for then she knew what pleasures awaited her in the bridal bed or whether she would have need of another lover besides her husband. In public, the lovers went no further than to exchange rings. Even if the lady was already married, the poet-lover could attempt to woo her, despite her husband's jealousy, for they paid homage to none other but the God of Love.

Maria had worn La Marche's ring for five summers at least.

La Marche's verse was worn-out, stilted and repetitive. He was stuck in a quagmire of clichés as seemingly passionless as a crow's cawing. The crowd jeered and railed against his tired rhetoric as if he were some skulking cur, forgetting both their manners and his birthright. So it often went with this game; I had seen even worse when the crowd became bloodthirsty.

A slight movement pulled my attention to a boy in the crowd whose startlingly handsome face was chalked with dirt. I saw that his right hand was hidden, but a slow movement of the attached arm at once alerted me to danger. He was drawing something, furtively, from out of an inside pocket. Someone started screaming. When I looked back to La Marche, his face was dripping with blood. Everything fell deathly quiet. Finally, La Marche's attendants came bursting through the crowd.

La Marche was standing, bleeding, staring blankly ahead. The thing the boy had thrown was not a deadly weapon, but a toad; it was with this creature's blood that La Marche's face was painted red. A large man in a leather apron bent and picked it up by its legs. He dangled it before the crowd until they shrieked with laughter. This was an insult of enormous measure; somebody would have to pay for this. For a commoner to throw a toad at a nobleman was a crime which would exact a severe punishment — if not death.

Surrounded by his attendants, La Marche could no longer be seen. I looked carefully about to be sure nobody was watching, then, satisfied, I stepped up to the nearest attendant and whispered my information into his ear. I told him I would later single out the boy by offering him a franc, for he was certainly poor. Then they could take and dispose of him as they liked and make a public example of him to demonstrate La Marche's power and greatness.

I could not say who the earwig was that told my lady the boy was to be taken. Had she not received this intelligence until a quart hour later, the boy would have left the château with La Marche's party. As it happened, my lady requested I go to her at once to take an order: she asked that I accompanied the torchbearer to the gates to meet La Marche's party as they departed for the château de Lusignan. That I asked, on her behalf, for the boy to be released, explaining 'gently' to the groomsman and attendants, that it would be better for all if the boy was left with my lady in order for her to punish him herself, since the offense was committed on her grounds.

'For I am sure you agree, Maryse,' she said to me, 'that the boy is young and should be taught court manners and given a second chance. You yourself have profited greatly from the kindness and generosity of our courtiers.'

I told her I agreed but that La Marche's party would not be pleased. My lady hesitated a moment, then, placing her delicate hand on my shoulder, said, 'If anyone objects to leaving the boy in my care, remind them that Hugh La Marche is my knight and, as such, he shall do as I bid.'

She told me I would not be needed for her undressing tonight as her sisters would attend her. She smiled at me, then left.

The wind was blowing fiercely as I rode out; the torchbearer lit the torches expertly and fast on either side along the path, for there was little time to lose. Some flickered, flinched, and then went out, but others flared up fabulously, lighting up the great, groaning trees of the château. La Marche's horsemen followed so close behind I could see their dark silhouettes and hear their banners whirring in the wind. Their faces were covered with cloth to keep the dust from their eyes and this, to me, was frightening.

La Marche's men released the boy only on the condition that they might attend his public punishment, and soon. The torchbearer quickly pulled the boy up behind him and galloped back towards the château dungeon. I rode behind him, uneasy in the enclosing darkness of the night.

Having been kept busy all morning preparing for the love-match, I had not eaten since breakfast and was feeling almost sick with hunger and fatigue when I reached home. I hoped my lady would have kept something by for my supper but found that she had not. Nor had she seen to it that a fire be lit in the attending-ladies' bedchamber, and so the chilling wind was rushing freely through the huge, gaping fireplace.

Angry tears burst forth from my eyes but I quickly brushed them aside; I would not go cold and hungry to my bed. I could hear the low talk of my lady and her sisters coming from the adjoining chamber and decided to go spy on them awhile.

The large keyhole always offered a close, if limited, perspective. I could see Lady Maria standing in the centre of the room. Her sister Aénor was seated on a low stool to her right, before an impressive fire. The youngest, Angelique, was not in view. These three women, according to the poet Bertran de Born, possessed "all earthly beauty". They were the daughters of Viscount Raymond II of Turenne and Élise de Séverac and were known as *Las Très de Torena*, or "The Three of Turenne".

Aénor, the eldest, had hair of such radiant gold it rivalled even the moonlight, which was pouring through the window. Her clear grey eyes, fringed with dark lashes, were as pretty as the lanterns which came from distant lands. In her youth, she was the most sought-after lady in the Limousin region, until she married dull Guillaume de Montvert at the age of twenty. She had since borne him two sons and a daughter and was not yet four and twenty.

There was a gap of around three years between each sister. Maria was now in her twentieth year, the same as I. Aénor and Angelique had both inherited their mother's golden tresses, but Maria's hair was the same rich mahogany colour as the viscount's, when he was a young man. All three sisters shared the same enchanting, grey eyes, but Maria's mouth possessed a disturbing sensuality, unique to her alone.

My lady was undressing and naked to the waist. One half of her body was glowing in the firelight. Her full, high breast, with the dark nipple pointed, was hanging as freely and temptingly as a ripe pear in a hidden orchard. A long crystal necklace was the only ornament she wore, as pure as herself, a charm she was never without. Its drop-like bejewelled locket was lying just short of her nipple now, as though they would kiss. My eyes ran down her long, carved body to her navel and neat waistband and up again to her pouting nipple. I was glad La Marche had never seen her naked, for then surely he would die for her.

When Aénor began to speak, I held my breath to listen.

'Maria,' she said, 'Hugh La Marche is human, is he not? Has not he declared his love for you these past seven years? How can you be so heartless after all this time?'

Angelique gave a little laugh, but Maria stayed silent and looked unhappy.

'Cannot you consider how he feels?' continued Aénor. 'He has loved you, steadfastly, these seven winters and how, now, have you returned his love? I warn you, Maria, not to tempt Fortune by thinking of none other but yourself.'

Maria then turned to face her older sister. 'Would you have me marry him, then? As you yourself married, uncertain of love but sure of wealth?'

At first Aénor said nothing, but studied the embroidery in her lap more closely. Finally she replied, 'I knew that Guillaume loved me as much as man can love and so I married him to end his suffering, for he is a good man. Besides, you must choose someone to marry soon or Father will do it for you.'

Maria then apologised for what she had said. Aénor stood up suddenly and a weird light flashed around the room. I blinked and saw more clearly. The same green light which had cast its ugly spell upon La Marche's verse had been curled up, folded, on Aénor's lap. What I had mistaken for needlework was, in fact, a bodice made of emeralds! It was this garment that my lady had worn to the love-match. The sickly green reflections which had so charged the general mood to my lady's advantage had been effected by this thing. A monstrous trick! What kind of person would use such artifice to alter the light in her favour?

Aénor placed the thing in a wooden chest and locked it with a key she kept close to her bosom.

CHAPTER TWO

Next morning, as I and the other attending-ladies were assisting her dressing, my lady questioned me about the boy with the toad. I relayed the events of the night before, stressing the command that La Marche's men be invited to the boy's punishment. My lady nodded slowly, then asked if any of us present had witnessed the incident. We all replied that we had not.

'Well then,' she said, 'I suppose in the absence of an actual eyewitness, it will be difficult to prove 'twas he who threw the toad and not, indeed, his neighbour!'

We remained silent.

She continued, 'We cannot, in law, accept the testimony of a witness who comes from outside the court, as he may prove unreliable. Therefore, unless one of yourselves or another courtier *saw* it happening, the boy cannot be hanged.'

I knew the boy was guilty but I dared not say for fear of being branded as the snitch that told on him. Nobody would speak up against him and risk being assaulted by a common mob. I knew the boy would go free, which would be a grave insult to the count. 'Nonetheless,' said I, 'I must advise that he be beaten. Only this way can all parties be satisfied and proper order be restored.'

The two other ladies agreed with me.

After dressing, we went for a walk in the garden, as was customary. The oval-shaped enclosure with its high stone walls always put me in mind of a swan's egg. The ground was paved with grey-brown marble stone. We walked barefooted. We did two turns in silence and then my lady gestured that she would sit.

Viscount Raymond had this garden drawn up by a famous Italian artist at the time when he was courting Maria's mother, Élise. It was an entirely private space, his tribute to her. The heavy wooden entrance door required a key and the walls were too tall and dense to be in any place transparent. There was a fountain in the centre with steps to sit upon. It was rumoured that Raymond and Élise made love for the first time beneath its spouting font. A statue of Venus and her son, Cupid, adorned the spot; the deviant pair gazed down on all who entered here.

We were just dipping our toes in the water when an urgent knocking began at the door. Unhappy at being disturbed, my lady requested I tell the intruder to leave us in peace until breakfast. When I opened the door and saw the viscount's chief attendant standing there, I knew the matter was serious. My lady's father demanded an interview with her. She had to go at once.

I rushed to get her shoes. The others tidied her unruly hair into a netted bun. She told us to wait in her chamber until she returned. None of us had yet had breakfast, but she did not think of this.

After she had gone, I chided the others for not tidying up the mess in our chamber. They went about it and then I returned, alone, to Maria's chamber. They dared not disobey me; I was more their mistress than she. The other two were sisters and have not been with us long. They were the daughters of the court chancellor and were of marriageable age. It was hoped their sojourn here would put them in way of prospective husbands. At first I was grateful enough for their company and shared duties. I found that they were bland, but harmless creatures. I was not cruel to them but nor was I especially kind. After they left, I knew I would remain here.

The court had been my home for the past twelve years, since my father had died. At that time my uncle, Raoul, was newly wed to Maria's cousin, Isabelle. Because I was not high-born and my father was poor, I was meant to be a maid and nothing more. At the age of eight, my uncle plucked me from my village, my mother and five living siblings and brought me to live at court. I hadn't seen my mother since. Sometimes I had word from one or other of my siblings, but they were almost strangers to me now.

At first Maria played with me as if I were a new doll, but soon I was cast aside and forgotten. I cried always and hoped she would discover me again, but she did not. I comforted myself by watching what she did so as to profit from her good example. I hoped to win love this way, but I did not. Still, my efforts and quick learning meant I rapidly rose in rank from maid to waiting-lady, and so my heavier duties ceased and I received a good education.

Maria was generous with her things and gave me pretty clothes of hers to wear. In spite of this, I feared that love was not my birthright, as it was hers. I watched her throw the admiration bestowed on her away as carelessly as scraps were thrown to dogs. I, on the other hand, hoarded each morsel of attention I received as though it were my only sustenance. I craved the things she had but did not value like a plant which thirsts for drops of water and hungers for the warmth of the sun.

Maria's chamber was still warm after the previous night's fire. I added some oakwood and worked the heavy bellows to encourage the embers back into flame. I swirled around on the mosaic-tiled floor with its pretty pattern of birds and flowers.

The earthenware basin in which my lady washed was still steaming.

This water was brought to the château each dawn from a heated mountain spring some miles away. It was then reheated, slowly, over a pinewood stove and visited by the court perfumer who scented and frothed it by craft. Finally, I and the other attending-ladies carried it up the steep stairwell and placed it so that my lady's senses were freshly stimulated each morning as she woke. She loved this ritual and had a special interest in plant and flower extracts. The vapour rising from the water today carried a citrus smell which was both sweet and sharp.

The carved, dark wood shelves above the washing basin were lined with many fantastical and strangely tinted vessels. Most of these were gifts received from suitors and admirers. One, in particular, always took my fancy. It was a shimmering, jug-shaped bottle with a white-gold stopper given to Maria by La Marche on his return from his first crusade. It was composed of tiny pink and orange diamonds and when you looked up close, it gave the impression of a thousand different sunsets. Aside from its gemstones, it was priceless for the orange oil it contained, which was said to induce happiness.

My eye fixed on another favourite of mine, brought to Maria by an Arabian lord. It was an elixir the shade of night-sky blue in a glass bottle with an elaborate silver filigree heart clasp at the front. Its contents were supposed to bring pleasure to women. The silver seal had never been broken. I often wondered for what — or whom — she was saving it.

I heard footsteps coming up the hall and positioned myself under the window, as though I were busy contemplating the fast-flowing Aude below. I was accustomed to Maria's dramatic entrances and remained calmly poised as she entered and began her flustered speech.

'Oh, Maryse,' she said. 'I am so glad to find you here alone. I don't believe I have ever seen my father so angry or so determined.' She looked pale.

'I cannot think why your father should be displeased with you?' I prompted.

'Nor can I,' she declared. 'And yet it is so.' She carried on, breathlessly. 'He says that I have *strung* La Marche along for far too long and must end the thing at once. He says that if La Marche does not demand that the commoner who threw the toad be hanged, he is a fool. He asks if I have forgotten how dangerous and experienced the count's men-at-arms are.'

My lady let out a great, heaving sigh. I guided her to sit on the bed and let out her curly hair from its netted prison. I started combing it, gently; the porcelain comb I used had also been a gift from La Marche.

'The worst thing is,' she continued, 'my father has ordered me to marry at once — if not to Hugh La Marche, then to some other of his choosing. Aénor said it would be so!' She buried her head in the thick, crimson fleece which covered her bed.

I played the morning pigeon's part of cooing soothing sounds into her ear. 'Maria,' said I, 'it pains me to see you troubled thus. Do take heart. Your father may well have spoken out of temper. Tomorrow, you will see, the storm clouds will have blown over. Let it rest awhile and do not torment yourself.'

She shook her head. 'This time is different. I have never seen my father so determined. He says I must accompany him to the dungeon this very night. He insists that the boy be tortured in my presence.'

'How awful.'

'You will come with me, Maryse,' she pleaded. 'I do not think I could face it alone.'

I cast my eyes down modestly and answered, quietly, that I would accompany my lady always, in bad times as in good.

The torchbearer led the way to the dungeon with a blazing flame. We were a party of six in total — including the torchbearer, Maria and myself, with her father and two heavy men-at-arms just behind. We walked in absolute silence and you could hear the fallen leaves crunching under our feet.

Maria and I had both dressed in sombre black to fit the occasion. She wore a purple headdress of light linen, which was tied at her shoulder with twisted gold cord. The headpiece made her look very alluring, for it outlined her full, cupid's-bow lips. I noticed she had arranged a few tendrilled curls most artfully about her face.

The steps down to the dungeon were slippery with damp moss and the stench was rotten. There were but two cells. The first had long been occupied by a toothless hag whose devil potions murdered unborn babies in their mothers' wombs. It was whispered that these women sought to rid themselves of their babes, for they were either unmarried or too poor to care for them. And yet, when I looked now upon the hag, I was surprised to see no signs of evil upon her face.

'Maryse,' said Raymond, 'will you walk in with us? You may choose to remain outside or return to the château, if you wish?'

He spoke with some concern. I assured him that my only wish was to support my lady. We all entered the second cell.

I was, once again, startled by the handsome appearance of the boy. He was sitting down when we walked in. He stared at each of us in turn. It struck me his gaze was bold, for a commoner. I did not meet his eyes directly but looked at him only when his gaze was turned elsewhere. These large orbs were the colour of dark liquid amber, and his hair was again a darker version of the same. He had a generous-sized head and remarkably well carved cheekbones. I guessed that he was somewhere between late boyhood and early manhood. His limbs looked well-formed, even if he was slim.

We all stood awkwardly around him. Raymond eventually broke the spell by asking him to stand and face the men-at-arms. These two suddenly sprang into action as though they danced barefoot on hot irons. From there on, it all happened most quickly.

The torchbearer kept the torches alight while the men-at-arms took turns in using them. The flames were a vivid green, the beeswax having been soaked all night in a nettle mixture to heighten their sting. The boy was first stripped naked to the waist. He was hung upside down on a purpose-built wooden scaffold. Raymond asked the questions and, when the boy would not reply, the two men scorched his flesh until it shrivelled, blistered, blackened and burst open.

Maria shouted out in protest and had to be restrained, by myself, from taking some foolish action. She tried closing her eyes but Raymond forced her to watch. I whispered to her loudly that it would soon be over.

Raymond asked again the same questions and still the boy refused to answer.

'What is your name and where do you come from?'

The boy made no reply. Another torch was used and again he screamed.

'Are you refusing to answer the viscount Raymond of Turenne? Are you aware I have the power to hang you or to set you free?'

25

Still the boy made no reply and so another torch was applied to an open wound. His screams had grown most shrill.

'At least we know he's not a mute,' joked one of the men-at-arms. Raymond gave him a withering look. Maria had slumped to the floor. He ordered her to stand before continuing the interrogation. I thought she would not have the strength. 'Are you aware that you have been accused of assaulting Lord Hugh la Marche in an underhand and beastly manner? Do you deny this?'

Still the boy would not speak. Maria could take it no more.

'Father,' she said, 'I would rather you burn my own flesh than see him used so. Take me instead, for it was all done on my account.'

I could see she was in earnest and so could the viscount, for we knew her well. She had started to undo her bodice as though preparing for the punishment. Raymond raised one hand to stop her and spoke somewhat more gently than before.

'I am sorry, Maria,' he said, 'but we must receive some answers. We cannot afford to make enemies of the La Marche lords; they are too powerful.'

'Let me speak with the boy, then,' she pleaded.

'Very well,' said Raymond, who was visibly tired. He turned to the boy. 'If you do not answer my daughter's questions, you will be hanged at once.'

The torture stopped and the boy was pulled down. The men-at-arms were clearly exhausted and in need of rest and ale. Raymond accompanied them from the dungeon for some respite. Maria and I were left alone with the boy.

I stood by while she went to him. I noted her face was streaked with dirty tears which she did not attempt to wipe away. Her eyes were most unusually shot with blood and her hair was tangled. She gathered the boy in her arms and ripped up her headdress to serve as wrapping for his wounds.

His head hung low until she lifted it onto her lap. He stared directly at us. The light cast by his astonishing eyes gave me a queer feeling, as though they were two search-torches could see directly into my soul. I urged my lady to question him quickly before Raymond returned. She began, as her father had, by asking him his name and whence he came. When again he made no reply, she hastened to reassure him. 'If you deny the act of which you are accused, it may be enough to set you free. Just nod your head if you deny it,' she said.

'I do not deny it,' were the first words he uttered. 'I do not deny that it was I who threw the toad at Hugh La Marche,' he repeated, firmly.

Maria and I exchanged looks then.

'I do not ask you to confess,' she said. 'If you confess, you may be hanged!'

But he had confessed and we both knew that, in any case, I had been witness to it. We heard the sound of leaves crunching underfoot. The men were returning.

In a panic now, Maria turned to him. 'Why did you do it?' she asked.

He rested his brilliant lights on her a few moments. 'I did not like his verse,' he said.

Maria could not help but smile.

The men entered noisily and Raymond demanded to know what had passed. She told him that he had confessed to the crime but that the act had not been committed in a spirit of malice or treason, but rather out of an intemperate reaction to bad art. Raymond nodded sagely and looked at the boy with interest.

'I have a proposition, Father,' she said.

She suggested that, now they had learnt the truth, she would request a private meeting with La Marche to discuss what should be done. Raymond was easily persuaded that the La Marche lords — and not himself — could decide the boy's fate.

Raymond supervised Maria's missive to La Marche. It was dispatched that very night with the messenger's proud assurance it would have reached its destination by first light. La Marche would return to Turenne and dine with Maria the following evening. They would then put the matter of the boy to rest.

Maria asked that I share her bed that night, as her sisters were not at hand and she did not want to sleep alone. Greatly fatigued by the excitement of the day, I fell at once into a sound sleep.

I woke during the night to my lady's violent twisting of her person in the bed. She was sick in her wash basin.

I rose to clean the mess. Maria never could stomach anything horrible to see. I knew the day's events would affect her greatly and for a long time to come.

CHAPTER THREE

After attending a special service in the château chapel, we awaited the messenger's return with trepidation. Raymond, too, had slept badly and we all watched out for the first signs of dust rising on the road. True to his boast, the messenger arrived with good speed and welcome tidings. La Marche had accepted Maria's invitation and would return that evening with just a few men. Raymond could not have been more pleased — or relieved — and went at once to consult his wife about the evening banquet.

I and the other attending ladies were kept busy all day preparing for the banquet. La Marche's men would dine with Maria's parents, the viscount's two brothers and his nephews, as well as with various other nobles and advisors of the Turenne family residing at — or in the vicinity of — the court. Neither of Maria's sisters would be present.

Angelique had departed with Aénor for the château de Montvert the day after the ill-fated love match. She would not return until Christmas. While it was generally understood she was needed to help Aénor with the children, I knew that she was secretly engaged to de Montvert's younger brother, Richard. At the de Montvert estate, the lovers could conduct their affair freely, without any constraint.

Angelique was not free to marry until Maria had made her choice and — even then — as the young de Montvert had no land to inherit, it was not certain that Raymond would approve the match.

By eight o'clock all parties had assembled in the great hall. A magnificent fire crackled and spat and fresh, fat candles were burning on the long table which was set with fine, coloured linen. I was serving strong mead wine to the guests before they sat to eat.

La Marche was conversing in private chambers with Maria and Raymond while we waited on his men. He had brought but eight attendants and they were drinking thirstily of the mead after a good day's riding. One of these, a stocky brute, caught me by the wrist and whispered into my ear.

'I *know* you.'

'I know you not, sir, unleash me,' I replied.

His breath smelt sickly sweet from mead and he looked me up and down, hungrily. 'Don't you remember me?'

I swore that I did not.

''Twas you told on the filthy commoner that insulted my lord,' he said. 'Remember? 'Twas I you told. I never would forget such a pretty face.'

I denied it. He grew louder, more insistent and I knew the game would soon be up. I looked about to be sure no one was watching and ushered him, quickly, into the mead closet, closing the door behind us.

I asked if anyone else knew, but he said they did not. I asked him what he wanted to keep quiet and he said gold would do. I told him I'd no gold to give and then he asked for something more precious than gold. He asked if I was a virgin; I told him I was. He started lifting my skirts. I told him not so fast, that I would give him what he wanted but not until tomorrow, for I would be missed if I stayed away a moment longer. I handed him two jugs to carry out as though he were assisting me.

'Wait,' he said, as I opened the closet door. 'How do I know you're really a virgin?'

'You'll know,' I said. 'I'll meet you here tomorrow at five. It'll be quiet then and I'll not be missed.'

He was satisfied, for now.

When Raymond entered a short time afterwards, the hall fell silent while the guests scanned his face to guess his mood. I observed he looked somewhat more downcast than before but I did not linger long. I took a secret staircase which led to one of the family's private apartments. I positioned myself in a small, arched corridor overlooking the modest-sized hall where Maria and La Marche were dining. From here, I could see and hear everything that passed between them.

It was in this corridor I'd first fallen in love with La Marche.

I had been privy to the dialogues between these two since the courtship first began, but I had never witnessed anything like what passed between them then. It was like trying to follow the contours of the Aude in early spring after the melting of the winter snows, so swiftly twisting and turning and full of strange new objects it was. I allowed myself to be so carried along by it I almost forgot where I was.

It started normally enough, with the usual courtly — and conceited — greetings. La Marche told Maria she looked incomparably lovely. She told him he was the very embodiment of a perfect knight. The butler soon arrived with peacock soup served in tortoise shells, decorated with many eyes. This fellow was as deaf and dumb as an old dog and was thus a family favourite.

Maria and La Marche were seated at either end of the long table and so there was some distance between them. Normally they sat closer together. This table was an oak miniature of its counterpart in the great hall, although it could be said it was more finely carved. The table linen had been embroidered by Élise and her daughters. It featured many strange animals including a suit of chainmail armour sporting a goat's head which was decorated either side with green foliage; a sitting, brown bull with a thin gold halo which was wearing angels' wings and a prancing tiger with its red tongue sticking out, jumping through a ring of gold fire.

In the wake of the creeping butler's welcome departure, Maria was first to speak. 'I cannot imagine what you must think of me.' She looked at La Marche as though expecting him to reply, but he did not. She went on, I thought, sounding ill at ease. 'Of course you have heard that I oversaw the boy's torture myself. It was truly horrible to see. I shall never forget it.'

'I am sorry your lovely eyes were defiled by such a sight,' said La Marche, stiffly.

'As my father explained,' she said, 'the boy confessed to the crime — which is admirable enough — but most importantly, he bears no ill will towards you or any of the La Marche lords. In fact, he displays a decided naivety which I feel could, in time, be corrected.'

La Marche made no comment and he looked at his dish, not at her. They ate their soup awhile and drank some wine from delicate, rose-tinted glasses.

'Maria,' La Marche began, 'I must warn you now. My brothers and my father demand this boy be hanged. If it were only for myself I should not order it, but my kinsmen believe that our power will be diminished if this does not come to pass.'

'Surely, Hugh,' said Maria, 'you understand that if the boy is hanged I will have his blood on my hands? For it will have been done on my account.' She was beginning to sound distressed, as though she was no longer sure of her power over him. As if to clarify this, she added, 'Hugh, as my knight, I request you grant me this one favour. Do not allow the boy to be killed. It will come between us. Grant me this one thing.'

The butler had slid in again to remove the dishes and the two fell silent as he spread the next lavish course. My mouth watered at the delicious smells wafting my way. I had often wondered about the difference between the meals prepared for the family and those served up for the waiting staff. They would dine on duck and partridge drumsticks now with all manner of prettily carved vegetables and fruits, whilst I had eaten a meagre early supper of boiled chicken and raw onion. Surely all stomachs were equal and deserved to partake in fair measures of the bounties offered by land, air and sea? Did we not require the same air to breathe, water to drink and — by comparison — food for nourishment?

Despite the excellence of the food, they scarcely touched it.

'Hugh,' said Maria, 'you know the rules as well as I. If you do not grant me this one thing, how can I continue to call you my knight?'

'Do you really speak to me of *rules*?'

She paused awhile before answering. 'Yes … I had thought we could put this matter behind us and continue as before.'

'Ah, Maria.' His voice sounded choked. 'When it was you and I alone in the early days of our courtship, I was so full of hope. I thought I could show you a part of myself, when we were alone, that I do not reveal to anyone else. I have ever been shy… I had hoped to share my inward self with one person … with you.'

'I accepted your ring,' she said.

'When, finally, you accepted my ring, that never-ending summer that seems like a hazy dream now, my heart expanded with so much joy I thought I would die of happiness. Perhaps I should have died then.'

'Hugh, do not despair,' she said. 'It can be so again. We can put all of this behind us and start afresh.'

He continued, his voice heavy with tears. 'I have never known a woman like you. I shall never love truly again. I shall never love again.'

He spoke as though it were all over between them. Maria was white as a sheet. With much ill timing, she then asked, again, about the boy. It was clear to me that she cared more about the fate of this commoner than she did about the man who had laid his wounded heart out before her. It was clear she had never loved him.

La Marche spoke then with a harshness in his voice I had never heard before. 'It is rumoured that you cheated at the game,' he said.

She gave a surprised jump.

'It is rumoured you wore a garment made of emeralds which altered the light to your advantage. The people do not think ill of you for this piece of ingenuity; they prefer, rather, to think me a fool. This — and the toad incident — have caused me to be branded with the nickname Emerald. I am disgraced. The La Marche name is disgraced.'

I recognised my part in this unfolding drama and smiled. The attending-ladies, as I had known they would, had passed the intelligence concerning the emerald bodice to their father, who was chancellor for many of the surrounding châteaux as well as a lax-mouthed gossip. Maria tried to defend herself, but he would not suffer her lies.

'The boy is to be hanged on Friday,' he said. 'It is decided.'

In low voice, Maria uttered she was sorry.

He brushed her sympathy aside with a wave of his hand. 'I am to travel to Antioch and remain there until the scandal has blown over. There is talk of another crusade to the Holy Land soon. In Antioch I will be well placed if it comes to pass. I could be away for some years.'

I cried furtively. It had not struck me that the scandal would cause me to lose him. I felt great fear and foreboding, for he was the only sun in my dark world, and I knew not how I would go on without him. But I was glad, too, that Maria would not have him.

I remembered then my meeting with his man earlier and felt more trepidation. I would have to think on what to do, later. It occurred to me I could poison him by putting something in his wine, but I did not think I had sufficient knowledge of poisons. Also, he was La Marche's man and I did not want to commit treason against that lord. He might even be related to La Marche, for many of these kinsmen were blood relatives.

Maria woke me from my reveries with a feeble attempt to save the situation.

'You know that if you allow this boy to be hanged and if you intend on leaving France, you cannot remain my knight?'

La Marche just hung his head.

Maria slipped the little gold band he had given her off her finger and slid it down the table towards him. Clasping it, he got up to leave. There was no more to say.

Waiting in the mead closet for La Marche's man, I hid a dagger up my sleeve. If he treated me roughly, I would use it.

I was glad to see he was not drunk when he arrived. He treated me courteously and asked that I make myself comfortable. I accepted a cup of mead but as I drank, I secretly handled the dagger while we became better acquainted. It seemed he was, indeed, a cousin of La Marche's, and now I thought I saw some resemblance to my lord. Suddenly, he appeared more attractive to me.

We kissed passionately and I allowed him to take me. I felt a sharp pain at first, but it did not last for long.

'You really are a virgin,' he said, with heavy breath. After that I had a surprisingly pleasant sensation as we rocked together for some time until it was over. There had been no need to use the knife.

I and the other attending ladies all slept in Maria's bed the night before the hanging. We rose at first light to fetch my lady's scented water while she knelt down to pray. Even the fragrance of a thousand roses would not have served to lighten my lady's heavy heart. When we returned to her chamber, she was still clutching her beads and muttering Hail Marys. She asked us to join her and soon all four of us were praying together. I made sure to close my eyes tightly and pray with the greatest feeling. I wore a crucifix always so people would think me good and pious.

Maria took my hand in hers. I kept my eyes open and did not wink at all until they had produced some tears. When the bell sounded we were all close to hysterical, for we knew it was to summon the villagers to the hanging. We helped my lady attach some thin, black gauze to her headdress and drape it so that it covered her face. She could see out through this, but if she wished she could close her eyes to avoid the distressing sight.

I urged the women to move quickly. I had prettied myself up, since I might run into La Marche's man.

The hanging was set for noon. By a quarter to the appointed hour, all parties had gathered in the village square. The Turenne family and attendants were occupying the right side gallery of the back wall, while the La Marche lords and attendants were seated opposite, on the left. The public had gathered thickly in the square below and were making much noise and laughter.

All fell quiet when the boy, led by the hangman, walked to centre stage and stood beneath the scaffold. When the hangman placed the loop of rope around his neck, the people all cheered together. The boy's eyes were closed, which I thought was just as well. When suddenly the boy's eyes flew open, the people fell instantly silent. The hangman — as if performing in a circus — made a flourish with the rope, resulting in its pulling more tightly around the boy's neck.

An unsettling murmur ran through the crowd. I overheard two attendants whispering close by.

'They say the night he arrived a golden owl was sighted on the grounds,' said one. 'It is a very rare bird,' said the other. 'The owl himself is an omen of death, but the gold is said to signify alchemy.'

What nonsense, thought I. But a note of fear had crept into the crowd like a harsh-sounding bell. Sensing the changing mood, the hangman cleverly placed a sack over the boy's head, covering up his unsettling orbs. Some people cheered again and the hangman took a bow, which greatly pleased the audience. With slowly graceful and deliberate motions, he started pulling the rope so that the boy was soon standing tip-toed on a chair.

It would all be over now for the boy. La Marche's men looked on gravely, though Hugh la Marche himself was curiously absent.

Just as the hangman was making to kick over the chair, a great commotion began in the background. Some men on horseback had burst through. The people scattered away on either side as they galloped towards the scaffold.

'Stop!' they cried. 'Stop the proceedings at once!'

The hangman froze, his foot dangling in mid-air. La Marche's men had already made their way down to the square and were surrounding the horsemen.

'What is the meaning of this interruption?'

'We have received intelligence,' said one of the horsemen, 'that this boy is not a commoner. Hangman,' he commanded, 'remove the sack cloth from the prisoner's head.'

The hangman obliged and the horseman spoke again.

'This man is Gui d'Ussel, from the château Ussel-sur-Sarzonne. I am Ebles d'Ussel; his brother.'

La Marche's men stood helplessly by as Gui d'Ussel was led away. The crowd was told there would be no spectacle today and was asked to disperse peacefully.

Raymond took command, summoning representative lords from the La Marche and Ussel families to an impromptu meeting. Maria's presence there was also requested.

As we were seated up front in the gallery, Maria and I were last to leave. Just as we were entering the stairwell, Maria complained her dress was caught in something. Before we knew what was happening, one of La Marche's men had taken violent hold of her. Maria cried out as he ripped her headdress from her face.

I froze; I did not move to help. He pushed his face slowly up to hers and spat out threatening words. He called her a poisonous sorcerer. He said she was 'fair game,' and 'any man's spoils,' now, for La Marche would not have her. She managed to free herself by biting down hard into his arm. He laughed a false laugh and shouted after her that he'd see her some dark night when she was out hunting and treat her like the wanton that she was.

It was only when we were entering the meeting chamber I saw that Maria was bleeding from the mouth. Raymond demanded to know how this had come about. As Maria did not answer him, I quickly recounted what had passed. Raymond looked greatly disturbed by the account but said he would have to deal with it later.

Looking around me, I recognised the four La Marche lords present as Hugh's younger brothers. Also present was Ebles d'Ussel and another lord he introduced as his other brother, Peire. The boy, Gui d'Ussel, was clearly the youngest of the three.

Raymond asked all to be seated and offered them some ale. I saw that the La Marche lords would not look at Maria while Ebles and Peire, on the other hand, frequently stole glances at her. I moved about, refilling their cups as if I were invisible. Raymond asked the Ussel brothers if they were aware of the crime that Gui had committed. He wondered if they could give any explanation for their brother's reckless behaviour.

The brothers, Ebles and Peire, were both delicately handsome and softly spoken, but they shared not their younger brother's remarkable presence. They apologised for all the trouble Gui had caused. They explained that he had run away from home some weeks before and they'd had no idea of his whereabouts until rumours of a boy with owl's eyes held captive at Turenne had finally reached Ussel. They had set out at once to investigate and had been most aggrieved at the reports they had learnt en route about the toad-throwing incident at the love match. They felt sure that this was exactly like something Gui would do.

Raymond interrupted, wanting to know why Gui had run away from home. Ebles explained that, as the youngest brother, Gui had been overlooked regarding discipline and education. Gui was, it turned out, a good ten years younger than Peire, who was now five and twenty, fifteen years the junior of Ebles. He did not wish to excuse his brother's bad behaviour, he said, but he did feel as though Gui had been largely neglected as his parents were away much of the time. It seemed the young sapling that was Gui had been shaped by any which wind that blew in tempestuous gusts around the château d'Ussel. His parents, said Ebles, allowed all manner of persons under their patronage to wander, without check, around the court.

'Jugglers and actors,' he explained, 'to keep my parents and their courtiers entertained when they returned from their colourful trips. Among these entertainers were many of the poets they call troubadours. Gui has especially gone about with these troubadours since he was very young. We fear he has been influenced much by their ideas.'

'They have no rules,' added Peire. 'They make their own. They have no respect for authority or tradition.'

Raymond asked again why Gui had run away. Peire gave a brief description of Ussel-sur-Sarzonne which, although modest in scale, was situated in a fertile valley surrounded by soft fields of grains and corn which were set off by undulating meadows of poppy reds and lavender purples. The château was also bordered on all sides by an ancient variety of white oak, lending a year-round impression of snowy light. Not only were its lands generous and rivers flush with fish, Ussel was also rich in minerals and raw materials.

'Our father is a wealthy man,' said Peire, 'but he is greedy.'

'Therefore,' continued Ebles, 'when the rich, widowed duchess, Yasmin le Croix asked for Gui's hand in marriage, our father agreed to the match without consulting Gui.'

'When Gui refused to wed,' said Peire, 'our father demanded he either comply with his wishes or leave his house. Next morning, Gui was gone.'

Raymond turned then to the La Marche lords. 'I'm sure we all agree,' said he, 'the boy cannot be hanged now. Nor, however, should he be allowed to get off without punishment for the deed which he committed.'

He asked the lords what punishment they would suggest. They spoke among themselves awhile in tones so low we could not hear. Then the brother who was next eldest to Hugh La Marche spoke.

'If the boy returns with us, he will be in grave danger at the hands of all those who love our brother and have sworn allegiance to him. As we do not wish to feud with our prosperous neighbours, we suggest the boy remain imprisoned here for at least six months. When this time is served, he will be questioned and, perhaps, released.'

All parties shook on the arrangement and a cup was raised to future relations between the lords of Ussel and La Marche.

CHAPTER FOUR

The entire court had been given orders for the days to come. Ever since Maria had been threatened by one of La Marche's attendants, the viscount had been determined she be married most speedily. It was the only way she would be safe from assault; for when a lady like Maria was not betrothed, her chastity was always under siege. My lady was herself frightened enough to acquiesce easily to her father's demand.

Three high-born suitors had been invited to the château for the Twelfth Night celebrations. They would reside here for a subsequent five days, during which time they would each try their hand at wooing my lady. By the end of the week, she would have chosen her husband. Raymond was planning an elaborate period of feasting and play-acting, involving all the court, the visiting suitors, as well as the townspeople of Turenne.

The townspeople had been much put out by the events involving Gui d'Ussel and it was feared their mood was disgruntled still. It was enough to upset them that they had been denied the spectacle of his hanging, but the fact that Gui had got off so lightly, because he was not a commoner, had fired in some of them a spirit of rebellion. The viscount hoped that the days ahead would reconcile the court with its people.

On the eve of January 4th, the day before the arrival of the three noble suitors, all the town would attend a special mass. After the service some courtiers, accompanied by lute and recorder, would act out a surprise "Scene of Invitation". The scene would depict shepherds tending their sheep; they would be dressed in simple tunics of red or green with white tippet, pinched in at the waist. Their legs would be covered in white hose and their feet shod with black shoes — these peasants were clearly meant to represent the common man. Suddenly from on high, a herald angel would appear, bearing a scroll reading "Gloria in Excelsis". The angel would be dressed all in white, wearing wings of real feathers with dyed red tips. In the sky, above the angel's head, hundreds of painted, gold stars would hang. One very large star of stained glass would be lowered, spectacularly, on the eastern gable. It would be lit up all behind with torches. Mirrors were being placed all along the château wall to reflect the light of the holy star. The angel would then announce the coming of the three kings to visit Lady Maria — with a play on her name to suggest also the Virgin Mary.

All the people were invited to attend the Twelfth Night celebrations the following day at sunset. Raymond had informed them, in person, that the evening would also see a one-time revival of the old 'Lord of Misrule' tradition. In this practice, the people were offered a piece of cake which had a single bean concealed within. Whoever found the bean would rule over the banquet instead of the viscount. I could tell he hoped this transfer of power for one night would restore the trust between court and people. A meagre gesture, in my opinion, to make up for the poverty and hardship they would have to endure all winter.

My fingers were sore and cracked from plucking feathers for the herald angel.

Maria, Élise and Angelique were at another table, painting gold-leaf onto cut-out stars with fine, bone quills. They chattered excitedly over the preparations and made comments about the three intriguing suitors.

Angelique had returned from the château de Montvert the eve before Christmas; since that time I had scarcely exchanged two words with Maria, so occupied was she with her affairs.

The two other attending-ladies had been granted leave to spend the holiday with their own family. I endured a lonely Christmas and had been disappointed to receive only an orange from the cook as a gift. I scorned myself for the candle I had offered at Mass on Christmas Eve in the hope that it would bring some nugget of warmth to ease the coldness I felt inwardly.

Hugh La Marche had already departed for foreign lands; I spent much time lamenting him and was filled with a longing for him that was hard to endure. My inward suffering grew so extreme at times that I feared I would blabber my pain to anyone who would listen and put myself in danger. Thankfully, I held my tongue, and as the days went by my pain diffused and became a general hollow which I attempted to fill in other ways.

La Marche's man had forged an excuse to visit the château twice since our original encounter and I had, on both occasions, been willing to spend time with him in the mead closet. He praised my shapely figure and I craved more and more his touch, so I asked him to return again and bring me gifts and dainties.

I listened with great attention as Maria described her suitors. They had been selected with her consent, of course. Two of them were from neighbouring viscounties but the third was an Egyptian king, a foreigner, with whom we had never met. He was renowned for both his beauty and his wealth. Angelique studied his portrait closely, before remarking that, although he was most beautiful, he had an arrogant arch about the nose. Élise chided her youngest for judging the book only by its cover. Angelique objected, saying she was, in fact, attempting to see beneath the outer form.

They commented then upon the second portrait; it was of a local count named Elias le Font. He was not so young or well-formed as the king but he was quite nice-looking all the same. In the likeness, he had on his head a hat with an oversized and rather ridiculous feather. Angelique made all of us laugh by wondering aloud why the count had need of so large a piece of cockerel upon his head.

The third portrait was then produced; it was of Viscount Eble V from neighbouring Ventadorn. This man was older by two decades than the king, being all of seven and forty. He had been made a widower two years before, leaving the estate without an heir. Angelique wondered why Maria had consented to be matched with so senior a man. Maria reminded her sister that the present Eble was a grandson of Eble II who had patronised the famous troubadour, Bernard de Ventadorn.

'The present viscount carries on the family tradition of patronage,' she said. 'He himself informed me it is of the greatest importance to him. He is determined that his court should be a court of love like those of old. He says he wishes his new wife to possess the artistic tastes necessary to revive the Ventadorn name together with *fin amor*. He believes that I have just such a gift, for he has sometimes attended the love-matches at our court.'

'Indeed,' said Angelique. 'And was he present, do you think, at the *last* love-match?'

She referred of course to the infamous affair of the emerald bodice with which Maria had tricked La Marche.

Maria's response was curt. 'Well, yes, I believe he was.'

No more was said.

The three women worked awhile in silence, delicately placing the glittering leaf onto the stars that would adorn the Twelfth Night celebrations. Angelique, quite unexpectedly, broke the peace once more.

'Will he whom they call "The Boy with Owl's Eyes" be present at the feast?'

Maria and Élise both sat up very straight as though an invisible arrow had struck down through the table.

'For shame,' said Élise. 'Why must you ask so many questions? Of course the boy will not be present. Why should he be?'

Angelique, chastened by her mother's remark, said nothing but merely picked up another star. Two red-rose spots competed with the pale lilies of her cheeks.

Maria then spoke, gently, in her sister's defence. 'It is recorded that when the Lord of Misrule makes his wish on Twelfth Night, he often requests the release of all prisoners,' she said. 'It is just for one night and afterwards the proper order is restored.'

Élise looked cross. 'My father, the viscount of Séverac,' she began, proudly, 'had this game banned on account of the disorder it sparked.'

There were stories, she explained, stories of jewels being ripped from noblewomen's necks and afterwards paraded by goldsmiths' wives who sold the same jewels back to their owners for twice their original cost. It was rumoured that on Twelfth Night, certain married ladies of the court would allow themselves to be taken by common men of the town. Babies were born of these encounters; babies who were now grown men and women with whom Élise was acquainted.

Maria and Angelique exchanged looks of excited curiosity. I held my breath to listen. I was starting to greatly look forward to the Twelfth Night celebrations, despite my bleeding fingers.

Élise glanced in my direction and changed the subject. 'Of course, whatever the Lord of Misrule orders must be obeyed,' she said. 'Therefore, it follows that if he commands the prisoners of Turenne be released, they must be released.'

Angelique clapped together her hands. 'Well,' she said. 'I am glad! I *am* curious to see the boy. I have heard *most* fascinating reports. They say he may be an alchemist!'

'He is no such thing,' said Élise. 'He is Gui d'Ussel, the youngest son of the château Ussel-sur-Sarzonne. He has unusual eyes and that is all.'

Maria stayed quiet, but I could tell she was fiercely concentrated on the subject of Gui d'Ussel. She had attempted some meetings with him under Raymond's supervision. It was reported that he scarcely answered her questions, often turning in to face the wall. He showed as little interest in food as he did in speech and, when asked if he would like to exercise outside, he had refused. Normally, when she walked in, he remained all curled-up like a babe in the womb. But Maria was quite determined her conversation should be returned and so her visits persisted.

'Perhaps if he *were* released on the night, it would occasion some breakthrough. Perhaps,' Maria sighed, 'we would gain some useful insights into his character.'

'My dear,' said Élise, 'some people will ever be slow to place their trust in others. You never should imagine that others are the same as yourself: they are not. All creatures are made by Nature with such sweet variety as to promise each of us a lifetime of perplexity in the unravelling. Consider the human heart to be as carefully guarded as the centre of the melancholy artichoke. Do not attempt to unwrap it, if it wishes not to be unwrapped.'

'Perhaps,' Angelique said, turning to Maria, 'a lifetime of perplexity is just what you are seeking?'

When the Twelfth Night drew in, a slow, candlelit procession was made into the courtyard. The day had been cold, but bright. A deep-sea shade of blue was spreading like spilled ink across the pale parchment of sky and flecks of winking stars were starting to appear. Musicians on lutes and harps were playing soft melodies.

Maria was seated in full view of all, on a purpose-built podium in the centre of the courtyard. She wore a dress of royal blue silk with gold-flower design and the chair on which she sat was draped in a cloth of profound blue. She was as though a perfect, earthly embodiment of the heavens above. The people settled round her in a semi-circle, their candles flickering. The troubadour, Arnaut de Marveill then stepped out onto the podium and announced he would perform a composition he had written specially. A great cheer went up; then all fell silent as Arnaut started singing in throaty, but well-seasoned, baritone:

'Lady, by you and Love I am so swayed
That I dare not love, and yet I cannot refrain:
Part of me wants to flee, the other remain;
I am at once courageous and afraid.
I dare not plead with you to satisfy me,
But rather like a man wounded and dying
Who clings to life full knowing what's in store,
So despairing, your mercy I implore.
Where lineage and true nobility
Reside and merit is surpassing, there

Humility should also dwell, for where
There's worth, we should not meet with vanity...
Unless it's veiled by a sweet clemency.
I pray the mercy and humility
That you possess will lead you to want to aid me,
For I can't leave off loving you, good lady.'

When the song was sung, he bowed low before Maria and the people cheered once more. Candles were breathed upon until they went out and the gentle airs ceased. A trumpet sounded joyfully. On the eastern gable, the splendid, stained-glass star was lowered, casting its unearthly light.

There was a collective gasp then, when the Egyptian king entered on his magnificent black steed, weighted down on either side with bags of gold. He wore a blue-grey robe with gold pattern underneath an open, pink coat with white tippet; his head was decked with a filigree crown. He was a thing of great beauty himself, with large eyes and shining skin. When he reached the podium, he dismounted and, with a bow, poured a perfect pyramid of gold coins at Maria's feet.

Again the trumpet sounded and the next suitor appeared. He rode a white steed which had, in its saddlebags, many sticks of pale blue incense. His cloak was of pale blue also, with trailing sleeves. Upon his head was perched a tall hat, adorned with pink feathers. I recognised him as Count Elias le Font. He too dismounted beneath the podium but disappeared, momentarily, in a cloud of heavily perfumed blue smoke, only to emerge again in a pink garment embroidered all with leaves of silver. Maria's name appeared against the wood of the podium, etched with sticks of lightly-smouldering incense. The pretty trick earned him a generous applause.

Once more the trumpet sounded and in came the third and final suitor. He was Viscount Eble of Ventadorn. He came on foot and carried in his arms a casket of myrrh. He was dressed in a long, red robe with white tippet. He walked to the podium and knelt before Maria, placing the casket at her feet.

Maria bowed to each suitor, acknowledging their gifts and their right to compete for her hand. Leather drums were beaten with energy and caskets of wine, mead and ale were rolled into the courtyard on all sides. Silver trays of cakes were passed around.

Not a quart hour later, the cook's son, Merrick, offered a piece of cake to a sturdy, but rosy, daughter of the town. She frowningly refused, accepting instead a slice from another boy. Merrick downed the cake himself, chewing over-cheerfully to hide his unhappy heart. His mind being distracted, he was more surprised than pleased to find himself biting into something hard. With chubby fingers, he drew the curious object from his mouth; it was a bean of solid gold. He roared with laughter then and, before he could protest, his friends had lifted him high in the air.

'Hail, Merrick! All Hail Lord Merrick,' they shouted, passing him through the crowd.

He found himself deposited onto the podium, where the viscount was waiting with his family. Merrick's family was then called up and he was asked to choose his queen; he picked his mother and the viscount ceremoniously placed on their heads two wreathes of berried ivy. They were pronounced lord and lady of the banquet.

When asked to make his wish, Merrick consulted awhile with his mother before speaking. He wished for a month's supply of hard wood and grain for all present, if God be willing to provide. The choice was met with great approval and, I thought, relief.

It seemed that Gui d'Ussel would be safely kept away tonight.

Rows and rows of richly laden banqueting tables were wheeled across the courtyard; all courtiers and commoners would dine together, under the spread of stars. Merrick and his family took their place at the top table where the viscount usually sat. All others then made a haphazard scramble until the benches were full.

It was a feast the likes of which I had never witnessed before — not least for the splendid, themed dishes we tasted, but also for the view of all the citizens with faces becomingly aglow and eyes bewitchingly sparkling in the twilight. Most eyes turned back more than once to the three intriguing visitors.

The troubadour, Arnaut de Marveill was sitting at a nearby table, chatting unreservedly with the guests. An animated fellow, he entertained us all with stories and snippets of songs.

When night had disguised us with its cloak of blackness, all last remaining guards went down and we began to dance. Bodies were pressed so closely together that no one really knew or cared with whom they were dancing. I myself danced with a tiresome, but rich, old yeoman whose hands kept sliding lecherously towards my backside. He agreed to release me only after I had promised to let him come a-courting. I told him that, as I was shy and untested, I may well join a convent; but he could bring me flowers and sweet apples all the same and see what luck would bring. My speech excited him greatly, and he ran off at once as though in a hurry to gather up his finest produce for my pleasure.

Tired of dancing, I found again my seat and silently observed the dancers. Smiths with normally leaden limbs and halting speech were transformed into silent, but solid partners for flighty maidens. Weavers, millers, drapers, bakers and

carpenters flounced, above their stations, with squires'
daughters and even jewellers' wives. I even saw one young
gallant of the court stepping down an alley with a local farm-
hand.

Maria danced with each of her three suitors. The king, being
the boldest and most flamboyant in his movement, was
unafraid to throw his lady round. Next, Count Elias danced
with graceful, but dainty, steps, more conscious of himself than
of his partner. Viscount Eble was, perhaps, the most skilful of
the three, moving at least in rhythm with the music. He was
also the most considerate of his partner and Maria looked well
in his arms. Although his face was heavily lined with age, he
looked attractive all the same, being somewhat thin of hair but
strong of feature and of smile.

When the dance ended, Maria came to speak with Arnaut de
Marveill. He enquired after the prisoner, Gui d'Ussel, saying
that he'd been well acquainted with him since early boyhood
and expressing his sorrow at his current fate. When Maria told
him that the boy refused to talk, Arnaut asked if she would
permit him to speak some truths about him, in case it might
help. He told her that Gui had been a highly spirited, but
extremely passionate boy, who was both plagued and gifted
with unusual sensibility. He confirmed what Gui's brother
Ebles had stated before: that Gui had run away from home
after his father had ordered him to marry a rich widow.

There was, however, another important piece of information
which Ebles had — perhaps intentionally — left out. Many
months before Gui had left the château Ussel-sur-Sarzonne, he
had fallen into a deep melancholy which had been occasioned
not by the prospect of marrying the widow, but by something
much closer to his heart. Gui had tried — but failed — to
compose *fin amor* verse and, finding he could not easily do it,

had been gripped with a terrible sorrow. Arnaut believed that, when Gui had thrown the toad at La Marche, he'd done it out of a kind of death wish.

'Gui had lost the will to live,' he said. 'Perhaps he has not yet regained it?'

Maria nodded slowly.

'I tried to advise him,' continued Arnaut. 'But he would not listen. I asked him how he hoped to make art about love, before he had even experienced the art of lovemaking! Seriously, I told him not to be so unkind to himself, that it takes many years — without exception — for us to learn the art. I told him not to be disheartened at his first attempt.'

'What did he say to that?' Maria asked.

'Ah,' said Arnaut. 'His melancholy had already set in deep. He insisted it was not his first attempt; that he had been writing privately at his father's court for many years. That may be so, but he forgets that he is still a boy and that only when the work is tested, before a public audience, can it be truly modified. I advised him to be lighter of heart. The finest creative work is born of the spirit of play. I told him,' he laughed, 'that play also begets the most spirited lovemaking!'

'What did he say to that?'

'He said that he would rather die than fail to make the art, for if he cannot make the art, he sees no purpose to his life.'

My lady spotted me then and called me to her. Pressing her sapphire earrings into my palm, she asked that I not repeat what I had overheard and that I go fetch her indigo cloak, as it was growing cold.

When I returned, the troubadour was dancing with a buxom partner and my lady was now speaking with her father.

I placed the cloak around her shoulders and moved off again into the crowd.

CHAPTER FIVE

I was used as go-between Maria and her suitors. With so many private meetings to arrange, as well as public banquets, I scarcely had any time for myself. After spending such a solitary and forlorn Christmas, I revelled much in the company. I flirted with practice and wit amongst the attendants and soon was quite a favourite with many of them. But I did not have the time to satisfy my appetite with any of them, although I hinted we should meet again in quieter times. Maria's suitors, likewise, all received an equally divided slice of her time — but nothing more. It was agreed she would spend an entire day with each of them in turn. The other waiting-ladies, Angelique and I went also in attendance on the first of these outings.

On a promising but chilly morning, the dashing Egyptian king led us well-cloaked ladies amidst a crowd of jugglers and jousters to spend a day at picnic. We were, at first, marvellously entertained and awestruck at the manner in which the king and his attendants served us phials of sparkling wine whilst galloping fast on horseback. The king was as fine and distinguished a rider as I had ever seen, though Angelique observed that this, so far, seemed to be the singular talent that he brought always into focus. The youngest sister of Turenne did not appear to like the striking king, despite his many attractions.

'Fie, fie, dark angel,' said Maria. 'Must you always dig the kernel out of the casing? Perhaps the outward appearance of some things reflects also the inner substance, despite what the wise women say.'

'Know you of any poison which cannot be used for some good purpose?' asked Angelique. 'Or know you of any sugar which contains inside no hurtful properties?'

As if on cue, the king rode up beside us then, balancing a plate of sugared dainties. Maria politely refused the sweet.

But our day of fun ended badly when we returned to the château and saw how our great king treated his beautiful steed. The horse was stalwart, and he was tired and hungry after working all the day to please his master. When our grooms-boy went to take him, he grew nervous as he knew him not and neighed and rose up on his hind legs. The king's brow furrowed angrily; he did not attempt to speak gentle words to the animal, to cool his rising heat and calm his nerves, as Viscount Raymond would have done. Instead, he drew out a thin, black leather whip — the likes of which was forbidden in Turenne. The likes of which sent shivers down our spines.

It was clear the horse knew all too well the whip's vicious sting, for when he saw it he grew uncontrollable; rolling his eyes in a crazed manner and neighing to screaming-point. When the king applied the first lash, the horse looked bewildered. His master, for whom he had worked all day, struck him until he dropped to his knees. He beat the wind out of his belly until the screaming turned to heavy panting. Then he left him whimpering in the mud, his once shining eyes grown dull. The king himself then went in search of ale.

Next morning, my lady was so disturbed she had to cancel her rendezvous with the count. He accepted with a most obliging — and endearing — sweetness of manner. Maria spent most of the day in her bedchamber with Angelique. At midday, the count sent me with a message and a sack of lavender sprigs and ribbon. I reported that the count's own surgeon had been called to examine the horse's wounds and had affirmed that, physically, the animal was doing well. The news brought the sisters some small comfort and I helped them spend the afternoon plaiting the lavender into posies. Angelique asked Maria which of the three suitors she liked best, but Maria replied she had not yet decided.

'One thing I know for certain, it will not be the king!' Maria said.

'The count is quite the gentle man,' suggested Angelique.

'Indeed,' agreed Maria. 'And I am most grateful for his gentleness today. Though, he seemed somewhat absorbed in himself, I thought, when we were dancing,' she added.

'I overheard some interesting things from the count's attendants,' said Angelique. 'They think him a kind and considerate master, who has the rare and enviable quality of commanding respect quietly. He has,' she continued, 'one quirky, but understandable, weakness. It seems he has no hair at all upon any part of his body and that he is most conscious of this. When he is in public, the count wears always a hat with false hair attached. When he rides out, or hunts, indeed, or dances, he does so with dainty motions to make sure the hair does not fall off!'

There was some underlying glee in the manner of Angelique's report, but one could also tell she had sympathy for the count. Maria smiled and said she was always glad to receive new intelligence that brought to better light those things which were a mystery in others.

'Or,' said Angelique, 'which allows some welcome air to reach an itchy pate!'

'I *had* noticed he was scratching!' Maria said.

'And yet he is kind and nice-looking,' said Angelique. 'Also, *he* is not of an equal age to our father, unlike the viscount of

Ventadorn. How strange to imagine kissing a man who could be your own father!'

Next morning, Maria and I rode out with Viscount Eble to his expansive estate at Ventadorn. The day was brilliant, but again cold. The silk cloth we wore around our faces to protect against the freezing air was puffing in and out, making our breathing visible. The horses too were panting heavily as they laboured uphill for the last part of the journey. Château de Ventadorn was situated on a highly remote point at the top of a steep hill. It was surrounded by a forest of beautiful elm, and this was where we were to spend the day.

The path through the forest was broad and the penetrating sunlight made a shimmering dance of lights and shapes in the gaps between the trees. There was no breeze here, and so we untied our face-guards and breathed deeply of the green air. The horses brought us a long way in, then stopped before an iron gate, upon which was inscribed the words *Imaginatio* and *Phantasio*. Viscount Eble then worked a pulley to cause the heavy gates to open.

What struck me first as strange and impossible was that, even though I knew it was not yet noon, the light the other side of the gate was, unmistakably, that of the setting — and not of the midday — sun. Streaks of burnt orange and reds were lighting up the trees as though they were on fire. Next, I noticed the trees themselves were silver and not green-brown, as they had been the other side.

We trotted along a prettily curving pathway of smooth cobbled stone. Next, we came to the mouth of a large, heart-shaped opening, outlined by a cut-glass wall of emerald green. In the centre was a fantastic dragon-shaped sculpture in side-relief, composed of many orange and red rubies. It was this that mimicked the light of the setting sun! The words *Maria Domus* were written repeatedly around the edge of the creature's huge eye.

Suddenly it was clear to me that this was an allegory. The words on the gate signified choosing the gate to the imagination when going 'inside' the home of the viscount; the emeralds represented the bodice of gems with which Maria had tricked La Marche; the eye of the dragon was deep insight and understanding, referring to his comprehension of Maria's dedication to *fin amor* and his endorsing of her use of artifice in love-match; the dragon itself signified reaching the furthest point of fantasy and coming 'home' to Ventadorn. The rubies were an act of cleansing alchemy, transforming the virginal 'green' emeralds of girlhood into the formed 'ruby' of womanhood, through the purifying fire of marital love.

When I looked at Maria's face, I saw that she could not have been more pleased.

She promised him her hand there and then, under the dragon's gaze. Ventadorn held her tenderly as he slipped onto her finger a ring of crushed rubies, whispering words of love into her ear.

Next day at sunrise the early tolling of the bell, accompanied by the release of one hundred of the château doves, announced to the townspeople that Maria had made her choice.

Viscount Raymond was in high spirits as he bid the suitors adieu. The king bowed stiffly from his limping steed and Count Elias tried his best to smile graciously through his disappointment. The viscount of Ventadorn, though the eldest of the three by many years, was the most buoyant and light-hearted in his parting speech and steps. Maria smiled and waved to all, but reserved a more lingering look for Eble's eyes alone.

He seemed to me as kind and reasonable a lord as anyone could hope for and despite his advancing years, his motions were youthful enough. Raymond placed his arm affectionately around Maria's shoulders and told her he was proud of her this day. He approved the match and said he was glad to have gained Ventadorn as a son.

'I believe you have chosen prudently,' he said. 'Not only for the prosperity of all your family and future offspring, but I believe you will be happy, for you and Ventadorn are of an equal mind.'

Raymond asked then to know the wedding date; Maria informed him it had not yet been set. The faintest touch of worry brushed his face but cleared away again quickly.

'Well, that will do for now,' he said. All were dismissed.

CHAPTER SIX

Angelique had departed again for the château de Montvert, and so Maria requested my presence more frequently. She spent the next few weeks writing and receiving pretty missives and gifts from her fiancé, often asking me to read and judge the correspondence. I found much earnest admiration in Viscount Eble's lines although I could detect in them no great fire, but this I did not tell her.

One day, Maria summoned me to her. 'I believe, Maryse,' she said, 'that it is time we visited Gui d'Ussel and attempted to speak with him once more.'

She asked that I help her dress and, unusually, changed her outfit many times before she was satisfied. She chose, against my wishes, a new, silk dress of pink, more suitable for summer than for winter. As we left, she dabbed a strong rose paste on all her pulses, making herself as irresistible to the senses as a new bloom. I suggested the scent was wasted, as we were only visiting the dungeon.

'On the contrary,' she replied, 'I could not put it to better use. Rose contains great healing virtues, both bodily and spiritually, and as we both know Gui is sick at heart. Perhaps it will lift his spirits.'

As we entered his cell, I had the impression that, on hearing footsteps, he had retreated like a spider into a crevice, to face the damp wall. My lady asked the guards to leave us. I was reminded of the night he had been tortured when the three of us were left alone, but he looked much thinner now. His weaker frame made me less afraid of him; he was — after all — a mere boy.

At first, none of us spoke. I was tempted to shout at him and make him turn around, angry as I was that a prisoner should turn his back on two ladies of the court. I held my tongue, however, until Maria spoke.

'The troubadour, Arnaut de Marveill, sends his fond regards,' she said.

He turned, slightly, towards her. 'You have met Arnaut?'

Encouraged, she continued. 'Yes. He wrote and sang a special composition for … for the Twelfth Night celebrations.'

I wondered why she had not said the song had been composed in *her* honour.

Gui now turned fully round to face us. Once again, I found myself slinking from his gaze.

'He sang it himself?'

She had caught his interest. The great troubadours considered themselves poets, not performers; they rarely sang themselves. Sweet-voiced jongleurs were usually employed to sing at big events. It was some tribute to Turenne — and to Maria — that Arnaut had sung for her. Gui's eyes flicked over Maria's outfit but then returned and lingered on her face, and even on her lips. Many people made contact with the eyes, but some watched the lips of another when they spoke; perhaps Gui was one of these. Certainly he was listening to her now. I thought there was something studied about her manner, as though she had planned this meeting.

'He told me that you and he are long acquainted,' she said. 'He spoke a little of his art, how it is informed by love.'

'Love-making,' Gui corrected. 'Arnaut's art is informed by making love; he does not think it possible to write *fin amor* verse else. I myself believe it is his motivation, rather than his inspiration, for ladies fly at him like moths to beeswax!'

'I asked him to copy out the lyrics for me,' she said, drawing a neatly rolled parchment from her bodice. 'Would you like to see it?'

He brushed it past his nostrils, breathing its strong, rose scent, before unfurling it and reading aloud the title. 'Lady, by you and love I am so swayed.'

He smiled then. It was the first time I had ever seen this phenomenon and it transformed him. His normally round and staring orbs creased into two soft beams, as easy on the eye as morning light. Maria went up close to read the verse over his shoulder.

'It is well executed,' he said, finally. 'But it is so formulaic! Here are all the same tropes again. The poet loves in vain, a lady beyond his station. He begs her to end his misery, but at the same time says he is unworthy to be her lover. Is this really what you ladies want to hear?'

Looking unsure, Maria nonetheless attempted an answer. 'It's true the lady is exalted,' she said, slowly. 'But the knight, even if he is lowly, has a chance to win her love as long as he proves himself the worthiest.'

'Why must he prove himself?' Gui asked. 'Why should not the lovers be equal? Why should *she* not have to prove that she is equally worthy? Surely love does not distinguish between the sexes? The lady should be equal to the man who loves her, no more nor less.'

'But by the rules of *fin amor* —' Maria began.

'I do not comply with rules or conventions! Those worn-out clichés should be tested for the falsehoods they contain,' Gui said. 'It is the purpose of the love poets to express love truthfully. True love, surely, should be equal, no? Is not this what we should express? Love should not distinguish between age, religion or even class.'

'Then express it,' said Maria, simply. 'Write it down in verse. I shall return tomorrow with pen and parchment.'

'I confess that I have little else to do at present.' Again he smiled.

When she returned the next day, Maria and Gui discussed once more the troubadour's verse.

'It reads so like a prayer,' Gui observed with disapproval. 'You have noted, I suppose, the repetition of "mercy" and "implore" throughout? He begs her always to aid him! The poet is exactly like a supplicant to the Virgin. He sings of his ideal woman, but she is not of flesh and blood. It is an insult to both women and men!'

'On the contrary,' replied Maria, 'the poet's exalting of the lady makes her his sovereign. Where most of us live under the oppressive rule of our fathers, or our husbands, this reverses the rules, giving us the power to choose love freely. For this reason, it is imperative the lady keeps suzerainty over her lover.'

They carried on like this for hours.

Maria returned the next day and again the next, and they were always arguing over poetry. After that I stopped attending, as it grew too tedious.

I had my own troubles at this time and was much distracted. La Marche's man had contrived again to spend time at Turenne. We coupled every day in the mead closet and, sometimes, in my own bedchamber when I was sure all were away. Here we made love more freely, also more loudly. I found I often had to put my hand across his mouth to quieten him when he was crying out. He told me he loved me but I noted that he did not offer to marry me and, when I told him so, he grew cross. In fact, I suspected he was already married but even if he was not I would never marry him, for he was not rich. But I enjoyed our sport in bed and loved the sensations it sent cascading through my body. I asked him for some precious gem or metal as a sign of his devotion and was greatly pleased by the little cross of solid gold he bestowed on me, which he himself had received from La Marche.

But after he had gone, it emerged I may have taken too great a risk in allowing him to share my bed. Some vicious and unpleasant rumours were carried back to my ears by the two attending-ladies who shared my duties. I resolved not to see La Marche's man again and with that thought, I was struck with a surprising melancholy; I would, after all, miss his alert, jade eyes, his strong arms and expansive hands. But I would deny him to the death.

For I would have to silence these dangerous wagging tongues, especially before the stories reached my uncle, Raoul. I was so frightened by the thought of being turned out, penniless, into the streets; a disgraced cast-off with nowhere to go. For sure I would end up in some pox-ridden house of whores where I would live a short, disgusting life and die a slow, painful death, my face too disfigured for an open coffin, my reputation too evil for Christian burial.

In fact, as Fortune would have it, I received a visitor then who served my purpose well in disposing of these rumours. The rich old yeoman with whom I'd danced on Twelfth Night came courting with his basket of apples. I received the fruit gratefully, but told him I preferred cakes and bracelets. I played the new-born lamb's part with him and laughed inwardly at how excited he became at the mere fluttering of my eyelashes. As was customary, he soon asked permission of the viscount and Lady Maria to walk out with me.

After holding a brief interview with him, the viscount gave his happy, if amused, consent. In the eyes of the world, this would be an ideal match, for the yeoman was rich and I was ample-bosomed and ripe for breeding. Nobody would wink an eye at the great age difference between us, though some might find it humorous. For myself, I supposed it was the best that I could do, for I had always known that love was not my birthright. The recent shock I had received had urged me into securing my future, and so I was happy to entertain the yeoman and accept his gifts. But he had a big belly which wobbled like jelly, and his breath was foul. I resolved that I would never suffer him to touch me.

Maria showed little interest in my new courtship and I grew angry with her for her indifference to my future. While she was, every day, in correspondence with her rich, attractive fiancé, as well as having daily interviews with Gui, I was expected to make my bed with a fat and foolish man who saw me as little more than a farm animal ready for breeding. I would make my bed with the yeoman, but I would never lie in it. Once safely married, I would find my comfort elsewhere.

Deep winter had settled in and the ground was a constant sheet of white with night following fast on day's heels. Even during the daylight hours, all was darkly silhouetted against the snow. The only bit of colour was an occasional robin's darting ochre breast. Maria thus made a startling figure as she strode across the courtyard every day, warmly attired in her indigo cloak.

Maria's fiancé continued to send letters and gifts, but I noted she gave less attention to them now as she was always rushing off to meet Gui.

CHAPTER SEVEN

One morning as I was attending Maria's toilette, we were both summoned most unusually to an early meeting. I hurried through my duties and although fully dressed, we arrived at the great hall with flushed faces and untidy hair. Raymond was sitting alone at the great table. Some of his attendants were, as always, stationed motionless in the shadows.

'My dears,' he said as he rose to greet us, 'do sit and take some refreshment.' He indicated the Arabian silverware and I poured a glass of minted-blossom tea for each of us. I wondered if any breakfast would be offered to accompany the insipid drink.

'You may be wondering why I have called you here at such an early hour,' said he. 'I see, Maria, that you are dressed already, a tribute to your efficiency, no doubt, Maryse.' He smiled at me and I smiled back shyly. 'It may be, Maria, that you will soon exchange your present plain dress for a splendid gown of white and gold.'

My lady looked at him, confused. 'Father,' she said, 'is there to be an event at the château today?'

'There is, my dearest, there is,' he said. His manner seemed to me at once excited and somewhat embarrassed, or even guilty. He shifted in his chair and one of his men gave a little cough. His voice and manner changed then suddenly from that of a father and confidant to that of a ruler. He stood up tall. 'Maria de Turenne,' he said, 'you are to be married today. It is all arranged. Maryse will accompany you to the main living chamber, where you will find your wedding gown and jewels laid out. She will help you to dress and arrange yourself in your finery. Both of you must be in the chapel before the clock strikes nine. Viscount Eble, your groom, will be waiting, along with your mother.'

When I looked at Maria, I saw that her previously hot cheeks had blanched to an ashen pallor, her mouth had drooped and her body had begun to tremble. I had seen her like this many times as a child, whenever she felt an injustice was being done to herself or someone else. The look had preceded a violent outburst of passion. When she spoke next, her voice sounded strange, almost like an adolescent male's, lowered and cracked.

'But my sisters are not here, and I have had no time to prepare myself or make offerings to the Virgin,' she began.

Raymond brought his fist violently down on the table, making us jump. 'There will be no objections,' he said. 'I have been most lenient with you and it is all arranged. You may finish your drink and then you will go and do as I say. Do not attempt to escape, the doors are guarded all. There will be no more discussion.'

Raymond looked dangerously close to flying into a fury. A familiar sound of clinking armour reminded us again of the menacing presence of his attendants. If Maria lost her composure, I was certain one of these men would rush at her.

Before the clock struck ten, Maria de Turenne had become Maria de Ventadorn. I had arranged her yellow-gold veil artfully around her face so that any misgivings expressed thereupon would be concealed from her new husband. Ventadorn himself could not have looked happier and this, I was sure, would bring my lady some comfort.

After the ceremony I received a rare invitation to join the family for the wedding breakfast. We returned to the great hall where the bare table of just an hour earlier had since undergone an elaborate transformation. Raymond spoke to me kindly, thanking me for the fine job I had done preparing the bride at such brief notice. He said I must stand in for Maria's sisters today, so she would hardly miss them.

I partook fully of the breakfast feast whilst also taking care to fuss about Maria. Despite the delicacy of the food and complex flavours of the wine, she scarcely touched her plate. I noted that Raymond did not once look at her but passed the time in conversation only with Ventadorn.

Élise was splendidly attired in a brocaded dress of red and black covered with fashionable Arabian shapes. Her bodice was pulled so tightly I was sure it must be difficult for her to breathe; perhaps it was this that lent to her aspect such a vacant and distant look.

The women remained largely silent throughout, vaguely listening to the men as they discussed affairs of court. Tense and bleak were the silences which sometimes fell, for we were such a small party. I rejoiced inwardly at my ability to conduct myself with much ease and grace in such exalted company, for I had not been to the château born.

Raymond noted my good humour with gratitude, and it occurred to me that this event would earn me some future reward. Outwardly I remained suitably subdued, concerned about my mistress, but appreciative of my inclusion as a guest. I had long mastered the art of seeming to eat little by packing large portions into neat piles on my plate. With tidy, small motions, I managed to eat and drink my fill without displaying an unseemly appetite.

As soon as the last course was finished, Maria and Élise rose to leave, first looking to Raymond for permission.

'Of course, you must go,' he said. 'It will take some time to pack your trunk, Maria.' Still he did not look at her.

It was Élise who answered, but she looked at Ventadorn and not at her husband. 'My lord,' she said, 'Maria will not accompany you back to Ventadorn today. You understand that, given the hasty nature of your nuptials, we need some time to fit Maria with all those things required for a new bride. Nothing less would be seemly.'

Ventadorn had stood up and was nodding his agreement vigorously. Maria looked with some gratitude at her mother.

Raymond too had risen, but he did not look pleased. 'Sir, your bride will follow you directly, I will see to it,' he said.

Ventadorn bowed his acknowledgment politely, then turned his gaze to Maria. 'My beloved,' he said, 'today you have made me the happiest of men. I wish for no more than to embark on our life's journey together with all possible speed. But please, you must not rush simply to please me. It is no small matter to uproot yourself from the life you have led here at Turenne, surrounded by your loved ones. I cannot myself imagine leaving behind the forests of Ventadorn, with all their secret groves and whisperings, as I am sure it will grieve you to leave behind Turenne and all those special places and the people who have been your heart's companion since girlhood. I beseech you, take all the time you need to prepare. I shall be waiting for you with open arms.'

Ventadorn's eloquent speech was acknowledged with a little nod, but still Maria did not utter a word, only bowed to him, then left.

Raymond grumbled at the delay but was soon silenced by Élise's cold stare. For what bride in her right mind would choose midwinter as the season to enter into married life, when all around was death itself? No, it would be against the laws of Nature to attempt to kindle the fire of love on frozen ground. In spring, all would be renewed and all creatures would come forth to choose their mates in pools of bright sunshine to the background pitter-patter of musical April showers. This would be the natural time for Maria's arrival at Ventadorn.

After the wedding, Maria did not leave her chamber for two weeks. She pined for her sisters, especially for Angelique, who had not yet returned from Montvert. She wanted me always by her side for comfort. My lady rarely cried, and even now she did not cry but showed instead great turbulence of mind by the manner in which she paced about her chamber. This, coupled with her constant fidgeting, irritated me greatly and I had to bite my tongue often.

So concerned was she over herself that she did not once think of my needs or my present courtship, which I was neglecting. Finally, worn out, I confessed I found her much self-absorbed and asked to be excused for a day or so to conduct my own affairs. My request inspired some action on her part and she took to writing letters — one of which she asked me to dispatch.

The following morning found me on my way to the dungeon, happily breathing in the fresh air and clutching a letter addressed to Gui d'Ussel. It would not even have occurred to me to open it if I had not been waylaid by the yeoman, who insisted I go with him to take a cup of ale. I was happy to accompany him, and I fancied that the jovial atmosphere of the tavern would be a welcome change from the recent gloom of the château.

It was the first time I had stepped into a tavern. As a single lady, I could never have entered such a place, but the yeoman insisted on paying for a private, curtained *demi-chambre* where I would be unseen and unmolested. Even on our rushed way through the place, I caught the general ambience, the hustle and din of the main building. A huge, open space with crude stone walls was capped by a vaulted roof, crisscrossing overhead with beams as fat as tree trunks. A tall, open-flame torch was sparking, dangerously, in the centre and men in worn-out livery were roasting themselves around it.

Their chat ceased as I walked in, and I noted their eyes flicking from my face down my dress. The yeoman must have noted it too, for he put a heavy arm around me to show his possession. The foolish man half-smiled, half-grimaced, looking as swollen full of pride as a fresh-baked pastry, but also ready to charge at those who would undress me with their eyes. So confused was he between these two positions that, just as we were passing by the men, he stood in front of me and made me trip. I cussed him loudly and the men all laughed and whistled.

The yeoman suddenly started throwing his weight about, offering to fight each and every one. As this was going on, I spied some whores watching in the shadows; their faces blotted out, but their curly, brightly painted wigs glowing in the dark. It was a little early yet for business, but I guessed they were on the lookout.

Another woman in a poppy-dyed wig was moving about with a jug. She wore a faded velvet gown of cornflower blue, showing a great expanse of bosom. A strange duo had approached her with an alms bowl, one a fat, perspiring monk, the other a sickly looking adolescent boy in monkish garb too long for him. He was being supported by the monk, who seemed to prop him up as they stood. The monk was calling out a mantra.

'Alms! Alms for the sick! Alms for the sick child of God!'

The woman shook her head but she did pour a mug of ale for the monk, who drained it greedily.

'Mary-ze,' the yeoman then hissed at me.

I just had time to spot two pretty gallants leaning against a wall before being lightly shoved through beaded curtains. When I looked at the yeoman I could not help but laugh aloud, for he had hanging, just below his underbelly, a bulging pair of soft, red, leather purses which he was fiddling with and jingling. I quickly turned my laugh into a sneeze and he seemed not to notice. He looked around the chamber and tutted his approval, making comments as though he'd built the place himself, as though he had forgotten we'd just met on the road by chance.

'You see how elegant it is,' he said, gesturing roundly. 'I was sure we would be comfortable here. I have seen to it we will not be disturbed. It is such an advantage, is it not Mary-ze, that I can entertain you in so grand and elegant a chamber, just like those you're used to at the château.'

In fact, the chamber put me in mind of the woman's faded blue dress; it may have once been fine, but it had lost its lustre. It did contain the one, grand feature of a stained-glass window with cushioned window-seat and this, rather than on a low-stool, was where I chose to sit. Opposite me was a slightly peeling, gilded mirror on legs. To my relief, the yeoman sat opposite, not alongside, me, his bulging purse now wobbling in his lap.

Soon the woman in blue arrived and set a table down between us with two mugs of ale. Before she left, the yeoman had a word in her ear and when she returned moments later, she carried a plate on which were piled some curious-looking objects of brownish-red hue.

'A little bite to eat?' he offered.

On closer sight, I realised to my horror that these were shrivelled tongues. When I protested, swearing I would not touch them, the yeoman shushed me, hastening to assure me these were not *human* tongues, but only the tongues of baby harts which had been specially killed.

'A rare delicacy, very deliciou-ʒ,' he said. 'Not everyone can afford to eat such delicacie-ʒ. You are lucky, Mary-ʒe, that I can entertain you in the same manner you have become accustomed to at the château.'

He offered me the plate and I accepted one, as I was always hungry and they were only harts' tongues. I popped one in my mouth. As soon as I had done this, he gave a sigh of pleasure.

'It would be so nice to see you licking one, Mary-ʒe. These tender tongue-ʒ are not just eaten to curb appetite, they also create appetite, of a carnal nature, in young girl-ʒ.'

He was salivating now and I spat the thing out at once.

'Then I will not eat it,' I said.

He sulked awhile, but asked me to at least save some for later, so they would not be squandered. In order not to quarrel, I wrapped some loosely in a napkin and thrust them in my pocket.

When I looked up again, my eyes chanced to flick across the mirror and I received an icy bolt of shock. I thought I saw my face upon its surface, briefly, as a wasted, painted hag. When I gazed into it again the image had dissolved, but I was much disturbed. My thoughts turned back to my lady's recent wedding feast, when I had dined with her family in the great hall. I had been almost as good as an honoured guest, although I was only an attending-lady.

I thought of the precious gold and porcelain platter from which I'd eaten then, the rose-coloured glass from which I'd drunk and the refined conversation to which I had been privy.

I could not help but see my present situation in stark, unpleasant contrast to this day. I thought of Hugh La Marche and the passion I had carried for him. Then a novel thought arose in me. *Why must I squander myself on this old dog, even if I have no dowry? Why should not I strive for a greater life? Perhaps I am, after all, made for some higher purpose.*

The yeoman was much displeased when I stood up suddenly to go. He followed me out through the curtains, through the dingy tavern and down the street. All the time he was calling after me. 'Mary-*ze*! Mary-*ze*, come back!'

But I was young and light of foot, and soon I had outrun him. After a time I stopped for breath, and only then did I see the trail of bedraggled curs that had collected behind me. They sniffed me now as though they would eat me. A small boy laughed and pointed at me, saying I must taste good. I hissed at him, baring my teeth. I told him I would have *him* for my supper. With large, deliberate motions, I took one of the tongues from my pocket, unwrapped it and held it up for him to see.

The boy screamed and when I licked it, he ran off in terror. I felt a sudden rush of lightness and of joy and laughter bubbling up inside.

One by shrivelled one, I fed the tongues to the dogs.

By this time, I had also come upon Maria's forgotten (now dirtied) letter to Gui d'Ussel. The only thing to do was take it out, throw away the envelope and roll it up instead so it looked fresh. There was no shame in taking a drink with the yeoman on a free day, and I could tell Maria the truth about what had passed. In fact, as it was now opened, I saw no harm at all in reading it. One small advantage of growing up in the Turenne nursery was that I'd been taught my letters as well as the three sisters; Élise had seen to it.

Dear Gui,

You may wonder why I have not been to see you for so long. I have been ill. I know how well you will understand when I say this sickness is more spiritual than physical, and therefore all the harder to draw out. I wonder if your bright eyes will pierce through my confusion and help me discover a cure?

Perhaps you have already heard it rumoured that I have been engaged these six weeks past. I am sorry I was not more forthcoming with this intelligence, but we were so preoccupied with our arguments and I never could find the right moment to speak of it to you. Perhaps I did not wish to...

The engagement was to a good man, a truly noble one whom I respect, but do not love. I repeat again, for your eyes and ears alone, hear my voice when I say I do not love Ventadorn. I don't believe I would have finally married him had I not been forced to do so by my father. Yes, Gui, I have been married against my will since last I spoke with you. I know how strange this will appear to you, especially since... It was that kiss that brought me to my senses, for I have never known before what it is to love, although I played at it.

I only ask that you forgive me for what I have done, and believe me when I say I could not help it. It is with a cruel irony I see again the old argument rearing its ugly head: a lady is not free to choose her husband, though she is free to choose her lover. I hope you will see the truth of this now and not despise me for what I have done.

Please write and tell me that you understand.

Although my body will be borne away to Ventadorn this spring, my spirit will remain.

Yours,
Lady Maria de Turenne

I folded the letter carefully and thought for a moment what to do. I wondered what would happen if its contents were made known to the viscount. It may be that Maria would be disgraced. And yet the letter proved that they had only kissed, and this had occurred before her marriage. In all likelihood, the letter would simply be destroyed with a reprimand. I, however, would have gained the reputation as a snitch. I concluded that it would not be to my advantage to disclose the letter's secrets. But this was not the only reason I would not tell a soul of it.

It seemed that, after all, Maria and I were equal on some level. It seemed that, despite all my misgivings, love might not be Maria's birthright either; in spite of all her beauty, talent and high-breeding. *I had an equal chance of finding love.* And with the thought, I found great peace of mind.

Gui's face was turned away as he read the letter so that I could not gauge his reaction. I asked if I need wait for his reply, but he said no. I told him I'd return later to collect it.

A carriage had drawn up outside the château, and I noted one of Angelique's trunks being carried in. So she had finally returned to comfort her sister. I was truly grateful, for Maria was a burden in her present state and I could not endure her.

As I walked past her chamber, I caught the tone of troubled talk within and so I went to spy on them awhile. They were clasping each other tightly and Angelique was crying rather passionately.

'So it seems we are both of us married,' said Maria.

'Yes,' said Angelique. 'Father must be pleased, to have rid himself of two birds at once.'

Angelique repeated more than once that she was sorry, and I strained to listen more closely.

'You see,' said Angelique, drawing aside her cloak and pushing forth her belly. There was a small bump there, which could only mean one thing.

'And this is the reason Father hastened the marriages,' Maria said. 'For of course, the youngest could not be married without the other two going first, and especially not to a youngest brother with no fortune to inherit.'

Through her tears, Angelique again repeated she was sorry.

'Shush, Angel.' Maria stroked her cheek. 'You did not know. Besides, it brings me comfort to know that I have helped you in some way. And we both know Father would have had me marry Ventadorn anyway.'

I felt a sudden rush of envy towards Angelique, for she had married for love and she was soon to have a babe of her own to care for. I wondered then if Aénor, the eldest, had known of Maria's furtive wedding before the event took place. It was likely that she had and that she had even endorsed the plan, for she was shrewdly ambitious.

Maria's spirits improved with her sister's presence and, as always, the two were almost never apart. Angelique did not appear to care that her father refused to see her and took her meals in private quarters with Maria. Towards the end of her short sojourn, Raymond finally summoned both daughters to dine with him, perhaps as a gesture of reconciliation. I attended the sisters' dressing and only then did Maria find a quiet moment to inquire about the letter. When I told her there was no reply, she looked greatly troubled.

'But have you given him ample opportunity?' she demanded. 'I am sure you did not wait on his response?'

Offended, I assured her that I had.

'But then you have not returned since you delivered it, and he has had no means by which to send his reply,' she suggested.

Again, I quickly dashed her accusation.

Finding Maria much distracted, Angelique asked her whether she feared the imminent meeting with their father. Maria replied that she did not fear their father, but neither did she look forward to seeing him after what had passed. Again, Angelique began to cry and I was ushered from the room on some pretend errand.

In fact, I was as curious as could be to see what response Gui would make to Maria's ambiguous epistle. This intrigue was far more thrilling to me than the stiff love poetry they had discussed before.

Finally, my curiosity was satisfied.

As Gui did not possess a seal, his letter was simply rolled and tied carelessly with thread which even a child could open. I took it to the mead closet, where I was sure I would not be interrupted.

Maria, When at first I read your words I was tempted to deny I shared any of your passion, but this was a short-lived impulse, born of the sting of hurt. I can hardly say what my opinion of your marriage is, without the risk of insulting or belittling you. When put in the same position by my father, who wanted me to marry a woman I did not care for, I ran away. I cannot help but wonder why you did not do the same. Perhaps some part of you — even small — was tempted by the life of ease and security that Ventadorn will procure?

I offer you my friendship and penmanship, nonetheless.

I shall attempt to salve any wound to the heart I have received with the balm of poetry. I hope you will do likewise.

Yours with fealty, Gui d'Ussel

CHAPTER EIGHT

I awaited my orders with great trepidation. My uncle, Raoul, was positioned exactly opposite me on the 'men's' side. It was the first time I had attended a *Tenso* exchange, although I had heard of them. A private tent had mushroomed overnight on the château green. The tent was creased down the middle by a strange, gnarled-looking wooden pole, lightly caressed by premature vines. Élise and her two daughters were seated to the right of the pole. On the left, Raymond sat between the two Ussel brothers, Peire and Ebles. I had been only vaguely tutored in my role and was standing stiffly poised with a fat piece of ochre chalk, awaiting the entrance of the poets.

A poetic debate between Lady Maria and Gui d'Ussel had been Raymond's idea, eager as he was to mend the current rift between himself and his daughter. There was, of course, a strategic purpose too, for Gui d'Ussel had been a prisoner at Turenne these five months past and questions were being raised about his future. His brothers suspected that the only course for Gui was to become a troubadour, for their father would never again allow him to set foot in Ussel and he would have no inheritance. Besides, it was the only pursuit he showed any interest in.

My uncle was a tall, long-nosed and imposing man with a most unpleasant downward turn of eyebrow and of mouth. The starched, metallic cloak he wore was chequered underneath with black and grey, and he looked to me like some winged beetle perched on the brink of flight and ready to do battle.

As he was in my direct line of sight, more than once I caught his eye unwanted and was forced to attempt a familiar smile at him. He did not return it. Instead, his eyes cast over me a look of detached awareness, as if I were a pawn in his game of chess, as quickly disposable to him as useful.

I had not slept well, and a sound like a distant foghorn was beating methodically on my skull. When I looked for its source, I felt, rather than saw it, in the biting breeze that had found an easy passage through the tent. There was nothing to do but avert my eyes as best I could from my uncle's stare until the poets came. He whistled at me then, as if I were a dog. I crossed to him, quelling at once my rising anger before it appeared on my visage.

'Take your chalk,' Raoul said. 'Go and write these words in a half-moon at the foot of the pole: "*Be·m Pesa de Vos* — I am Thinking of You."'

I lingered, expecting further instructions.

'Go!' he ordered.

The torchbearer had arrived and once or twice we almost bumped into each other, so busily engaged we were upon the ground with our tasks. A sweet scent of beeswax was filling the air and easing my aching head, but it was only on looking up I noted multifarious torches beneath glass covers dotted all about the tent. These exuded not only light and charm but warmth as well.

I stepped back to survey my work and found the writing looked artistic, lit up as it now was by a row of flames. I glanced at Raoul, but he showed little interest in my artwork.

'Maryse!' Élise called me to her. 'My daughters came without their cloaks and now they are cold. I have been trying to call you this past half hour at least!'

I answered somewhat crossly back. 'Madam, you can surely see that I am heavily occupied. If your daughters are cold, nothing could serve them better than a brisk walk to the château to retrieve their cloaks!'

They all looked at me, surprised. I rarely, if ever, spoke up to them that way. But my uncle's presence had unnerved me, and I was much out of spirits.

'Of course,' said Angelique. 'Forgive us please, Maryse, for our thoughtlessness. We can see that you are occupied. Besides, I begin to feel the heat from these torches. I am sure I will not have need of a cloak, is not that so, Aénor?'

Aénor blinked her beautiful moonstone eyes at me before agreeing magnanimously with her sister, adding that I should join them once my tasks were completed.

I nodded my acceptance and moved swiftly back to my post. Raoul was studying me and I feared he had overheard the exchange, though that was most unlikely.

'Ring the bell, the bell!' he yelled at me.

I saw no bell. I looked about me in a panic but still saw none. With long, swift strides, he glided over close to where I stood and pulled on a rope I had not noted there. The bell sounded a short melody, after which the poets made their entrance.

Raoul sprang forth to lead them in. Stepping between them, he managed to manoeuvre Maria over to the left whilst guiding Gui to the right. Then, batlike, he swooped back to his spot and stood as still as a statue, his long, tasselled shoes pointing out gracefully.

They brought no parchment with them, for they had memorised the verse. Despite the fact we were a small, familiar crowd, Maria was shining with the mysterious, captivating aura she oftentimes inhabited. Her sumptuous locks were beaded with turquoise gems, and her eyelids had been darkened to set off her eyes like jewels against her alabaster skin. She wore her indigo cloak open and clasped at the bosom with a pearl brooch. Underneath she wore a dress of raw silk coral which gathered like waves at the hem. The torches about were causing miniature, shifting lights to sparkle forth from the crystal necklace she always wore. She could, indeed, have been a creature made of some impermeable metal, extracted from the sea like glittering treasure.

Gui d'Ussel seemed grown from boy to man. His hair, too, had lengthened and was sweeping across his forehead and down his shoulders like a soft, fur mantle. His brilliant eyes burnt brighter than the torches all about. Although it had been offered, he had refused rich attire; but he wore his dungeon cloak of wool as if it were his natural skin. He moved about with a vitality and prowess akin to a young, Pyrenees bear, with dangerous beauty sparking from his eyes.

Maria looked younger than her years, and I noted her frame had shrunken of late. Though standing firmly grounded and flawless of gait, her lips were parted and she wore on her visage an expression of open vulnerability, which added to her appeal. All were looking towards her expectantly, for it was she who would start the debate.

It was Maria who had finally challenged Gui to the exchange. At first she had not wanted to, for she had been distressed at the coldness of his letter and her visits to him had ceased. But when she discovered that he had slipped back into a terrible melancholy, her heart bled for him and she was compelled to see and encourage him as she had done before. They had spent the past four weeks in preparation and though both their spirits had been lifted in this time, it was unlikely they would meet again once today was over. The first of the spring flowers were pushing their way up through the dark earth, and Maria would soon be spirited away to Ventadorn. Gui, too, would presently be released into the wild Languedoc hills. So it was little wonder if Maria hesitated to begin.

When she began, it was more like an incantation than a song. Her voice was strong and filled with compressed energy.

'Gui d'Ussel, I've been distraught
Since you gave up singing. In
Hopes that you'll make a new beginning
At this, and since you know about
Such things, I ask you: when a lady freely
Falls in love with a gentleman, should she
Do as much for him as he does for her
According to the tenants of amor?'

It seemed to me a fine opening to the debate; certainly Gui must answer precisely. In order to be fair, the men were adjudicating on Maria's side, the women on Gui's. As soon as Maria had finished, I noted Raymond and Gui's brothers were chalking something onto hand slates. When they held these up, I saw they had numbers on them. Raoul then added up the total and called out.

'Lady Maria has received twelve points out of fifteen in the opening verse.'

Raoul then strode across to the curious pole and chalked in twelve out of fifteen grooves on the bottom left: Maria's side. So this was how it was to be done! I noted there were six sets of lines on either side, each with fifteen grooves, and concluded there must be six verses in total. I would have to follow my uncle's lead and do the same for Gui.

When he began, Gui surprised us all by singing and not just chanting. His voice was sweet and rich, like figs on a summer's day. I had hoped he would not be good, for he was already so lofty and I did not want him to succeed. Nor did I care much to see Maria win, however, so I could carry out my task with perfect indifference.

'Lady Maria, I thought I'd given
Up debates and all those other
Forms of song, but when you order
It, how can I refuse your bidding?
Here is my opinion since you ask me:
A lady ought to treat her love exactly
As he treats her, with no regard to station
In friendship rank is no consideration.'

I did not think there was anything remarkable in his verse, which sounded to me just like normal conversation. His delivery was somewhat erratic, even if his voice transported one to summertime. I had to wait a longer time than Raoul to receive the ladies' votes, but when they did arrive they were favourable to Gui; he too had twelve points.

I moved across and seamlessly chalked in the grooves so the poets were equal on both sides. I even made a little flourish with my dress as I stepped back into place. Maria did not show any displeasure, even if she felt it. She drew the attention cleverly back to herself by walking about with long, easy steps and seeming to ponder her reply, even though she knew it already by heart.

'Gui, the lover should request
All that he desires, humbly;
And the lady should comply
Within the bounds of common sense:
And the lover should obey her commands,
Treating her as a lady and a friend
Equally; she, however, should regard
Him as a friend but never as her lord.'

The men took longer than before to mark their slates. They would have liked to dispute amongst themselves awhile, but they were not allowed. I was not sure I fully understood the argument myself, but it sounded like Maria thought the lady should never allow her lover to have power over her, and this seemed correct to me. I would never allow a lover to rule over me.

Finally, the collective vote was eleven; the brothers Peire and Ebles gave a generous four points apiece, but Raymond gave only three. Luckily, the poets themselves could not see the individual scores, for I was sure Maria would be cross with her father for voting against her otherwise. Raoul marked the pole again and Gui stepped forth, somewhat too hastily.

'Lady, here the people say
That when a lady wants to love,
She owes the man an equal share of
Honour, since they are equally
Smitten: and if it happens that she loves
To excess, then her words and deeds should prove
It; but if her heart is treacherous or fickle,
With a smooth face she should disassemble.'

Now, if I understood correctly he seemed concerned about the man not receiving true love, although he gives it. I had not thought on the emotions of the *man* before, for I was always thinking on myself. But then I remembered Hugh La Marche and how Maria had been treacherous and fickle with *his* heart, and I thought Gui's words sounded true.

Maria paced about now as though in fighting spirit, and could hardly wait for me to chalk in Gui's ten points before making her retort.

'*Gui d'Ussel, when they begin,*
Lovers do not behave like that;
They join their hands together and get
Down on their knees to try to win
A lady's favour: they say,
"Grant that I
May be your man and freely serve you, lady,"
And she accepts; to say
She should receive him
As a servant and an equal's treason!'

To hope to be received as a servant and an equal is treason! Surely I, a servant, was also striving to be an equal. Was I not in many ways an equal? I remembered the first time I had heard Gui speak about the troubadour Arnaut de Marveill's verse. Then, he had stated that true love should transcend religion, *even class*. If this was so, I could one day marry a nobleman like Hugh La Marche! This thought was indeed treason. But treason was most thrilling. Of course, I knew that none of this really applied to me, for courtly love was restricted to ladies of noble birth and the knights or troubadours of lesser titles who ran about after them. It was really of *these* men and women that Gui d'Ussel was speaking. This kind of love was not *my* birthright.

Maria's score was also ten this time, and now the chalked grooves were reaching high up the pole. There was only one verse to go, on Gui's side. He stepped forward, striking an unusual and arresting first note.

'*It's truly a disgrace to argue*
That a lady's greater than
The man who loves her, lady, when
She has fashioned one heart from two.
You must either say that the man exceeds

86

The lady in love (scant praise), or else concede
That with respect to honour they're the same:
The lover only owes what bears loves name.'

It was all very well for this boy to say the lovers should be equal, but what, indeed, did he know of equality? I could teach him much of inequality, but he showed as much interest in me as if I were a ladybird. No, he had eyes only for Lady Maria and wanted, presumably, to be treated as *her* equal. But he was not her equal, for she would be the rich and powerful wife of Ventadorn and he would be a penniless poet at best.

If Maria were to return Gui's love without reserve, as her equal, she would be diminished and impoverished. But it was only verse, after all, and I supposed his argument was good enough for fantasy. Still, I was surprised when he received twelve points; it seemed he was to win by just one point!

Maria took her defeat in good spirits, smiling and clapping along with the rest of us. But she did call out to say the debate would be continued in the future.

The torchbearer quite unexpectedly stood forth, setting fire to the wooden pole and we all, nervously, stepped back to watch. The flames did not quite touch it, but danced rather around it, leaving the wood unharmed. An ancient, Arabic script appeared beneath the flames and we all gazed at it, mesmerised, until the fire died down and the letters faded away. The vines hanging loosely about the pole had suddenly produced ripe grapes and two unusual, beautifully plumed birds alighted on the pole. Gui picked a burgundy bunch, offering it to Maria; she accepted the offering and they shook hands.

All of us were content to stand about in silence, eating grapes. The air about the place felt warm now and was sweetly scented, and my mood was strangely altered for the better. I was filled with an inward peace and contentment, which was rare for me, and I did not even mind the menacing presence of my uncle.

CHAPTER NINE

The warm glow of contentment I had felt at the close of the love-debate lasted for some days after. During this time, Angelique was once again resident at Turenne. Her belly had grown round, and all the people knew she was married and with child. They wondered, as I did, how the couple would make do, for Richard Montvert had no land to inherit. Unless he could earn a living somehow, they would be dependent on others for their keep.

It was no great surprise then when the viscount announced that he would accompany Angelique back to the château Montvert, where he would help them make arrangements. Aénor and Maria's advantageous matches would surely help secure the couple's future, though I was not sure exactly how.

I noted some tension brewing between Maria and Angelique. I was glad of it, for it made my lady more attentive towards myself. Perhaps now that her journey to Ventadorn was looming, the stark reality of her position was causing Maria to lash out at those around her like any common animal in pain. I wondered if, in time, Maria's passions would curdle like sour milk, or turn from fiery flames to dampened ash. Perhaps it was the fact that she and Gui would soon be parted that quickened Maria's temper. Or maybe she was simply envious that Angelique had married for love and she had not. Whatever it was, by the time of Angelique's departure, the two were barely speaking.

It struck me I would not wish to be in Maria's position. For she would have to leave the man she loved and make her bed with another. Still, it would be no different really from the grief she had inflicted on Hugh La Marche, and so I thought that she deserved it.

Her suffering was surely no greater than what I'd felt when Hugh la Marche had departed for distant lands. I had learnt a great deal about love since then, and I knew for certain I would never again allow myself to be carried away by my passions. Instead, I would control myself and be strategic; it was the only course for me. I would aim high and retain always power over men until I had gained my desires.

I had, therefore, little sympathy with Maria's plight, for she was snivelling over a boy she could never marry, unless she wanted to forever relinquish her power and live in squalor and obscurity.

With Viscount Raymond gone, rules about the château were greatly laxed. It was for this reason he had not specified the date of his return, but only assured us it would be soon. This way, he hoped we would be on the lookout for him always and would not misbehave.

After winning the tenso exchange, it had been decided that Gui d'Ussel would serve out the last few weeks of his sentence in relative comfort. He was to be given a bare servant's loft, where he was expected to work on the verse which would be his livelihood after release. He would remain strictly confined to this chamber and would not be permitted to wander elsewhere. Two men-at-arms were placed at his door to keep an eye on him in case he tried to escape, though this was considered unlikely as he had nowhere to go.

Raymond was eager for Maria to be dispatched before he left, but Élise insisted her daughter remain as her sole companion until his return. A roll of pressed linen had just arrived from Rennes, and we would be kept busy preparing it for Ventadorn's great table. Once this task was completed and the chill March wind had given way to softer, April breezes, Maria would go to Ventadorn.

The next day, Élise, Maria and I spent all morning and afternoon dutifully stitching patterns of forest ferns and leaping fauna onto the fine cloth. When eventually our fingers grew tired of the tedious handiwork, we sought some other means of diversion. Élise suggested we visit Gui d'Ussel in his new accommodation.

'I do not see why he need be *entirely* confined,' she said. 'When your father directed he be kept out of sight, I am sure he did not mean him to be kept out of *our* way. No, I am certain that your father meant him to be kept out of the *public* eye, in case the sight of him would stir up trouble. It would be pleasant entertainment, would it not, to hear him sing again. Maria, you should ask him to recite his compositions for us. In return, we shall take some things to him so he does not feel so bleak and alone.'

Élise was all brisk busyness now as she ordered the cook to prepare a tray and sent me with Maria to procure some wine. I could sense Maria's growing excitement; her colour had risen and her eyes betrayed inward turbulence. Although I hated to admit it, I too felt my spirits soar at the prospect of hearing again the voice of sweet summertime. Our needlework was abandoned into a random, misshapen pile and would not be resumed again until the first dust from the viscount's carriage rose up on the road.

We arrived at his door bearing a miniature feast. Élise excused the guards, bestowing on each of them a generous helping of food and wine as well as a small purse of gold. When we entered, Gui was positioned at his writing desk. After his initial surprise, he smiled at all of us in kindly fashion, offering up his only chair for Élise. The room was indeed bare, but he found some cushions and arranged them on the floor for us.

At first, the conversation was stilted and no one knew of what to speak. We informed him of the viscount's departure, though he said he had already heard of it, of course. Élise then asked him how he fared and he replied, formally, that he wanted for nothing. It was only when she complimented him on his tenso performance that he grew really engaged.

'Did you not think,' asked he, 'that I answered too hastily on the second verse? I am sure my voice was shaking the entire time!'

His self-absorbed questions irked me, but Élise encouraged him and Maria told him it was all simply a matter of breathing more deeply. I noted he addressed Élise most of the time and scarcely glanced at Maria.

After a time, though, they lost their shyness and were tripping over themselves with important things to say, or so they thought. Happily, the food and wine was shared out evenly between us. Although Gui's candles were lit, he had no fire and so the room grew cold as evening fell. Élise and Maria were given blankets to wrap around themselves, but there was none for me.

As night drew in, Maria and Gui sang out their verse like a pair of greedy nightingales eager to attract each other's notice. The singing served to warm my heart but did little for my toes or fingertips.

It was late when we returned to our own bedchambers. When at last I slipped into my bed, words of fevered love were drifting through my head like ghostly echoes. In the spirit of the moment, Élise had assured Gui that while the viscount was away, rules about his confinement would be relaxed enough to allow him to walk around the grounds in the early morning or late at night, when the gates were locked and he would not risk being seen by the townspeople.

When I awoke next morning at first light, my whole body was aching dreadfully, and I could not stir. I attempted shouting out to the other attending-ladies, but my voice was so weak it did not even carry through the thin curtains separating our beds. I was forced to wait until the dim creatures guessed something was up and ventured in to me with foolish timidity.

Crossly, I managed to whisper they must prepare my lady's bath alone and explain to her that I had taken ill. She would be surprised, for I was hardy and rarely indisposed. When they had left, I chided Fortune angrily for playing me this dirty hand just when the viscount was away and I could have had some fun.

Despite the fact the bed was piled with blankets and I was soaked in perspiration, my very bones were chilled and I was convulsed with shivers. As well as a throbbing pain between my eyes, my stomach was so nauseous I had no appetite. This terrified me, as I knew the illness must be serious to put me off my food. I had just drifted back to sleep when the graceless sisters were again at my bedside, discussing loudly whether or not to wake me.

'You see I am already woken, you loud-mouthed warblers. If in future you wish not to wake me, take my advice and do not enter at all, for you are too large to be discreet and too gaping to be silent. 'Tis little wonder no husbands have been forthcoming!'

That silenced them. They stared at the floor until I spoke again.

'Since you *have* woken me, you may as well report whatever it is you came to say!'

'Oh yes, madam, we thank you,' said the first. Their simplicity was so complete, the more crossly I spoke to them the more they tried to please me.

After an exhausting explosion of sneezing had subsided, they told me that Maria had insisted they turn their duties temporarily towards my better health. They were to answer my bidding and I was to be supplied with anything which might alleviate my suffering. She would go herself directly and order the court physician to come and examine me.

First, I asked for the fire to be built up grandly and kept generously fed by day and night. Next, I requested a special menu to be sent up from the kitchen, explaining that as my stomach was so upset, only very refined and special foods might tempt me. In fact, by the time the food arrived I was asleep.

Over the next few days, I was visited regularly by Maria and Élise. I could barely speak with them and could not conceive of tasting the hot dishes they offered, though they forced me to drink some fluids. The physician diagnosed a fever and ordered all who saw me to wear protective masks as he feared it was infectious, carried either on the breath or by small droplets emitted when I coughed or sneezed. He bled me to remove the infected blood and this left me weaker still.

The sisters were temporarily relocated to the attic. To be extra vigilant, the physician forbade Maria and Élise to come within twenty yards of me, a prohibition completely ignored by Maria, who came right up close, even removing her mask to better speak with me.

I was so feverish I could not distinguish night from day, nor tell how many days or weeks had passed since I'd first taken ill. I had every luxury I could think of brought to my bedside, including my very own tub of rosewater, but I could not really enjoy it as I was always sore and tired. I cannot tell how many days and nights passed before I was well enough to get out of bed alone and walk about the chamber.

Fancying I heard the voice of a throstle or a nightingale outside, I went to the window to investigate. As I was too weak still to draw aside the heavy curtains, I stepped rather to the other side of them so I could observe the trees and river below. The change of scenery hit my senses like a welcome rush of fresh air. Having just woken up, I could not tell if it was break of day or twilight, but I was glad of the gentle lighting and found my eyes could focus on many pleasantly familiar objects without too much strain.

I was just admiring the mysterious outline of the silver birches when an unnatural-looking shade of blue suddenly arrested my attention. In a dreamlike trance, I watched the curious object moving about like some large, exotic butterfly between the trees. At last it alighted, as it were, and stayed static for long enough for me to recognise it.

If my eyes did not deceive me, it was Maria's indigo cloak. Its owner was attached to it and she was not alone. Behind her, in the trees, a shadowy figure lurked but I could not make out who it was. The blue and the shadow appeared to intertwine, then fell apart again abruptly, before she ran out of the woods alone, back towards the château. I knew then that it was dawn, for the light was turning up fast with every passing second. As Maria passed directly below my window, I saw her face so clearly I could tell she had been crying.

I crawled back into bed and did not wake again until the sun was dipping in the sky. It was Maria's voice that stirred me.

'I did not wish to wake you, Maryse,' she said. 'Go back to sleep.'

I told her to stay, that I was feeling better. She took me by surprise then by wrapping her arms around me and holding me close, speaking into my neck.

'I am *so* glad! I cannot do without you, Maryse.'

It seemed she needed me now as never before, and I was glad my faculties had returned so I could think ahead.

'Father has returned,' she said, 'and is insisting that I go to Ventadorn. Mother cannot argue with him any longer, and so I must face my destiny and go.'

Her tone, although dramatic, struck me as resigned.

'There is something I must speak to you about,' she said, resuming her more formal voice. 'I know you have been courted these past months, and I have even met with your intended.' She paused, as though wondering how to proceed. I remained motionless, devoid of expression, feigning weakness still, if necessary.

'I find myself in an awkward position,' she began. 'You see, I wish only for your happiness, Maryse. And although I would be lost without you, if it is your intention to marry I would never stand between you and happiness. However, I would give *anything* to have you come with me. As it is, I am to travel to Ventadorn alone and friendless. It is, as you know, a vast estate and though I am sure it will come to be my home one day, I cannot yet *conceive* of that as I am ... so ... *pained* at heart.'

She paused awhile, gathering her composure.

'Let me speak plainly, Maryse. I am frightened. I do not wish to leave my home. I do not wish to go to Ventadorn. There, I will be a stranger amongst strangers, an exile. I will not be loved by Ventadorn's vassals as he is loved, for *they* have not chosen me. Although they must be courteous, I will not even know if they truly like me. I will always be a foreigner to them, although I will forever play the diplomat. But the thing of which I am most afraid is this: I fear that I will never again be able to truly be myself. You have known me since I was a girl, Maryse, you are a part of my childhood. With you by my side, I would not be so lost in this new life.'

As I listened I noted, yet again, her whole concern was with herself. She had only referred slightly to my impending marriage, returning all too quickly to her own affairs. I deliberately said nothing, only looked vaguely pained, as if in sympathy with her plight.

'Maryse,' she began then, slowly, 'I cannot presume to know your feelings. Correct me at once if I am wrong, but you do not love this yeoman, surely?'

I was surprised she called him 'yeoman', as I hadn't thought she even knew his profession. It was the first time she had mentioned him to me, and I was curious as could be to see what she made of him.

I saw my opportunity then, as clear as glass. 'He may appear coarse to one such as yourself, but he is kind to me and … generous. You see, Maria, I am not in such a position to *choose* my husband freely.'

I knew this would strike a familiar note with her and sure enough, she agreed with me at once.

'It is just as I thought, then,' she said. 'You do not love him, but you see no other course for yourself but to marry him and live comfortably. I would never propose that you come with me if I thought I was breaking up a love affair. It is true that we are not getting any younger, Maryse, but I believe you could do better than this *yeoman*. At Ventadorn you may meet with another who takes your fancy, and I would never stand in the way of a match made for love.'

'My lady —' I rarely used the formal title with her — '*love* is all well and good, but one has to eat. I am not like you, I have never considered love to be my birthright. I must think to my pocket before my heart. It is the saddest truth, but I do not know if I can afford not to marry the yeoman.'

I was surprised at how natural my speech sounded, despite the fact my heart was beating fast. It seemed I was on the verge of striking a deal. Maria considered what I had said; then, as if a thought had just struck her, she spoke with some excitement.

'As mistress of the estate, I would have some power and I have some fortune of my own. Maryse, what if I said I would see to it that you are paid a proper wage? You would not have to share your bedchamber and if you fell in love you would, of course, be free to go.'

It was an exceptional offer. As I had already broken with the yeoman, I had nothing to lose and everything to gain. Of course, I still did not jump at it but dissembled, rather, a disturbed expression and said I would have to think on it awhile. I assured her of my undying allegiance but said my conscience was troubled regarding the yeoman. Although I did not love him, I said, I would in time have come to care for him and so to break it off was no small matter. Also, the compensation that she so generously offered *in gold* (I craftily added) meant little to me compared with these much weightier concerns, but they would at least be of practical value and make her proposal feasible.

I noted Maria looked drawn, pale and tired, yet her eyes exuded a peculiar light I had not marked before. She noted me studying her, I think, for she suddenly blushed and turned away.

'Think on it, Maryse,' she said. 'But let your decision be hasty enough, as my departure is imminent.'

I promised her I would not ponder it long.

She went to leave then turned back. 'I would dearly love to have my friend with me on this journey,' she said.

The words were uttered with such sincerity I was touched and strangely saddened all at once.

'Maria,' I called after her, 'I will come with you to Ventadorn with all my heart. I cannot conceive of doing otherwise.'

CHAPTER TEN

The day was still newborn by the time we set off on horseback. Ventadorn and his attendants went before us. We wore thin headscarves to keep the dust off our hair and light, pink gowns of silk.

It was midday by the time we reached the forest's edge. The mournful sounding of a horn stopped us in our tracks. Two more notes followed closely behind, signalling a hunt. The air bristled with watchful listening and in the distance, sure enough, we heard the barking of hounds and collective thud of horses' hooves.

'A hunt,' the men declared, gazing longingly after the sound.

Ventadorn rode up beside Maria. 'Dearest,' he said, 'would you mind taking your luncheon here in the glade while my men and I join with this hunt awhile? I feel it would do the men much good to send their blood coursing through their veins this way and spend it thus rather than fighting in the tavern later, as they often do! We will not be away long, and you would benefit from some refreshment.'

We were more than content to be left to our own devices. As soon as the men rode off we removed our headdresses and kicked off our footwear, spreading our picnic things out on the grass.

The sensation of warm sun on my face as I ate was indeed pleasant. The trees around were large and well spaced-out and many were in budding leaf. The elm — I believe — was sprouting a pale green, baby leaf which had yet to turn thick and velvety. Many of these leaflings were drifting lightly through the air, catching the sunbeams and sometimes landing weightlessly on our hair. The goddess Flora had cast her spell here too, for the ground was as full of flowers as the sky is of stars.

Upon one branch a single bird was singing sweetly, and in my heart I was glad to be young and free and excited about what the future might hold.

My uncle Raoul had summoned me to him the day before I left. At first he had questioned me about the yeoman. 'Your future is no great matter of concern to me,' he'd said. 'I believe I more than carried out my duty when I took you from a life of certain poverty and placed you in a position of advancement beyond your family's furthest imaginings — though I guess their imaginings are limited enough.'

He stood up, suddenly very tall, and started pacing back and forth. I did not know whether he wished for me to speak so, to be safe, I remained silent. As the silence extended, I grew uncomfortable and felt compelled to break it.

'Uncle,' I said, 'I am eternally grateful for the kindness which you and Aunt Isabelle so happily bestowed...'

Here he interrupted me, swinging around. 'Enough! If as you say you are *eternally grateful*, I simply cannot comprehend why you never informed me of your engagement to this yeoman, nor, indeed, sought out approval for the match from I, your closest kin at court. Imagine my surprise when I learnt that you were to break with this intended I'd never heard of and accompany Lady Maria to Ventadorn.'

When I went to defend myself, he shushed me again.

'You have done well, Maryse,' he said, 'better than I would have expected, coming from such a milk-blooded father. I am, however, *gravely* disappointed at this latest oversight.' He paused. Afraid now to speak, I simply nodded. Alarmingly, his voice was almost cheery when next he spoke. 'So, you are to accompany Lady Maria to Ventadorn?'

I nodded, carefully.

'Very good. There you will be always in attendance, as you are here?'

Again I nodded.

'Excellent. You will return to Turenne only once twice per year, I expect, at Christmas or for family occasions.'

This last was spoken as if to himself.

'To make up for your recent insult to myself and your aunt, you shall gather any intelligence you discover concerning the courtiers of Ventadorn and their activities. You will report your findings solely to myself whenever you return to Turenne. Mind, I do not wish to receive any missives from you about which silly gallant you may fancy and his dress or eating habits. Likewise, you may omit any common banalities about who sings, plays, rides or hunts the best at court.

'I simply ask that you make it your business to see and confide in me — your kindly uncle — those things which happen covertly, behind the fortress walls. Who is courting whom; whose wives make cuckolds of their husbands; who observes the rituals of our Church with fervour and who ignores them; with whom does Viscount Ventadorn like to do his business.

'There is nothing untoward in my request. I am merely curious and should like to compare the happenings in all the different châteaux hereabouts. I am sure I have earned the right to such confidences from my own niece?'

I nodded vigorously.

'Very well,' he said, dismissing me with a wave.

The men were soon returned, flushed and panting from the exercise.

We were climbing upwards now, and the ground became less densely clad with flowers and trees. We came to the place where the path diverged in two, where in the winter we had gone through the iron gates. This time we did not take that route but went instead on a more difficult, windy path which led always uphill.

'I have a surprise for you, ladies,' Ventadorn called back. 'It is not much further, we shall soon be there!'

Maria looked as though she were in no mood for games. I hoped the surprise would involve some food and rest, for I was tiring of the journey. We emerged out of the forest and onto a windswept plain. Nothing could have prepared us for what we saw then.

'The sea! Oh, the sea!' Maria cried out.

The hugest expanse and depth of water I had ever seen was stretched out all around as far as the eye could see. It was the mottled turquoise of blackbirds' eggs with shards of brighter light playing across the surface, dazzling to the sight.

Our horses lined up nervously before it. Ventadorn cautioned that we were standing on a cliff and pointed out the waves beneath, which were licking and biting pieces of the earth on which we stood and dragging them back as sacrifices to their master, the Sea.

The castle of Ventadorn was as though carved out of rock, standing as it was on the exposed cliff top, with caves and arches for cellars and dungeons. I remembered that, as girls, we had sometimes come upon the sea in tales or drawings, and Maria would always beg her father to take her there, but he had refused, saying it was too far. It seemed that Fortune had designed to make it all the more spectacular when her wish was finally granted.

The guards shouted their orders for the drawbridge to be lowered, and soon our horses were trotting down the avenue of the château de Ventadorn. Servants, male and female, young and old were lined up, gawking at us, the new arrivals. Some lords and ladies too had turned out to observe us. Comments were made and murmurs of approval went round concerning Maria. She was deemed to be more beautiful in the flesh than the poets had depicted her in verse. I was not worth much comment but was stared at nonetheless as a novelty, after they tired of gawking at Maria. I was not afraid to outstare them, for I had little to fear or hide from anyone.

I noted that the servants' attire was not nearly as neat or clean as at Turenne, and I was shocked to see at least one young female with long hair hanging loose. Élise would never have tolerated such slovenly habits. Even the lords and ladies were much less elegantly dressed; their clothing was of linen, not of silk, and their colours were muted, not vibrant, like ours. Neither did the folds of the ladies' gowns move gracefully with the body as ours did.

Maria requested we be shown at once to our chambers and our trunks be carried up. She was escorted to the viscount's grand bedchamber; I was to sleep next door to be always close at hand. I was pleased with this arrangement and glad that Maria was keeping her promises. It was unusual for an attending-lady to be thus privileged, and it seemed it had already caused some ruffling of feathers, for I overheard comments from the servants as we were passing through. I was certain these comments were directed nastily at myself, for they were made out of my lady's earshot. I responded by taking on an air of great importance, as if I were some person of note. I would soon put them in their place, these court frights, with their untidy hair and shabby clothing.

Being so far away from home amidst total strangers had planted a seed of recklessness in me, as if I were invisible. I revelled much in the mixture of resentment and curiosity I detected in the expressions of those around us and wondered how I could take advantage of their fears and envies. I was surprised when, as soon as we found ourselves alone in the viscount's bedchamber, Maria dragged off her headdress in a fury.

'This is *intolerable*,' she began.

'What ails you, Maria?' I asked.

'I had not thought I would be forced to share Ventadorn's bed the very day of my arrival. I had thought I would be given time before… We do not even know one another!'

I pondered the situation. She had been allowed many weeks of liberty at Turenne before Ventadorn had laid claim to her, so surely he had waited long enough. Yet still it *did* seem unpleasant that she should have to lie with a man she did not know. She was a virgin, after all, and so, of course, she was afraid.

'I have heard,' I began, 'that it is not all that unpleasant for the lady.'

She glanced at me with amusement. '*That* is not really what concerns me most,' she said. 'I simply cannot abide this whole arrangement. That a woman should be forced to marry at all and then that she should be kept in chains within that marriage, beginning with the bedchamber, chains of convention and expectation. Why cannot I freely choose where and when to lie with my husband? You'll see, Maryse, if you walk about tonight after we are retired; you'll hear the bawdy whisperings. They'll not be happy until the sheets are soaked in blood and an heir has been conceived. It is all so barbaric, such poison to love. Ventadorn and I don't stand a chance in such a climate.'

I dared not respond. It was most unusual for her to speak so freely with me, but who else had she now?

She read my unmasked thought. 'My apologies, Maryse, I am not good company today. I am much disturbed.'

We unpacked her things in silence, beginning with her precious vessels. Her earthenware bathing tub had been bundled like a baby into the luggage carriage. She'd wrapped these up herself when I'd been ill. It had been left to me to pack her clothes and fabrics only; she'd not entrusted any of her valuables to my care, nor to any other servant's either. I wondered now if this was because she feared the dipping of soiled fingers into her pure oils, or perhaps she knew — too truly — that none but herself would pack her things with real care. Indeed, when the two ungainly attending-sisters had offered to help me pack, I'd laughed at them outright. As if I'd let their long, pale, awkward fingers near my things, and my meagre possessions were not *nearly* as fine or costly as hers. So caught up was I in musing thus that I was unprepared for what happened next.

I was liberating another of her objects when, unexpectedly, I uncovered the clear glass perfume bottle of night-sky blue elixir which was meant to bring pleasure to women. Out of Maria's extensive collection, this item was my favourite and I'd spent many hours, all in all, thinking on it and wishing it were mine.

'The seal!' I cried. 'The seal has been broken… How has it happened?'

It had a special love-heart clasp of silver which had been expertly undone, as far as I could tell, by a small hand too. It was impossible that it had happened by accident; it was too neatly achieved.

'There is some liquid gone from it,' I said, turning towards her for an explanation.

'I have noticed sometimes, Maryse, a tendency in you to be nosy. I should not need to explain the use of any of my ointments to you or anyone else. But since you ask, it would hardly be surprising if I chose the day I lie with my new husband as an apt enough occasion to try the potion?'

I had given too much away and had been put quite firmly in my place.

At the evening banquet, I dined alone and friendless. Ventadorn and Maria rose early to leave the hall. I followed them not long after and was amazed to see a crowd already gathered outside their door. The stone walls of the castle were as full of holes and imperfections as the servants' clothing, so it was easy to find a chink through which to spy on them. I watched the others watching for some time before making my presence known. Here at Ventadorn, it seemed that men and women went around together more freely than they had been permitted to do at Turenne. Both sexes watched together now, and much commentary was made as Maria removed her outer garments. The men were growing frisky, while the women's focus was more on the sumptuousness of her clothing than on the succulence of her skin.

'I wonder if the old stud is still up to the mount,' one of the men jeered. The women tittered, enjoying reducing the great lady to the status of a well-bred mare.

'*My* filly will not escape me long,' said one lad, grabbing a pretty girl around her waist. Though many laughed, the girl did not enjoy the jest but swore at him, scratching his arm.

'Shush,' an angry hiss went round. 'Do you want us to be caught and sent away, Rosamund? Miss the pleasure of seeing her broken in?'

The girl stalked off down the corridor, saying she wanted no more part in this. One or two more agreed, suggesting the couple be left their privacy, but no one else moved an inch.

'Why is he whispering so long with her; what is there to talk about? Get on with it, man,' one said.

'Wait! He's laying her across on the bed! He's kissing her neck, now her mouth, oh! He's cupping her breast. No, he's not forgot what to do!'

'Look, she's closed her eyes. Wait! She's up again, what's she doing? Ah! She's undoing her bodice, oh! Wait, what's that? Oh, she's removing the chain from her neck, in case he breaks it, I suppose, when he's straddling her!'

Maria must have removed her crystal necklace; I had never seen her without it. At this point I thought it was time to show myself. 'What's happening here?' I said, innocently.

'Nothing, Lady,' said one of the women, awkwardly.

But they became brazen again too quickly, not wanting me or any other to spoil their fun. One fellow stood squarely before me.

'We just came to see if he needed assistance.' He winked at the others. 'Thought if she proved too modest — or too fast — I might offer to lend a hand, or another part of my anatomy!'

I stared coldly through the tired jest. 'How inventive,' I said. 'How gallant.'

I bided my time, not quite knowing how to handle them. I was eager to establish my authority but knew the men were fired up with drink and lust, and the women, for their part, would happily see a new rival drowned.

'Please,' I said, assuming a gentle air, 'I have not introduced myself. I am Lady Maryse, closest companion and confidante of the viscountess of Ventadorn. I am pleased to make your acquaintance.' I extended my hand. Sourly, they introduced themselves, afraid I would report back to Maria, no doubt.

'Do not let me disturb your viewing,' I said. 'I would not watch myself. The priest at Turenne warned us to avoid such sights lest our soul caught fire through our eyes and we were damned to burn everlastingly in hell. Goodnight to you all.'

I watched with glee from my bedchamber as they crept off one by one. Soon the corridor was empty, and I went out again to spy awhile in peace.

Next morning when I knocked on Ventadorn's door, he came himself to greet me. He did not look like a man who'd been making sport all night with his new wife.

'It was late before we fell asleep, and I fear I've overslept,' he said, wearily. 'Maria has taken ill; it must have happened in the early hours, for she was well last night. She cannot stir and complains of aches and pains. We must call for a physician.'

Poor Ventadorn looked beside himself with worry and was only slightly comforted after I saw Maria and vouched that she suffered from the same illness I had overcome just recently. We'd been told that it was catching yet, typically, she had taken no precaution.

The physician soon confirmed what I had said. He asked that Ventadorn remove his wife to quarantine so the entire court was not infected. As I was deemed immune, he also suggested Maria share my chamber so I could wait on her.

While the physician was carrying her next door I gathered up her things, making sure her costly bridal nightgown and crystal necklace were out of thieves' way.

Maria did not share my strong constitution and so her illness lasted much longer than mine. Still, her life was not in danger and the physician assured us that, with plenty of rest, she would be as good as new by summer. For this reason, we saw no pressing need to inform her family.

Ventadorn was sickened so with worry that he hung around constantly outside the door. He was not much of an outdoors man, even at the best of times, preferring to stay indoors writing records of the counties and peoples hereabouts. When he did go out, it was only to take a stroll along the cliff; I sometimes observed him from my window, a solitary figure with few attendants, gazing pensively out to sea. He seemed to be an inward-looking man and was certainly concerned about Maria.

When an urgent message arrived from Turenne demanding Maria's immediate return, Ventadorn refused to disturb her. It was true she was too weak to undertake the journey, and he feared the news would shock her further into ill health. Angelique and her new husband had resettled at Turenne after Maria had departed. It seemed that Angelique had lost her child soon after and was seeking comfort from Maria. Ventadorn did not think the tidings serious enough to risk Maria's health, and so we left her be.

I examined Maria's necklace up close. It had been a gift from her parents on her fifteenth birthday, and she had never since that day removed it. It had a little locket with a clasp which, when tried, came apart easily. Inside there was a lock of dark gold hair. My first thought was that the hair belonged to her mother, or perhaps to Angelique, for it was much too light to be the viscount's. It struck me then it was not pale enough to belong to Élise or her golden-haired daughter, unless its colour had darkened over time. As this seemed a likely possibility, I did not think on it again until later that evening, after sunset.

I'd taken my supper alone in my chamber and was pleased to find my wild boar steak was of a superior quality to the everyday victuals at Turenne. Perhaps there was more to the château Ventadorn than first met the eye. Or maybe I was specially privileged as Maria's confidante, a pleasant thought indeed!

I was just draining the last of my wine when Maria cried out faintly in her sleep. Thinking she had waked, I went to her bedside but found her eyes still shut. She was muttering something over and over, and I strained now to listen.

'Gui d'Ussel,' she said. 'Gui d'Ussel.'

I hurried to soak a cloth in rosewater and drenched her forehead to bring the fever down. I would ensure that Ventadorn and all others kept away until her delirium had ceased. Ventadorn must never overhear her speaking the boy's name thus.

A thought as sharp as a needle's point struck me then; what if the hair inside the locket belonged to Gui d'Ussel? It was a perfect match for colour. Only then, strangely, did I recall the night I'd waked and wandered from my sickbed to the window and watched Maria, cloaked in indigo, fluttering through the trees. My thoughts turned to the elixir of night-sky blue which had been opened sometime between my illness and our arrival at Ventadorn. I wondered what had really passed between the two of them while I was ill in bed.

PART TWO

CHAPTER ELEVEN

Château de Ventadorn, 1204

Maria cuddled her newborn jealously, challenging the midwife's orders to release him to her. Finally, being separated from its mother, the little creature roared and Maria looked greatly pained.

'Take care of my cherub,' she called after the midwife. 'Do not let him get too wet. Don't leave him long without his robe. When he cries, comfort him; tell him his mother waits for him.'

Nearly three years it had taken her to conceive, but she had at last pleased even the malcontents by producing a healthy boy and heir. Not four and twenty hours had passed since he had entered the world, yet his baptismal ceremony had already been prepared, in case of sudden death and eternal damnation. Before Maria had finished her speech, the midwife had borne the bawling child away, so fearful was she for the little soul. I followed her out, arms outstretched, carrying the infant's robe of white linen and seed pearl which had been Ventadorn's own. As Maria looked so distressed, I hurriedly assured her I would see to it that the child be brought back quickly.

I myself was wearing a costly gown of pale, shimmering blue with lace trimmings and was conscious of how the string of sapphires round my neck made my blue eyes sparkle. My hair, only lightly covered with a band from ear to ear, had been soaked all night in lemon juice to give a special silken sheen. Tied loosely at one side, it was falling in soft coils as far as my bosom. I'd had my gown cut subtly low in front, so when I bent forward a tempting crevice appeared between my breasts. My waistband, though expanded with good eating, was shapely still and my skin much softened from the plumping out. With head held high and back nicely straight, I ensured my gait was graciously attractive as I displayed the infant's ceremonial gown.

It was for Lord Merle-Beaumont's attention I had attired myself so alluringly. He was Ventadorn's keeper of the treasury as well as the newborn's appointed godfather. His sister, Marguerite, was godmother. They greeted the midwife and myself at the chapel's entrance, and we handed our charge to them. I had hoped the lord would glance towards my bosom, but he was nervous and distracted, so I received only a customary nod from him. I was not disheartened, for I knew he would be more relaxed later, at the celebration, where I would see to it that we drank a cup of wine together. His sister took the child and I made sure that when I passed the gown to him, my hand lingered a moment on his arm. Perhaps he would not notice the touch at present but later, in solitude, the recollected intimacy might bring him a tinge of pleasure.

Six pageboys lined up on either side behind us and the doors were flung open as the procession began. I was not usually timid, but a rare sensation of unworthiness flushed through me as I stepped into the holy place of ritual. All eyes turned towards the infant as though it were a tiny bride. Ventadorn walked up front with Marguerite, babe in arms. Merle-Beaumont came next with the midwife. I followed after them, partnered with a knight, and together we stood for fealty. The twelve pageboys followed, carrying small, embroidered cushions with various gifts, representing the values of the château and its lands.

The great stone baptismal font had been lowered from the ceiling until it hung, suspended, a few feet off the ground. Made of twinkling, pink sandstone, it was covered with ugly faces, supposed to ward the evil eye off the newborn. I did not believe in such superstitions, but I very much enjoyed studying the distorted sculptures.

Water was flowing out from the font and pouring into many dug-out, floral shapes in the floor like little reflective ponds. Lilies and rose petals floated on the water's surface, infusing the air with sweet perfume. The walls about were supported by high arched columns of light sandstone, carved with tiny stars and shapes. Between the arches, rows of crystal windows looked out onto the lush, green and yellow foliage of spring, drawing the colours of growth and rebirth into our chapel to aid the general mood of lightness and joy.

The priest muttered a Latin creed and lifted the child up high for all to see. Then, scooping water generously with a large silver spoon, he wet the babe's head. His name was then pronounced. Eble VI of Ventadorn had no idea yet of the privileges Fortune had bestowed on him by birth as he roared at the top of his lungs in protest at the unexpected shower. The godparents stood forward to recite the prayers they were expected to teach the child.

Beams of sunlight cast a flattering, golden glow upon their faces, making the brother and sister seem a good ten years younger than their actual years. The little bags and shadows usually resident around Lord Merle-Beaumont's eyes were temporarily shaded out, and in this light I had no difficulty imagining him as my lover, despite his advanced years.

As soon as the ritual ended, I requested that little Eble be placed into my arms so I could return him to his mother. Ventadorn told me to wait while he announced refreshments in the round tower. He then insisted on accompanying me back to the grand bedchamber where Maria was anxiously waiting.

I entered first with little Eble, and Maria's eyes grew wide with pity for him.

'He's perfectly well,' I assured her, 'just a little red-eyed after bawling. He's well now, you see?'

As she inspected him the midwife entered, noisily. Only then did Maria spot her husband standing in the shadows.

'Eble!' she exclaimed, pleased. 'I did not see you!'

Their journey of mutual affection had been bumpy and slow-reached, but it seemed they'd reached a happy understanding now. At the start she'd shied away from him, despite the efforts he'd made to draw her close. Even after she'd recovered from her illness she'd continued to share my bedchamber, only going to him occasionally, on request. He asked me to persuade her to rejoin him, but I told him straight that Maria was wilful and had ever done as she pleased. In fact, it served me well to have her stay with me; I was considered a person of some consequence, since she confided in me alone.

Ventadorn, I believe, grew jealous of me, for he asked me to keep away sometimes so they could be alone together. But I ignored his request and this he did not like. He was a just and generous man who treated his wife with great care and attention. Though some liked him for these qualities, I thought him weak and was unnerved by his persistent, stifling devotion to Maria in spite of her coolness towards him.

In time my indifference towards him turned to dislike, for I could tell he did not value or like me as the viscount of Turenne had done. Maria did, in time, warm to Ventadorn. On finding out she was with child, the bond had deepened even more between them.

'Dearest,' she said, 'I wondered if I might ask you something?'

At this moment, with little Eble gurgling in her arms, she could have requested any impossible thing and he'd have agreed to it.

'You know that since my ... confinement, I've had to put aside our plans to offer residence and patronage to some gifted troubadour who might lead our Court of Love. Though I've not been consciously thinking on it, a name has occurred to me quite unexpectedly. If you agree with my choice, then I wondered if you'd help me draw up the terms of patronage?'

She was speaking with some excitement, and Ventadorn responded with equal enthusiasm.

'I have no doubt your choice will be excellent, for there is no one whose taste can equal yours in matters of *fin amor*. Who is it, dearest, you wish us to invite?'

I too was curious to know but Maria teased us a little first, pausing and smiling, smoothing little Eble's collar.

'It is the Monge de Montaudon!' she finally declared.

Even I had heard of him. He was the infamous, but gifted monk who sang of loving the comforts of the château much more than his hair shirt.

'Ah, the Monge! Indeed! An unconventional but excellent choice; his satirical verse is causing quite the ripple amongst his peers!'

'Do you think he'll come?' Maria asked.

'I should hope so. I've heard much good of him; word of his talent and wit is travelling fast around the courts, and he is in high demand. Of course, he has no fixed abode and he is always forced to travel from court to court. He's well paid, but I'm sure he would welcome a permanent dwelling place and a regular income. Who would not? We shall compose a letter to him this very day!'

Little Eble had fallen asleep in Maria's arms, and she passed him to the midwife who carried him from the chamber.

'I must return to our guests now,' said Ventadorn, 'but I will come back presently and we will put our heads together.' He kissed her lightly and walked to the door, swinging around suddenly. 'Oh, I just remembered,' he said. 'Last I heard, the Monge was travelling with a young protégé. You know, I heard his name but I've forgotten it! I believe it is the same fellow you had imprisoned at Turenne that time?'

'Gui d'Ussel?'

Luckily, Ventadorn was standing too far away now to see Maria's blanched face.

'The very same! It seems,' he continued, torturously, 'this Gui d'Ussel is showing remarkable ability. All who hear him are in awe of him, and the Monge has taken him under his colourful wing these past months. We shall invite him too.'

Then he was gone.

'Oh!' Maria cried. 'I cannot have him here, Maryse, and yet I wish to see him so much... I do not think I could *bear* to have him here at Ventadorn. I am not free now as I was at Turenne. What would he make of me now that I'm a wife and mother?'

Maria had taken me more and more into her confidence since we'd come to Ventadorn, but she had never spoken so directly of her feelings for Gui d'Ussel before.

She asked that I open wide the windows. The view from Ventadorn's chamber looked dramatically onto the sea as it crashed into the rocks below. Today the water was reflecting the sky's swiftly passing strokes of sun and cloud. Just now a murky charcoal was prevailing, edged with angry foam. Wearing only her light nightgown, Maria threw back the bed linen, went to the open window and gulped in mouthfuls of the salty air.

'Maria!' I was fearful. 'You'll catch cold! Get back to bed.'

She was not strong like me. But she ignored my request, as if she had not heard me. I knew it was useless to entreat, so I took a fleece from the bed and wrapped it round her.

'Why is it every time I am contented, as I was just now with my husband and my sleeping babe, something *always* occurs to stir up my passions frighteningly? I received such a shock just now, at the mere mention of his name, it feels as if some great damage has been permanently inflicted upon some vital organ.'

'Maria,' I could not help say, 'why cannot you maintain the peace of mind you had before? Why must you always allow yourself to be so affected and carried along by every new turn of events? It is not good for your health.'

But unlike me, she had never minded about her health.

'Why?' She looked at me for a moment, before turning back to the sea. 'Because I am like the ocean; I have such depth and turbulence of passions that I fear myself. I wish to live in peace with my kind husband and beautiful son, but I'm afraid my nature will not allow it. For sometimes I am calm and quiet and utterly content and then, suddenly, I am as restless and tormented as a raging storm.'

I knew what she said was true, for I'd known her since she was a girl and she had always been this way. But still I did not understand it; I did not believe she could not choose to change her ways, as I had done, to control her passions and her future. She would have to rein in her intemperance now that she was Viscountess of Ventadorn. I did not hesitate to tell her so.

'I thank you, Maryse,' she said, 'but I cannot alter my very being. It is for this reason I am afraid of the harm I could cause myself … and others.'

I saw no use in arguing with her further and was eager to get back to the celebration and find Lord Merle-Beaumont.

'Is my hair still neat?' I asked.

She told me I looked very well and urged me to rejoin the party.

Lord Merle-Beaumont stood at least a head taller than those around him. I did not go to him, of course, but stayed across the room and practised nonchalance. I fell into easy conversation with the château fletcher who, knowing few, was grateful for my company. Though seemingly engaged in conversation, I did not really heed what the fletcher said but only nodded and encouraged him so I could go on standing with him.

Many times I glanced towards Merle-Beaumont to see with whom he spoke. Finally, he looked my way and our eyes met. Proof, I believed, that he thought of me! The sound of tinkling laughter distracted us then and we looked to its source: Lady Rosamund, the Fair, was drawing attention. But I did not worry, for I knew I had little to fear from Rosamund. She was just a girl of six and ten and too highly desirable to be a pleasing prospect for the aged lord. A girl like that had her choice of any noble, and Merle-Beaumont was too sensible and humble to ever consider her.

I, on the other hand, had a soft, matronly appeal and with studied gestures was drawing his interest subtly and, I fancied, artfully. I'd been taking great care of my appearance and placing my finest assets under his nose at every opportunity. I was certain he watched me when I was not looking, for I had almost caught him out sometimes. Last week, for example, I'd feigned bumping into him in the chapel. Of course, I knew he'd be coming at that time, for he was predictable in his devotions. As he walked in, I made sure to seem hard at prayer. Eyes shut tight, I'd placed myself under the yellow-glass window where I knew the light was flattering, and I'd worn the cross of gold La Marche's man had given me, falling to my bosom. As he was a pious man I knew he'd not resist the sight of me, praying aloud that Maria might produce a son. When I opened my eyes I fancied he was staring, before he quickly turned away. I feigned bashfulness that he had caught me praying thus. When I rose to leave, he bid me a warm adieu.

As one of Ventadorn's closest advisors, he worked in the inner chambers every day and so I naturally came in contact with him often. But since his wife had died some months ago, I'd set my cap at him and placed myself where he would see me. I'd heard that he was rich, for he had inherited a great estate nearby and he was thrifty. As he had only daughters, it was whispered he would want to remarry and try next for a son. I'd heard the stout lass they called Lady Adel say she'd like to try with him, for he was rich and she was lusty. But she had three chins and two large moles, and I did not think she'd stand a chance with him. Still, she was a lady so I was wary of her all the same, afraid she might climb on him some night when he was feeling lonesome. I'd no doubt I'd have the skills to rouse him, but I wanted him to think on me in terms of his future wife and not just as an easy bedfellow.

My greatest fear was that I'd not be considered personage enough for him to marry as I'd been born poor. Yet I was independent now. Maria paid me generously and I carried my new status well, holding my groomed head in dignified and lofty manner. Surely no one would bother questioning my pedigree only to marry a wealthy lord, for Merle-Beaumont was neither count nor earl. I fancied my chances well, and so it was with confidence that I eventually strode over close to where he stood.

I bowed, slightly, showing my even teeth. I'd already planned my opening address.

'It is so warm in here, I can scarcely breathe!'

'May I offer you some refreshment?' he asked on cue.

I looked as though the thought had not occurred to me. 'Perhaps a cup of wine, but only if you're taking one yourself.'

He stepped aside to pour the wine but just as he was returning, the stout maid Adel made an advance towards him. Quickly, I started coughing loudly so that he rushed back to relieve me.

I smiled inwardly as Adel flashed me a thunderous look. I had his full attention then, as planned. I began with a discussion on the christening ceremony, as though I were as devout as he, showing off I understood the Latin so he'd think me well bred. I alluded more than once to my love of little Eble, brushing my hand lightly across his arm, suggesting I'd like to practise for a son myself. I believe he was enjoying our chat and it would have continued had Ventadorn not interrupted us. He asked me help to serve the wine. I was peeved, suspecting it to be a deliberate slight, intended to show me up as a mere servant in front of the lord. I bowed, excused myself and went about my business, but I was angry with Ventadorn. I wondered if he'd spied my strategy but decided this was unlikely. Still, I'd not forget his unkindness and would be sure to tell Maria of it.

I rose early to prepare Maria's bath. It was the first time she had bathed since giving birth, and she'd given orders for the tub to be lined with special seaweed before the water was added. I did not like to handle it, for it was slimy and seemed to me a dirty thing, but she insisted it held rejuvenating properties.

As she bathed, I told her a little of my displeasure over Ventadorn's interruption of my conversation the eve before. She questioned me about the lord, asking if I had an amorous interest in him. Caught unawares, I almost replied my interest was more in his gold than in his goodness, but stopped myself on time. Instead, I said I thought him wise and pious.

Maria pondered this, commenting, 'You should not be ashamed to like the lord; I see no great impediment to your starting a friendship with him.'

I could have hugged her then. I noted again some sadness in her aspect which was frequently present since our arrival at Ventadorn.

'It would bring me great pleasure, Maryse, to see you fall in love,' she said. Looking into my eyes she said, firmly, 'Love is *everyone's* birthright.'

I felt a sudden pang of shame, for Maria really was nobler in her heart than I.

A strange look came into her eye then, the same I'd seen shortly before we'd left Turenne. 'Love *is* every woman's birthright,' she repeated, slowly, 'only it is not always easy to keep it after it has been gained.'

I guessed she was referring to Gui d'Ussel. I told her that it was easier for the likes of her to gain it, than for the likes of me.

She promised she would help me try to win the lord's affections. She'd have me bathing in scented water every day, she said, until I was quite new-born. She said she was sure the lord would notice me.

I was pleased and told her so. She turned the subject then to another matter, closer to her heart.

'Eble has penned a letter inviting the Monge and ... Gui d'Ussel to come and compose here under our patronage,' she began, carefully. 'I told him I wished to add some final word to it, so it has not yet been dispatched. I could refuse to have Gui here... There is still time to think up some excuse, or remember some old grievance at Turenne which would disable the plan. I find, however, the more I think on him, the more I am compelled to see him. I don't believe there will be any trouble. I am the wife of Ventadorn and mother to his child... Gui is young and talented; he will have all manner of young ladies following him...'

I could tell this last thought caused her pain. Her earlier kindness had warmed me, so I told her she was not without admirers herself. In fact, she *was* still captivating. The years at Ventadorn had drawn out a softness in her manner which had not been so evident before. Every day, excepting when she'd got too big with child, she took long, brisk walks along the cliff, often venturing dangerously close to the brink. I rarely accompanied her, for I liked to use the best light for needlework and did not share her love of the outdoors. Still, sometimes I observed her from the window, her dark hair flying loose, a mysterious figure, moving amongst the rocks, sometimes singing, or with a distant look, removed.

I was not the only one who watched her thus; on more than one occasion I'd shooed away bunches of brazen young men who'd gathered at the upper windows to gain the best perspective.

'You are still beautiful,' I said.

She smiled, grateful for the compliment, but said that she did not mind. 'I am a mother now and love my little boy more than any man,' she said. 'I *am* afraid of rekindling the fire which used to rage inside me,' she went on, after a thought. 'I do not wish for any man's love, apart from my husband's, but I fear these embers — always slowly burning — could reignite … on sight of him.'

'But if the fire is given no fuel — surely it will die out cold?' I said, meaning that if Gui did not return her love, it would die out naturally.

'You are right,' she said. 'I must put the interest of the court and the future of *fin amor* before my own fears. He is a gifted artist and I shall be proud to be his patron.'

Over the coming weeks Maria took up again her long walks by the sea, and her strength and good spirits returned. She bathed each day in the jagged-edged seaweed. When she finished bathing, we'd tip the water out and fill the tub again. After she'd added some sweet-scented potion, I'd hop in. She fussed over my toilette and my dress, searching amongst her own nice things for some fabric big enough to fit me.

She was a great deal smaller than I, especially around the waist. She sent for the dressmaker to adjust some gowns and advised me how to paint my visage to best enhance my features.

These frivolous arts amused us and our laughter sometimes carried down the corridor to where Ventadorn stood waiting. We were careful to hang heavy gauze around the tub and dressing area in case anyone came spying.

'It is not fair on him, I know, to let him wait so long,' she said of Ventadorn. 'Yet he does test my patience by hanging about so idly. I wish he were not so *very* attentive. It would be natural, would it not, Maryse, for him to show more interest in the outdoors?'

I agreed at once, observing that the only interest he seemed to show was in my lady's whereabouts. I knew that Ventadorn only hung about thus because he was afraid of losing her, the wife whom he adored. But I could see the possibility of a breach in their precarious bond and I was happy to encourage it.

'I am sorry for him,' she said, 'but sometimes I feel smothered, and all I want to do is run outside and cry out my vexation to the winds. I would like to cry out my longings sometimes, too.'

What longings were these, I wondered? Since mention of Gui d'Ussel, Maria had been more restless in general and less tolerant of her husband in particular. I had some faint remembrance then of the longing I'd carried once for Hugh La Marche. But that was long ago and it had been replaced by ambition, which I knew now to be more important.

Maria never had given much consideration for the hurt she could cause to those who loved her, and it struck me she would end up hurting Ventadorn as well.

'Then other times,' she continued, 'I love to sit quietly by the fire with him and little Eble. I am a happily married woman,' she concluded. But I was not convinced.

It seemed to me Maria's longings had risen up afresh since we'd received word that Gui d'Ussel would shortly be arriving at Ventadorn. The letter to the troubadours had been dispatched and the invitation had been accepted.

When the first of the altered gowns arrived, Maria made me try it on and look at myself in the glass. I was pleased by the strong, fine-looking figure I saw there, with my own hair and a full set of teeth. I turned, proudly, for Maria's inspection. She was as pleased as I at the effect; the emerald-coloured gown set off well my creamy skin and would surely attract the lord's attention.

CHAPTER TWELVE

The day the troubadours came was the hottest so far that year. I'd been up since dawn, collecting eggs from wherever the château hens had deposited them around the grounds. The troubadours were to have omelettes for breakfast, and I was looking forward to some hard-boiled ones myself. I mopped the perspiration from my brow; it was not yet nine o'clock and yet the sun was baking hot. Having stayed up late the night before, I was tired and short-tempered.

Picking up a fat stick, I set about beating some birds out of the scrub. When they ran out, I flapped my skirts and shouted at them until they ran about quite wildly. Focused as I was on the fowl, Gui d'Ussel had ridden almost upon me before I noted him. He gave me such a fright I let out a small cry. The Monge was riding slowly up behind him. This was how the troubadours entered Ventadorn, without ceremony, to the unmelodious squawking of befuddled birds.

I stepped aside as they passed by, barely remembering to curtsy. Gui's glowing orbs alighted on me and an old, familiar feeling of dread swept over me. His handsomeness was even more startling than before, for he carried himself now with manly confidence and grace. We exchanged a nod of recognition, but I quickly averted my gaze towards the Monge.

Many of the court women had gathered and stood gaping now at Gui; he would have his choice of any one of them. The Monge saluted broadly as he passed and looked a friendly, happy sort of fellow. They made a contrasting, even a humorous pair; the one lean, striking and inward-looking; the other round-bellied, red-cheeked and curious.

They'd arrived a little earlier than expected and although Ventadorn was standing at the door to greet them, Maria had not yet appeared. I knew she hadn't slept the previous night; she'd told me so when I'd helped her dress. She'd been greatly agitated and I wondered if she'd calmed down since.

I did not want to miss the first moment when herself and Gui locked eyes, so I hurried after them to where Ventadorn stood waiting. After their horses were led away and their baggage taken, Ventadorn invited them to a late breakfast. It seemed Maria was already positioned in the great hall.

At first sight of Gui, Maria betrayed no sign of inward turbulence; their greeting was slight and formal. During breakfast, Gui remained largely silent, letting the Monge soak up the attention. True to his reputation, the Monge chattered almost continuously, whilst managing still to eat ten eggs! A lively fellow, he had a way of noting the peculiarities of each personage, making some clever witticism regarding them, but without real offence. He was not kind to them, but neither was he cruel. His language was so roundabout and clever I could not always follow it.

'We are grateful to be here,' he almost shouted. 'One wearies of the road. We spent a long six weeks at Limoux for the spring tournaments. Their youngest son, Richard, had his first joust. He took the heads off a great many of the *rosa alba*. Still, at least his brothers' heads remained intact, though perhaps not for long! The troubadour Arnaut de Marveill was there with us — a fine fellow, despite the fact we had to listen every evening to his whingeing. It seems his lady *still* refuses to comfort him, and after twenty years of listening to his complaints, who can blame her!'

Ventadorn laughed aloud. 'Yes,' he agreed, 'it is perhaps time poor Arnaut changed his tune. His tropes are well worn out. I hear great things, though, of his namesake, Arnaut Daniel? It seems he's airing the old verse and giving it a fresh, new twist. A welcome change, I'll warrant. What have you heard of him?'

'Arnaut Daniel is well enough,' the Monge bellowed. 'He has on his head a fine, thick mane of curls and wears the most intricate collars. If only one could understand a word of his pretentious verse!'

I watched Maria closely, for I was curious to know how she'd manage herself. To all appearances, she remained perfectly poised. I noted, however, that when Arnaut de Marveill's name was mentioned, her eyes flicked over to Gui who also glanced her way and seemed to blush. I recollected then the Twelfth Night celebration at Turenne at which Arnaut had sung and how, afterwards, they'd argued passionately over his poetry. Apart from the silent exchange, they hardly seemed to know each other.

After breakfast the troubadours were shown their new quarters and I accompanied Maria to the inner chambers to find little Eble. At her request, we diverted a moment to my bedchamber, closing the door behind us.

'There was such a distance between us ... and yet such closeness! Do you recollect, Maryse, the time when he was tortured and we were left alone with him? How his head was laid in my lap, although I knew him not? Yet somehow it's as though I've always known him, for he is so familiar. Why do you think it is so?'

She was pacing, feverishly.

'I cannot say,' said I, briskly. 'Perhaps you only *fancied* that you knew him, for he is so fine-looking.'

She did not seem to hear. 'Seeing him there, in this great hall, I could not help but picture him at Turenne... I *grieve* for

Turenne, Maryse, but his coming here is like a part of my lost home returned to me.'

Truly, Maria suffered much from her exile here and felt the loss of her old home keenly, despite her love of the sea. If she'd not been so wilful and waited such a long time to marry, she may have settled sooner. I did not indulge in such melancholy reflections, for I had profited well from the move to Ventadorn. Perhaps another reason I did not lament Turenne was due to my untimely and unhappy transference there as a small child.

'Do you recall,' asked Maria, 'that joyous evening we passed reciting verse in the loft where he was imprisoned? I was so euphoric afterwards I did not sleep for hours!'

I recollected how cold my nose and toes had grown that eve and how I'd woken ill.

'What do you think of his eyes, Maryse, are they not *profound*?'

I answered I did not like his eyes one bit; I believed, indeed, they could be dangerous. I said I did not think it wise to look directly into them for they may have a power which fascinates, like snakes in lore.

Maria laughed a small, light laugh; I did not know why. 'I had forgotten,' she said, 'how afraid the townspeople were of him at Turenne. I wonder if it will be likewise here.'

'One thing is certain,' said I, 'the ladies will not be afraid of lying with him.'

Maria looked at me, upset. 'Maryse, please try to refrain from speaking so basely of him. Remember that he is a nobleman and a great artist and should, as such, command your respect.'

Rebuked, I suggested coldly that we go retrieve her son, for he'd been much neglected that day.

Over the following week Maria and I saw little of one another. It was not long, however, before she was again in pressing need of my service. One day, just as I was about to take my midday nap, she called me to her.

'Maryse, I'm glad to see you.' She indicated for me to sit. She herself remained standing. 'Now that the troubadours have settled in and their terms have been decided and drawn up, we're ready to start making preparations for their formal welcome ceremony. I thought to run a few ideas by you. The scorching summer heat dictates that we must feast outdoors and that, perhaps, we commence either early morning or late evening. We will, of course, invite the villagers hereabouts. What think you of inviting children? At first I thought it would be wise to do so, so that their mothers could attend. But now I think on it, I worry that a child might easily stray along the cliff top here and stumble to their death below. I do not see how we can make the place secure enough, do you?'

I said I did not think it wise invite the children. Mothers of young bairns should either stay at home or find some relative to mind them. Maria often asked for my advice in matters such as this as I could foresee danger where she could not and had a much more practical turn of mind.

Château de Ventadorn was vast, but its outdoors could not easily accommodate large groups due to its hostile surrounds. On one side its jagged-edged cliffs dropped down to the sea; on the other side a thick forest of tangled elm made the way impenetrable this time of year, apart from a single horse track. Aside from the wild expanses of forest and sea, there was only one narrow strip of lawn to the back of the château which was, in fact, a sloping hill. This was the obvious choice for an outdoor feast, but Maria was not sure if it would do for the ground was so uneven. It would not even be possible to erect a podium where the troubadours might stand to perform. The Monge and Gui d'Ussel would sing that day for their excellent supper, and the villagers would understand the meaning and importance of fostering such talent.

The date for the troubadours' welcome feast was set for June 21st. As the day drew close, the maddening summer heat was causing me to grow most frisky. The careful guarding of my reputation became a troublesome task not easy to endure as more and more young knights flocked to Ventadorn to join the celebrations. At times like this I wished I were a scullery maid or, better still, a shepherdess so I could ease my agony by falling in the long grass with some sturdy rider. The heat between my thighs was rising fast and needed to be drenched with some man's seed. I did not know if I'd be able to withstand the pain much longer.

Since coming to Ventadorn, I'd often had the leisure to watch Maria preparing simple potions that could be brewed to raise the body heat or calm it down. Taking a basket, I went outdoors to find some water-mint to grind into a cooling paste and massage into my lower parts. As I walked through the massive doorway, my passage was interrupted by a tall, broad-shouldered fellow standing in my way.

'*There* you are. I've been looking for you,' he said.

My eyes squinted against the light. He placed a heavy arm languidly around my shoulders; I caught the tainted whiff of beer upon his breath. He gazed at my shape, pointedly.

'I've been watching you, m'lady,' he said. 'Thinking how nice it would be for you and I to get better acquainted.' There was no mistaking his meaning. 'Would you drink a cup of ale with me?'

I allowed myself the pleasure of running my hand along his strong arm before answering that my service was required elsewhere. Heat was surging fiercely betwixt my thighs, but I forced myself to turn away.

I spotted Lord Merle-Beaumont's tall figure standing at the gates. Fortunately, he was speaking with some newcomers and had not noted my exchange with the handsome squire.

Next moment, Maria was upon me. 'Maryse,' she said, glancing at my basket, 'I see we have the same idea! I was just going to gather some *pommes d'amour* and *lavande* from the shore. We can go together, if you like. What are you seeking?'

I mumbled that I hoped to find some water-mint; that I would go with her. I regretted the missed opportunity to speak with Lord Merle-Beaumont, but it could not be helped now.

'Do you not find this heat insufferable?' I ventured to ask.

'You'll find it is much cooler by the sea,' she said. 'The breeze is quite refreshing!'

That, at least, would be a welcome relief.

I was not pleased at having to climb down so many steps, dressed in well-spun silk. Maria did not seem to mind her skirts being ripped by rocks, but she could more easily replace them.

'Had I known we'd be coming this way, I'd have changed into something coarser,' I complained. She heard not this comment as she was already too far ahead. Despite the fact she carried a stack of baskets, she scaled the sharp decline much faster than I. It was true that when we landed we were rewarded with a delicious breeze shimmying off the sea. She smiled at me.

'I *know* you do not love it as I do,' she said, 'but perhaps today you could embrace it?'

When I looked about, I was quite dazzled by the brilliant shades of the plants and flowers covering the rocks.

'I believe more species have emerged even in the past few days,' she said, examining the rocks. 'Perhaps it is the intensity of the heat, or maybe,' she smiled shyly, 'it's because I've been singing to them.'

'That's very nice,' I said, peevishly, 'but my hair grows quite wild in the wind. Unlike your own, mine does not curl so beautifully, but only tangles and looks dull.'

'Forgive me, Maryse,' she said, 'it was thoughtless of me not to advise you to wear your headdress. I suppose I am so used to going without it here.'

It was true that both of us had long abandoned the customary wearing of our headdresses.

'Would you like to gather some fruit and herbs with me, nonetheless, for our Festival of Love?'

The activity was not so unpleasant once I'd set my mind to it. Before long, our baskets were full. I tasted a wild apple, enjoying the sharp, thirst-quenching juice sliding down my throat.

Maria had not spoken to me of Gui d'Ussel since the day of his arrival. Perhaps she did so now because we were far away from the prying eyes and curious ears of the courtiers.

'I've been instructing him every day,' she said, 'just like when we were at Turenne. His voice is rich and his verse true, but he suffers much from melancholy and from trepidations concerning the performance. I am attempting to help him overcome his fears. He is the same Gui,' she smiled, 'tremulous and unsure, although he appears so lofty.'

'Ah. Does he suffer still from his ... melancholic disposition?' I chose my words carefully, knowing Maria would be angry if I implied I thought him weak-willed or self-indulgent. My question pleased her. I suspected she thought his temperament made him special in some way. But I knew better. She had always been so wayward too that I supposed they were alike in many ways. They were like a pair of unruly infants, refusing to take responsibility for their lives.

'He said he was much afflicted with melancholy since leaving ... Turenne.' She paused, continuing, 'The only distraction from his pain was poetry. Seeing me again, he says, has been like balm to his wound.'

She looked not at me as she spoke, but I could see her eyes were lit up with joy. I felt a sudden rush of envy then and spoke a little rashly.

'It is a pity you are married already then, for maybe you would have chosen Gui d'Ussel instead of Eble de Ventadorn to be your husband!'

The bold remark had slipped out before I thought. I held my breath, not knowing how she'd take it. She turned towards the sea; I could not see her face. Her body stiffened but she uttered not a word. Fear gripped me and a muffled, conch-like sound filled my ears. It was really treason to speak as I had done. If such a statement were overheard, I'd be beaten or turned out. Finally, she turned to me.

'You must not say such things, Maryse,' she said, but in a gentle tone. I was much relieved. 'You know as well as I what little choice I had, for you were there when I was forced to marry.'

Her eyes darted back to the azure blue water. After a time she spoke again, so softly I could barely hear. 'No, we ladies are not free to choose our husbands ... though some may say we *are* free to choose our lovers.' She paused awhile, adding, '*That* is all very well, but to put such a theory into practice would cause much pain to all.' Turning again to me, she said in normal voice, 'We must return now, little Eble will grow impatient!'

The similitude between our plights then struck me forcibly. Maria's marriage to Ventadorn had secured her wealth and status but also, strangely, freed her to procure a lover under the terms of *fin amor*, of which she was an advocate. I too sought to secure my future by marriage with Lord Merle-Beaumont, and only then would I be free to indulge my secret fancies.

I determined again to be careful; I would encourage the squire no more at present. For both of us, it seemed, marriage and love were not to be compatible. Our lives were therefore destined to be duplicitous if we were to pursue our desires. My life so far had dictated I study well the arts of dissembling in order to survive, so I was well equipped for playing at the game. Maria, on the other hand, was a guileless sort who followed her own nature blindly without thinking on a strategy before.

In short, I knew it would not be so easy for her to conduct a clandestine affair. Likewise, it seemed that Gui d'Ussel possessed an open, impulsive and impassioned nature which would not abide by rules or conventions. Relations between these two would surely lead to trouble. I concluded I was better off than she; for I was crafty and subtle in my double dealings while she lacked the qualities necessary to thrive in such shady environs.

'I suppose we should go back,' she smiled at me. 'Did you say you wanted water-mint? I think there's some by here. What did you need it for?'

I told her I had no more need of water-mint; our walk along the shore and conversation had been as refreshing as a bucket of iced water poured over my head. She enjoyed the comment much.

'By the by,' she asked, 'have you seen Lord Merle-Beaumont today? I believe I noted his eyes drawing towards you last week in the banquet hall. That burgundy gown suited you well. We must dress you up prettily again tomorrow, for I'm sure it will be a marvellous occasion to flirt with him!'

CHAPTER THIRTEEN

I rose next morning at cock crow to the promising crescendo of horses' hooves outside. From my upper window, I observed the early arrival of many sumptuously dressed nobles, followed on foot by a train of plainly attired villagers.

I rushed at once to prepare my own toilette before attending to Maria's. A sound night's sleep had benefited me well, and it was with some satisfaction I inspected my clear eyes in the glass. I stepped into the dress I'd had prepared and pressed. The mauve, linen gown was cut low at the front but embroidered with tiny, white rosebuds to suggest overall a feminine but provocative purity. Around my neck I tied the daintiest string of pale green seashells.

Just as I was applying the faintest hint of blush to cheeks and lip, the maid Claryse arrived to braid my hair. Claryse was by far the deftest in such arts and always was in high demand at feast times. Normally reserved for the high-born ladies, Maria had promised to send her to me so I could make the best impression with Lord Merle-Beaumont.

The chamber quickly filled with the sounds of merrymaking and I was eager to be outdoors. I hoped Maria would have no use of me.

On sight of the viscount and Maria, my sense of well-being evaporated. They were much flustered and sent me about so many different tasks I was sure I'd find no time for breakfast. I cursed them inwardly, for of course they had not thought on that. Still, I was accustomed to such treatment and so, with a grumbling stomach, I carried out the work. Afterwards, when I stopped at one of the hall mirrors to tidy myself, a pair of glowing eyes bore into mine. I froze to the spot; Gui d'Ussel was standing alongside me.

'Maryse,' said he, speaking to my reflection in the glass, 'I'm glad we have found this opportunity to speak for we were, of course, acquainted at Turenne. I hope you fare well?'

I had somehow lost my tongue. Nor could I find my feet to move so I continued standing, open-mouthed and mute.

'I suppose you have met the viscountess Maria this morning?' he inquired then. *Now* I began to see why he'd stopped to address me. 'Would you be so good as to inform me of her whereabouts?' he asked, drawing in closer. I stepped back apace. 'It is *imperative* I speak with her this morning,' he said. Still I did not answer; he took his leave abruptly.

I watched then as he passed by others and noted how they shied away from him. Ladies, though they stared after him, approached him not, for he had hanging about him a remarkable intensity. It struck me he must lead a lonely life, but I was not sorry for him as I had ever been alone and friendless in this world. He'd seemed agitated, whether fearful or furious I could not tell. I hoped he'd not get in the habit of stopping me thus; a devil would hardly have had so unpleasant an effect on my nerves. I did not ponder the encounter long, for I had my own affairs to manage.

I turned my thoughts again to Lord Merle-Beaumont and whether he would like my braided hair. Satisfied at my figure in the glass, I wandered out to the lawn, where I was sure I'd spot his head above the crowd.

After much deliberation, we had fixed on the bumpy stretch of hill they called 'the lawn' as the only safe place to host the outdoor event. Hunks of ancient trunks had been sawn off fallen trees and smoothed to act as rustic benches on which whole families could sit, spreading their picnic things. Some elms were dotted round the green, providing a natural shade. The troubadours' podium was likewise whittled of wood which had been prettily carved with verse and painted a festive green and red. Their stand had been set on the west end against a backdrop of forest, providing ample shade for them and their instruments.

Despite his towering height, I saw no sign yet of Lord Merle-Beaumont. The courtiers and nobles of Ventadorn were closing in on the best seats whilst the commoners stood back, waiting their turn. Dressed as I was in costly fabric and looking every inch the lady, I hoped to be invited to take my seat with the best of them.

The Monge was already in place, tuning his lute and charming the small crowd gathered at his feet. He was dressed all in white with long shirt and bulbous pants; a turban of black and gold was wrapped generously around his pate. His cheeks were their usual florid hue and his bubbling laughter was both frequent and infectious. The troubadours would be as shining stars today, with everyone wanting to bask a little in their glowing light. There was no sign of Gui d'Ussel. I wondered fleetingly whether he had found Maria and why he'd seemed so agitated before.

'Maryse!' a man's voice called.

Swinging around, I saw a figure with thick, yellow hair waving in my direction. It was the squire who had flirted with me the day before.

'Come here, Maryse,' he called.

I was surprised he knew my name.

'I have reserved a cosy spot for you,' he said, gesturing beside him.

Had I not been seeking Lord Merle-Beaumont I'd gladly have sat with him, for he was well positioned on a spacious round bench, surrounded by knights and a few ladies. I knew not what to do and paused a moment to decide. I would perhaps be compromised if I accepted the invitation, for the squire with yellow hair had made his attraction clear. On the other hand, I was not sure that another invite would be forthcoming amongst a high-born group.

I did not wish for him to get the wrong impression, so I called my thanks but turned him down. Perhaps encouraged by my hesitation, he left his party and started coming towards me. Again he attempted to persuade me to sit with him. I assured him I would like that, only my lady was expecting me.

The falsehood had escaped my lips before I'd thought on it. Alarmingly, he then offered to accompany me to wherever the viscountess was seated. In fact, I was sure Maria would not sit down today but would stay at the forest's edge behind the podium to better encourage the poets. The more I insisted I'd do just fine alone, the more he persisted by my side.

Just then I spotted Lord Merle-Beaumont, but instead of walking towards him I walked swiftly away so he would not see me with the squire. The latter's presence was a great nuisance and I cursed myself inwardly at having started the day on such a clumsy foot.

There was little I could do but let the squire trot alongside me as I tried to think on a plan. Maria would be visibly confused if I presented myself to her. For this reason I steered him away from the poets into the thick of the crowd, where I was quite sure we would not find her. There was no smell of beer upon his breath today, and the squire turned out to be an entertaining and courteous companion. I brought him through the crowd until we reached the eastern gable and could go no further.

'She is not here,' I sighed. 'She must be indoors with her child. I must go to her. Do please, sir, return to your own company. You risk losing your fine view otherwise.'

Just as we were parting, a harsh, crashing noise rattled us to the bone. It seemed to have come from the direction of the round tower. We crept up close until we could hear voices arguing within. Placing a finger to my lips, I cautioned the squire to be quiet as we moved round the back to where the tower windows looked out to sea. Before I'd had a chance to peer inside, I'd recognised the voices as Maria's and Gui d'Ussel's.

'Step back,' I commanded the squire, who was closing in fast on me, 'this is a domestic matter.' Something firm in my tone planted him to the spot and he advanced no further.

I watched for a few moments what seemed to be a heated argument between Maria and Gui. I noted too some fragments of a costly vase which I deemed to be the source of the earlier crashing noise. *Just like them not to think on the cost of their passion.*

'Do not speak of paltry things,' I heard Gui say.

'What would you have me do?' Maria responded.

'Nothing,' he replied, 'your fate was sealed when you chose this gilded cage over my poor offering of love.'

I listened no more but hastened back to the squire. 'Come,' I said, 'let us return to our posts. There's nothing for us here.'

'I believe you have found your lady,' he grinned, but not unpleasantly. I could not deny that it was she, for he had heard her voice. 'I am sure any debate between the viscount and his wife is no concern of mine,' he added, lest I should think him disrespectful or treacherous.

I smiled, relieved. So the squire had mistaken Gui's voice for Ventadorn's.

'No doubt they will resolve the matter soon,' he said, eager to please.

When we returned, all the seats were occupied and I was forced, after all, to sit with the squire. The Monge was entertaining the guests well, and the people were all doubling over with laughter at his jesting verse.

Our company consisted of eleven, including the squire and myself, six knights and three ladies, one of whom was Rosamund the Fair. The knights all vied for her attention, joking and squabbling but careful of their code of chivalry. I wondered why the squire paid any heed to me with such a beauty in our midst.

It was her hair which first arrested the eye; spun of threads the colour of sunshine, it was like some glossy tail that drew the eye with every movement. Her eyes were as deep and mesmerizing as the rock pools below and her lips were a pouting cherry. Her smile and — even more — her laugh was like the lighting of a gentle flame in one's heart. She possessed also a seemingly flawless temperament, for she was timid and unassuming and unconscious of her power. Considerate of others, despite their class, she did not like to gossip. She was virtuous, too; it was rumoured she was determined to keep the flower of her virginity closed to any man who was not first her husband. But men could smell the sweetness of that fruit and went about half-crazed for her.

Her father, Sir Walter, was one of the most esteemed knights at court and a hero of the last crusade. He had come to Ventadorn shortly after the fever had taken Rosamund's mother. Sir Walter was greatly feared and respected, for he was a magnificent swordsman who trained younger knights in chivalry and battle skills. But he was viciously protective of his daughter. Although they all desired to push fair Rosamund down in their feather beds, not one of them would dare to touch her. With her beauty and youth combined, her father hoped she would draw at least a count, if not a king. Rosamund herself did not endorse her father's plans but hoped to marry for love, whether the man was rich or not.

The Monge was tiring and the crowd was growing restless.

'Where is the other one, the handsome one?' someone called. For still there was no sign of Gui d'Ussel. After a time some chanting started up and the crowd was calling for him.

Attended by some men-at-arms, the viscount slipped off to investigate. Muttering an excuse, I left my own perch and hurried back towards the tower to find Maria and Gui before the viscount did. I almost ran right into Lord Merle-Beaumont, standing as he was under a shady elm.

'Maryse.' He bowed, courteously.

'I cannot stay, forgive me!' I replied, breathlessly.

I saw some men-at-arms heading from the château towards the tower. I crouched down low in hopes they would not spy me and crept around the back to rap upon the windows, mouthing my warning. Maria looked up first and froze when she saw me there. The men were marching fast towards the tower door. It seemed Maria heard them, for she grabbed Gui by the arm and made a dash for it, exiting by the window just as they were entering on the other side.

The three of us then hid in a thicket until they had carried out their search. After discussing our options for a moment, Maria and Gui parted ways. I advised Gui to return alone through the château where he could make a late, dramatic entrance from the forest side. If questioned later on his whereabouts, he could claim an attack of nerves. Maria and I would wander back the other way, through the lawn, as though we had been picking flowers.

'You take too great a risk, Maria,' I said, angrily.

So far, the morning had not passed well. I was unnerved and tired and conscious I had missed yet another opportunity with Lord Merle-Beaumont. Still, I helped tidy up her hair and dress, fearful her dishevelled appearance would cause suspicion.

'You take too great a risk,' I repeated, more worried for myself than for her. For what would happen to me now if Maria was cast off? I'd not made friends with the viscount or any others at Ventadorn. I'd surely be cast out with her, and what would be my chances then of making a good match? I had a horrid vision of myself, penniless and dirty, running about on errands still for Maria and her lover, Gui d'Ussel. Despite the heat, I shivered. 'What about your son?' I said. 'Do you not think on him?'

She swung round towards me. 'I *am* thinking on him,' she said, fiercely. 'That is *precisely* what I have been saying all this while to Gui. But he does not understand; he believes I invited him here so we could be … together. He says he would not have come otherwise. He accuses me of deliberate cruelty for refusing to…' She did not finish, but I knew she meant for refusing to lie with him.

'He could have his choice of any lady here,' I said, huffily. 'Why do you not tell him so?'

'I *have* told him so,' she said, walking briskly away from me.

I sat down heavily upon the grass and accepted a glass of ale from the nearest peasant.

When Gui d'Ussel finally made his entrance, a bolt of energy darted through the crowd and sent everyone applauding. The exhausted Monge had gratefully stepped down, letting the younger troubadour take centre stage. Dressed in his usual earthy attire, Gui's remarkable looks alone assured a godlike presence. It was the ladies who were cheering loudest, their menfolk looking sulky.

For many years to come it was rumoured that when Gui d'Ussel made his first appearance, Cupid's arrows rained down on Ventadorn. For sure, throughout the day, many women swooned for love of him; perhaps some men did too. Although I did not care for him, I noted how his haunting voice played upon the heartstrings in an unsettling manner. Despite my better judgment, my eyes wandered back more than once to the squire with yellow hair.

I wondered if Gui d'Ussel was in fact some demon sent to tempt us all. I was not alone in believing he was dangerous, for I overheard some remarks about his strange eyes and whether they were 'wholesome' or 'demonic'.

'They say he does not even attend at Mass.'

It was true I'd never seen him enter a chapel door, even on saints' days when all were in attendance.

At midday, all the guests moved indoors to escape the brilliant sun. Loud utterances of approval could be heard as we filed through the doorway. Ventadorn's spacious floors had been lined all with silk instead of straw, in honour of the Festival of Love. Lavender hung all about in huge bunches, soothing tired heads while gently stimulating the senses. Baskets of pomegranates were passed about to quench the thirst and satisfy the tastebuds, playing upon them with a touch of sweetness.

For the high-born, this was a mere reminder of their habitual pleasures, but for the peasants, this was both a rare and welcome respite from the harsh realities of daily life. They looked about with awe and gratitude, and it struck me that if my uncle had not taken me to live at Turenne, I'd have been unaccustomed to such dainties too. But the thought brought me no comfort, only bitterness, as I did not really belong to either class.

Men and women parted and went to different quarters to relax or gossip, sipping minted tea and refreshing themselves with fragrant water and scented oils until the sun had started its descent and the troubadours had again taken up their instruments. The Monge and Gui d'Ussel had been joined by all manner of musicians and jongleurs who looked set to play and sing the eve away. Venison was roasting on a spit, filling the air with delicious aromas.

Feeling light of body and of heart, I stepped out with the rest in happy anticipation.

Maria and her husband were seated on an ornate wooden throne just right of the musicians. She stood to chant her opening address; she'd changed into a splendid silver dress and her hair was decorated with a tasselled scarf of heliotrope. The near-transparency of her gown outlined her perfect form and many of the guests gasped in awe. Her eyes seemed luminous, like moonlight on water. She peppered her speech with verses written by herself — and others — in the language of Love. The clarity and passion of her words drew many a tear from the eyes of young and old, high-born and low alike.

As Maria spoke, I noted Gui d'Ussel was staring at her with a fierce intensity. Worried, I glanced to Ventadorn to see if he had noted it, but thankfully he only had eyes for Maria. Once her speech was over, Ventadorn pulled her towards him and kissed her full and long upon the lips. The guests cheered.

Afterwards, the Monge and Gui d'Ussel sang some verse in harmony and couples formed to dance. Then many musicians joined in, creating a fun, full-bodied music which brought us all to our feet, quickly choosing partners.

I noted a young woman sidling up to Gui d'Ussel when he had stopped to rest. She presented him with the white-gold ring I'd earlier seen fair Rosamund removing from her finger. The woman then pointed Rosamund out to Gui d'Ussel and he bowed graciously to her. He had accepted her ring. I looked to Maria, wondering if she'd seen the exchange. I was certain she had seen it, for I caught her looking furtively at Rosamund, catching my eye briefly, before turning away.

Later that evening when all had departed, Maria called me to her. I agreed that all had passed off very well.

I felt all contented and aglow, same as I had felt after the *Tenso* at Turenne between Maria and Gui. Judging from their aspects, many of the guests had left with the same lightness about the heart. But I could tell Maria was much disturbed and I knew why.

'Maryse,' she interrupted my chatter. 'I have been thinking on it for some time and … I've decided to return to Turenne for a visit. Little Eble is strong enough now to be without me awhile. Angelique, as you know, has not been well and I have felt much separated from her. I feel the need to see her keenly.'

She did not say it, but I knew it would also be too painful for her to watch Gui d'Ussel falling for another. Or perhaps she was generous enough to realise he could not fall for Rosamund if she were present.

I said I thought it wise and proper for her to return home for a visit. Apart from two short trips at Christmas, she had not returned at all, though she was often homesick. Also, it was true that Angelique had been left sickly and weak after her miscarriages.

Maria was grateful for my endorsement and asked if I'd accompany her. I said I would, and gladly; I had some confusion of my own to sort out over the squire and Lord Merle-Beaumont.

CHAPTER FOURTEEN

The church bell was striking midnight as we entered Turenne and the ground was glistening wet after the rain. Soon the château came into view, its line of ancient trees all lit up by torches. The torchbearer met us at the gates and our carriage rolled down the avenue past the pleasing spray of rustic leaves suggesting the changing season.

'It's *good* to be home,' Maria said with feeling.

I too was looking forward to the break away from Ventadorn, though I worried that my comforts at Turenne would fall short. I resolved not to help carry our luggage up as I had done last time.

The weeks preceding our departure had been challenging for us both. Rosamund the Fair had placed herself so boldly in the way of Gui d'Ussel that he could not help but note her. With all her youthful petals still intact, she had no need of paint or artifice to enhance her beauty; such practice would be as futile as painting a flower. Rosamund and Gui, in fact, were not an impossible prospect and all were speculating as to whether Sir Walter would allow the match.

When asked directly whether she thought Sir Walter would approve of Gui d'Ussel, Maria forced a smile but made no comment. Gossip was such fodder at the court it was even rumoured the pair was secretly engaged. I knew the story was not true, for I had watched for signs of love between them, but Rosamund kept to her own bedchamber and never met alone with Gui d'Ussel. Still, I noted how distressed Maria had become and how she preferred to stay indoors now, playing with her son and avoiding other company. She greeted our departure with relief.

I too had been eager to depart, for I was in a most surprising muddle. Although I'd set my sights on Lord Merle-Beaumont, the squire with yellow hair had been persisting most annoyingly in my thoughts. It was not only that I wished to make sport with him in bed and fancied how he'd plant in me a pretty babe with yellow hair like his, but having passed the festival day with him, I missed his pleasant manner and easy conversation, for I did not have another friend.

I knew I must not succumb to passion as I had done before with Hugh La Marche; such weakness would be foolish, given how much I'd learnt since then. Still, I thought it wisest to remove myself from his sights awhile lest I forget my ambition.

The Turenne family had gathered on the wide steps to greet their daughter. Viscount Raymond stood in the centre with Élise. To his right were Angelique and her husband, Richard de Montvert. It was with some displeasure I noted too the long figure of my uncle Raoul standing alongside some servants bearing torches.

Maria flung wide the carriage door, disembarking before it had fully halted. I grumbled at the untimely disturbance. Embraces were exchanged and Angelique, as usual, shed copious tears. The youngest daughter had grown thin and her clear eyes were shining, not only with tears, but with the glazed light I've often noted in the eyes of the sick. Maria must have noted it too, for she held her sister longer than the rest.

'Maria,' I called to her, impatiently, 'shall I descend and order our things sent up? It is growing late...'

She ignored my request completely, as if she had not heard, and I exited the carriage alone. Only the viscount stepped forth to shake my hand; he had aged and was a bit unstable on his feet. After enquiring briefly about affairs at Ventadorn, he had our things sent up. Maria and I were to share the attending-ladies' bedchamber, for Angelique and her husband now occupied her old room. Angelique's lady had been temporarily lodged in the attic.

Maria's earthenware basin had travelled with us and next morning I rose early, as usual, to prepare her bath. Passing by Angelique's chamber, I heard voices from within and stopped to spy awhile through the large keyhole.

Angelique had not yet risen and was chatting with her husband as he dressed. Richard was not in view but I could see her clearly. She wore a heavy nightgown of rose-coloured linen which set off well her fresh complexion. With her delicate frame and peachy skin, she could have been a girl of five and ten. Her white-gold hair was tumbling over her shoulders and she was twisting a thick strand between her fingers.

'*Must* Raoul and Isabelle dine with us today? Maria has *just* arrived and I did so wish the family could be alone together for once. It seems that Raoul is here so often now, and you *know* I do not like him...'

My heart sank, for I knew she was speaking of my uncle and I did not wish to see him either.

'It is only for today,' Richard replied, 'then it will be over. They will disturb us no more and you will have your sister to yourself.'

'Still,' said Angelique, 'I do not understand it. How is it they were invited to dine with us today? I do not think you like him either, and yet you seem to pander to his wishes.'

Angelique's familiar boldness made me smile. Her body may have been weakened, but she'd not lost her spirit. When she was younger she'd been nicknamed "the spirited one", for she would always speak her thoughts directly. She was lucky her husband did not beat her for it as another would.

Fond of her ways, Richard only gave a little laugh. 'Raoul hinted at it so strongly last night, it would have been an insult not to ask him,' he said. 'Besides, he is Maryse's uncle and will wish to speak with that maid,' he added.

'Ah yes, I had forgot,' said Angelique.

I was curious to see if they'd discuss me any further, but it seemed that Richard had finished dressing. I thought he made a movement towards the door, so I skipped off.

Angelique's lady was waiting at the bottom of the stairwell. I knew the perfumer had already been by the scented fumes rising from the water.

'Shall we carry it up to Lady Maria?' I asked.

'To my lady Angelique's,' she said stoutly. 'The sisters would like to have their ablutions together and Angelique is weak, so it's better if Maria comes to her.'

This lady was devoted to her mistress and as she was hefty both of body and of mind, I thought it best not to argue with her. I asked her how she liked her attic room and if she'd mind my going there from time to time.

'As you please,' she said.

Maria's old chamber had lost some of its charm. Despite a steadily crackling fire, it lacked the luxuriousness I had so enjoyed before. Perhaps it was that all Maria's pretty objects had been removed to Ventadorn and the shelves were now lined with Angelique's medicine bottles. I found it strange, also, to note evidence of a male in a chamber which had belonged to the maiden sisters.

Maria entered practically on our heels; the sisters barely heeded our presence as they embraced and started chattering.

Angelique's lady set down her things silently, then bowed and left. I lingered a little, hoping to be included in the fun, but I was not.

'Thank you, Maryse, that will be all,' Maria said.

An old familiar feeling of hurt and anger rose up in me. It was as though Maria had forgotten all I had done for her now that her sister was by — had forgotten our shared confidences. It was as though I was a child of seven again, cast aside like a used doll.

In a huff, I climbed up to the attic where I hoped to spend much of the morning avoiding work.

As I entered, I realised it was the same chamber Gui d'Ussel had stayed in shortly before his release from Turenne. It was the first time I'd been back here since the night long ago when he had entertained us with his verse. It struck me that much had changed since then. The mood had been so carefree then; Maria and Gui had sung together as joyously as a pair of songbirds, their hearts bursting with love. I recalled how Maria had looked happier that night than I had ever seen her since. Laughter had reigned then at Turenne, but now the mood was gloomy.

Where were those words of love that had drifted round the room like smoke, entering our eyes and — through the eyes — our hearts, like some hallucinatory spell? I cast my eyes about the chamber, sure that I would find some hidden slate with words of love engraved just as they'd burnt into our hearts that night. I'd been so feverish afterwards I'd fallen ill for many days. What of the love between Maria and Gui — what had it come to now? What did it mean that it had come to nought?

I cast my eyes about, but all I found was the sensible attire of Angelique's lady. No secrets, nothing hidden... There was nothing here, no evidence of what had passed that night. Again

I concluded that all this *fin amor* was mere illusion, designed to fool the mind and trick the heart.

I thought again of the squire with yellow hair. I cursed myself, forcing my thoughts to return instead to Lord Merle-Beaumont. Love had no worth or staying power; it was as puffs of smoke. Gold, on the other hand, had lasting value.

Just as I was settling down to some needlework, I heard steps along the corridor approaching fast. To my great alarm, the door flung open and my uncle was standing suddenly before me.

'I was told you'd snuck off here,' he said.

'Uncle, so nice,' I stammered, 'hardly *snuck*, I'd say…'

He raised a hand, halting my speech. 'Since you did not seek me out, your kind uncle thought it best to come to *you*. Now —' he perched on the edge of the bed — 'do tell all.'

So flustered had he made me that I pricked myself and blood was trickling from my finger, staining the light coloured fabric.

'Clumsy,' he said, following my gaze. 'The garment is perhaps for the new-born heir of Ventadorn? Do tell me how he fares. Is he a healthy child, likely to live, you think?'

I babbled on then, like a brook, so unnerved was I and eager to please.

After he had gone, I couldn't even recall all that I'd said. He seemed most interested in Maria and Ventadorn, asking if they'd slept together since their child was born. I said I thought not and mentioned the possibility of a breach between them. I told him of the recent Festival of Love and how the Monge and Gui d'Ussel had been received. I told him of the girl, Rosamund, and how the courtiers were speculating over her match with Gui. He asked me how Gui was liked at Ventadorn and if they called him by his old nickname, "the boy with owl's eyes". I said the people feared him, even if he hardly spoke and some suspected he was devilish, for he never attended at Mass.

Raoul seemed most interested that Gui did not attend at Mass, I did not know why. I was pleased to have struck some chord that was of interest to him, though. He asked me then to take note of Gui's movements, where he went, with whom he met. I said I would and gladly.

'Thank you, Maryse, you have been most informative,' he said, pressing a gold coin into my palm.

Left to my own devices until dusk, I gathered up my things and descended in search of food and beverage. On my way to the kitchen, I passed through the small corridor where I'd been hidden when Hugh La Marche had broken his engagement with Maria. Hearing voices below in the family dining chamber, I peeped through the banister. Maria and Angelique were seated at the dining table, sipping sugared tea from painted glasses. Élise and Aunt Isabelle were standing by the door, as though preparing to depart.

'No need to rise on my account,' Isabelle said, as the sisters curtseyed, stiffly.

'Well,' said Élise, after she'd gone, 'I thought she'd never leave!'

'The whole day wasted!' Angelique said, mournfully.

'Now, now, do not become upset,' said Élise. 'It is not good for you. You have your sister now for the whole evening. I'm going for my nap. Maria, do not tire your sister out with idle chatter.'

'Idle, Mother? Hardly!' Maria protested.

'I wish Mother would not fuss so,' sighed Angelique when Élise had gone.

The sisters reclined to a long, low scarlet couch which was rarely used. They began at once an intense discussion, as though continuing a conversation started earlier.

'Your health, you know, is everything,' said Maria. 'There's no point in giving birth to a healthy bairn if you're not around yourself to help it grow… I don't trust these physicians; their methods are not tested and I suspect they're flawed. Besides, they are all men; they do not really know the workings of the female body… Their main concern seems to be getting you with child, which I do not agree with! You need the advice of a wise woman with experience in these matters. She'll look not only to the health of your unborn child but to your health as well. I believe I know such a woman, for I dealt before with an herbalist steeped in such knowledge. With your permission, I'll summon her.'

'That would be well enough,' said Angelique, 'only I am not permitted to see such women. Besides, why do you think the physicians' potions are no good? What do you know of these things? *I* am hopeful their cures will work, for I am desperate for a child!'

'I examined the bottles in your chamber,' said Maria. 'I am familiar with the remedies and I tell you they won't work. I wonder if these men really have your best interests at heart or if they're willing to sacrifice your health solely to produce an heir.'

'It's true that my fate seems to be in the hands of men and never women. Why *does* that Raoul hang about so?' asked Angelique. 'I believe he brings ill luck, for all has gone against us lately. Sometimes I believe there is some greater power at work causing us adversity. I know you may be right about this wise woman, but our father and Raoul would not approve and I have no desire to stir up further trouble.'

'It could be done in secret, then,' suggested Maria. 'They would not have to know. I ask you just to consider it, no more at present. Has it affected your relationship with Richard that you have not produced?'

'Not one whit,' Angelique replied. 'It has perhaps made us even stronger, for we have had to face the challenge together...'

'Ah,' said Maria, 'in that case, you are fortunate.'

Angelique looked at her closely. 'I trust that all is well between you and Ventadorn?'

'It is well,' Maria said, brightly, 'though he has perhaps some insecurity that makes him watch me more than usual. He fears I do not love him as he loves me... But all is well besides.'

'*Do* you love him as he loves you?'

'Not quite the same,' she said. 'I bear a different love for him than he bears me.'

'Do you? Different in what way? Do you still desire him as a wife should desire her husband?'

'He is perhaps more like a kindly uncle than a husband sometimes...'

'An *uncle*! My goodness, that is bad!' laughed Angelique.

'We are sometimes passionate with each other,' said Maria. 'It was better before my son was born. I am at fault, for little Eble has consumed most of my time. I miss him much!'

'And your husband, do you not miss him?'

'Of course... But if you observe nature, you will see that all things in this world burn brightly in their turn, then fade, then burn again brightly and fade again... It is the natural cycle. It is the same with the love between a husband and wife; it is not possible to sustain a raging fire at all times,' said Maria.

'Such a view coming from you!' Angelique exclaimed. 'I cannot believe it! Of all people, you whose very blood is inflamed with passion! You whose mind was chiselled into shape by the old love-poets? To express such moderate, lukewarm views now, I cannot believe you mean it!'

Maria did not respond but simply closed her eyes and tucked her feet under her skirt. I wondered if she would mention Gui d'Ussel then, but she did not. It seemed to me the breach between herself and Ventadorn had been caused not by the birth of her son, but by the presence of that troubadour. Perhaps her heart had always belonged to Gui, even if she would not admit it.

Studying her a moment, Angelique gushed forth an apology. 'Forgive me! I do not think before I speak. Mother is always chiding me for it! I give an ill-considered view and say what I should not. I should not presume you are the same person you were before... Of course we all must change ... and adapt to what life throws up.'

Angelique's voice was brim-full with tears. Maria took her hand.

'You are honest, Angel,' Maria soothed, 'for that quality, you should never be rebuked. Our mother has conformed too much and is too restrained. She could not have been otherwise, for she must live by our father's rules. Such is the fate of women; we live by the rules of men. *You* are true to your own nature, and I have always admired you for it. This is why I respect your opinion greatly. Perhaps I am not being entirely true to *my* nature, but don't forget, although I was betrothed to Eble, the marriage was forced untimely. Sometimes I blame our mother for not intervening, though I know she could not... Like her, I am destined to be torn between my own nature and my role as Viscountess of Ventadorn. You understand my fate?'

Angelique nodded, tears rolling down her cheeks. 'It often occurs to me,' she said, 'perhaps had I not been with child, Father may not have forced your marriage. If that is so, it was all for nothing! I lost the child and another one besides! Sometimes I think God is punishing me for my recklessness by taking my babies away... I don't deserve the blessing of a child. I see now clearly how my thoughtlessness affected you. I've learnt my lesson, but it is too late. Our actions are as chains; if one end is tugged upon, it pulls along all those we care about.'

'You must not think like that,' Maria said. 'Father would most certainly have married me to Ventadorn anyway, even had you not been with child. He was worried for my security and — of course — his own. It is as I said; women are not free, we live by rules imposed by men. This is why I must insist on your consulting this woman about your condition. But we will do it secretly, it is the only way!'

I'd have liked to listen for longer, but my stomach was growling fiercely so I continued on my way to the kitchen. The larder here was not so well stocked or so fine as at Ventadorn; Élise kept a strict, watchful eye over household expenditures. I had to admit, there was none to rival the viscount and viscountess of Ventadorn for generosity and hospitality.

CHAPTER FIFTEEN

On a cloudy, black night, Maria, Angelique and I set out to meet the medicine woman in the woods. Happy to be included, I led the way with a muffled lamp, wrapped to detract the wakeful eye. We hoped that any sleepy observer would mistake it for a common firefly. Maria had picked the woods as the safest venue, for the château was unguarded on that side. Still, there was always a sentry on watch at intervals from an upper corridor, so we timed our flight to coincide with his movements. My heart beat wildly as we ran into the woods.

The woman was waiting beside a weak fire and — to my surprise — she moved at once to embrace Maria, holding her warmly to her chest. She seemed a peasant woman by her garb and Angelique too looked aghast at the familiarity.

'Maria of Turenne!' the woman exclaimed, then, 'Or rather, Maria of Ventadorn! We are so grateful for what you did,' she added, mysteriously. 'I never did thank you, for you left Turenne so suddenly... My sister, she is well since her release; she has been reunited with her husband and children, poor things... I am so happy you have summoned me to help; I would do anything for you. Just tell me what I can do for you and for your sister.' She glanced at me slyly, whispering something to Maria, who laughed a little.

'She can be trusted, certainly,' Maria said. 'She is my ... friend.'

I was grateful for the term, even if she had hesitated.

'In that case,' said the woman, 'only say the word and it shall be done.' She looked at Angelique. 'A cure for your sister first, I see.'

There was nothing remarkable in her noting that Angelique was sick, for it was obvious by her pallor.

'A love potion for your friend?' she said then, smirking in my direction.

I started, surprised, but I did not protest.

'And for yourself?' She looked closely at Maria. 'You have no need of a cure, I see, you are not sick... And you have had a healthy child just recently... No love potion, either, for all those you desire, desire you in return. What then...? Ah, I see you are not happy, but I cannot tell why...'

Maria interrupted her, fearful perhaps she would guess too much.

I was impressed with the woman's insight and excited by the mention of a love potion. It could be used to draw Lord Merle-Beaumont's love to me. Still, I thought she had a cunning look about her I did not like or trust.

'My sister, you see, is in the greatest need,' Maria said. 'I require nothing for myself. My unhappiness is occasioned by my sister's illness. Look you now to Angelique and that is cure enough for me.'

The woman nodded. 'It shall be done,' she said, 'with the greatest pleasure.' She added, curiously, 'My family will never forget the kindness you showed *our* sister. We are forever in your debt...'

Maria interrupted her. 'I helped your sister and now you are helping mine. There are no debts, only kindnesses between friends.'

The woman reached into her sack, pulling out a thick piece of fabric which she unfolded and spread on the ground. She motioned for Angelique to lie down and began prodding her belly, asking where she felt pain. None spoke during the examination. Maria was intensely focused on the procedure

162

and all was tense and solemn. Finally, the woman got out a variety of pretty, coloured powders and began measuring them out into a bowl.

Maria looked at her inquisitively.

'Eggs,' explained the woman, briskly, 'dried and ground. They all have different uses. Not just to encourage fertility; they strengthen the female organ and ease cramps in the abdomen. Your sister's suffering should begin to ease directly.'

'Eggs?' Angelique sat up, nervously. 'What *kind* of eggs? Oh, please tell me they are not the eggs of something horrible! They are not *lizards'* eggs, are they? I know stories of such *revolting* things put in these potions...'

'Only birds' eggs ... nothing to fear,' the woman mumbled.

She added a yellow liquid, mixing the powder into a fine potion before offering it to Angelique to drink.

Angelique looked at Maria with an air of mock disgust. Maria smiled, nodding her encouragement, motioning for her to drink. Dramatically, Angelique lifted the bowl to her mouth; her lips curled slightly with displeasure, but she bravely drank the lot. The woman then thrust the last few drops on the fire, which flared up into a brilliant yellow flame.

I blinked and cried out, for I thought I saw a child being swallowed up in the flames.

'Don't be afraid,' the woman said, 'it is only the potion conjuring images.'

Angelique was growing sleepy and the woman moved her closer to the fire.

'The medicine will make her sleep,' she said.

I was not convinced it was the medicine and not the brilliant fire was making her drowsy, for my own eyes were blurring in the heat. She asked that I watch over Angelique while she spoke with Maria alone. Again, she told me not to be afraid of what I saw in the flames.

'It shows different things to different folks,' she said. 'Take heed of what you see, it may be useful.'

Their conversation was carried out in tones too low for me to hear, but I heard the clinking of glass and saw the furtive exchange of objects passing between them. I wondered, fleetingly, if Maria was acquiring some self-serving potion would help her with Gui d'Ussel, but this was most unlikely. It struck me that Angelique would need this same potion ministered again and Maria was receiving instructions on how to play physician to her sister.

The strange fire was burning ferociously, warming me to the very marrow. I had resolved not to look into it, for I did not like magic, but the dancing flames were mesmerizing and drew me in anyway. I saw many strange scenes and creatures in it which gave me an unpleasant sensation. It seemed to flash forth pictures from my life. I saw La Marche's man and how we'd coupled together; himself crying out in pleasure, myself squealing in delight. When he turned his naked self around, he suddenly became the squire with yellow hair. I could not tell if my own fantasy was reflecting onto the fire, or if the fire was projecting its fantasies onto me. Either way, I did not like it, especially when I saw myself aiding a raucous crowd to shoot down a golden owl of spectacular beauty.

Angelique stirred, her pretty opal eyes slanting open then widening on sight of the astonishing fire. She gasped. At first I was afraid she too could see my shameful actions in the flames, but soon it became apparent the woman had spoken truthfully when she'd said the fire showed different things to different people.

'Where am I?' Angelique called out. 'I see our father half-crazed, our mother in mourning ... where are my sisters?'

Maria rushed to her. 'Don't be afraid,' she said. 'This woman is our friend, remember? She has given you medicine which made you drowsy. How are you feeling?'

Angelique said nothing, but pointed at the fire.

'It's just a reflection,' explained the woman, 'on your life, past, present, future, all mixed up, like a waking dream, nothing more. But sometimes it can show us something useful, something clearer than a dream. Some knowledge in advance can be useful.' I thought she stole a glance at me. 'Not always, only sometimes,' she said again, 'it shows us something useful about ourselves. Some people have self-knowledge and reflect naturally upon themselves. Others do not have this gift and sometimes they must be shown, as in a mirror, a reflection of themselves.'

I did not like the way she was slyly referring to me. Nor did I like what the fire had shown me, for I did not understand it; therefore, it was not useful at all.

She thrust some water on the fire and made the images disappear. 'Now,' she said, 'your friend has need of a love potion? Tell us of the man that you desire — is he a good man?'

I told them all about Lord Merle-Beaumont and how I'd set my sights on him. I told them how his goodness had first attracted me and how I'd help produce an heir for his estate if he chose me, for I was strong and able and kept my figure plump and shapely. As I spoke, the woman prepared a mixture in her bowl.

'What's in it?' asked Angelique. 'It looked like you threw some common leaves in there!'

The woman coughed, ignoring the remark. 'I perceive you are a lusty dame,' she said, turning to me, 'and would satisfy well this lord or any other. Take heed, you must drink only half this potion or you will grow too frisky. The other half should be poured into the cup of the man you desire above all others. Choose carefully; the charm is strong and will not wear off lightly. Be warned that, though it will cause your man to lust for you most hungrily, it will not produce lasting love in the heart. This is an effect beyond the reach of magic.'

'Is not lust and love the same for men?' I asked.

The woman laughed.

'I do not think men find any great difference between the two!' said Angelique.

'For sure one can be easily mistaken for the other!' Maria agreed.

The woman packed her things up quickly, urging us to make haste back to the château.

I woke with alarm in a pool of weak sunlight. Eyes foggy with sleep, I rushed into my clothes and half-stumbled down the narrow staircase. In all my years of service I'd never missed my morning duty, apart from the rare occasion I'd been ill. I looked about for Angelique's lady, but finding no one, I hurried back upstairs to call Maria.

Passing Angelique's chamber, I heard voices and stopped a moment to spy. On looking through the keyhole, a dazzling green light caught me unawares and blinking, I stepped back. Just then I heard a noise behind me; Maria was walking towards me.

'I was just coming to call you!' I cried, over-brightly.

Surprised, she halted. 'Very … well … Maryse,' she said, as though an idea was just striking her. 'Has my sister risen yet?' she asked, with a bemused smile.

I cursed myself for acting suspiciously and giving away the fact that I'd been spying. 'I believe so, yes,' I replied, meekly.

The chamber door flung open and a fantastically dressed Angelique stepped out, pulling us both inside. 'Look what stole in at first light!' she cried.

Maria gave a little gasp but I was struck dumb with awe, for Aénor stood before us, resplendent in a garment of sparkling green jewels. I recognised at once the infamous emerald bodice with which Maria had tricked La Marche. Seeing me, Aénor quickly drew Maria's old indigo cloak over her finery.

'We've been dressing up!' Angelique explained.

Glaring at her sister, Aénor then added for my benefit, 'Only *play* things of course, nothing *really* costly.'

Our eyes all turned together to the open trunk. My mouth fell open. I had never before seen it so fully exposed, its contents spilling out. There were many pretty gowns and trinkets in there, but that was not what made me catch my breath. The chest was brim-full with exquisite gems of every shape and size conceivable; some as smooth and clear as eagles' eyes; some big and jagged-edged like chunks of coloured granite; others rich and opaque like deep, lush petals.

Only for play, my eye. They were costly jewels and no mistake.

My drooling must have worried them, for they quickly closed the trunk and locked it up.

'We've been dressing up all morning,' Aénor addressed Maria, 'to amuse ourselves until you woke. I was surprised to find your cloak in there. I thought it was your favourite? Have you tired of it? If so, I might borrow it.'

She referred to the indigo cloak Maria had always worn at Turenne. It was true it was strange she had not taken it to Ventadorn.

'Here.' Aénor handed the key of the trunk to Maria. 'It's your turn to mind it. Don't be careless with it, like the time you lost my tooth.'

Maria cast her eyes to heaven. 'I was *four*,' she said, tucking the key into her bosom. 'It's good to see you, sister.'

They embraced.

'You may wonder,' said Angelique, 'why we've been taking out our old things. You see, when I woke this morning I felt like dancing! I had forgotten how much I love to dance!'

Of the three sisters, Angelique was by far the most skilled in the art.

'Married ladies have little time for dancing,' sighed Aénor.

'That's why,' Angelique continued, excitedly, 'I had an idea! Why not have a dance here at Turenne, just like when we were girls? Who knows the next time we'll all be together again…We should dance and make merry while we can, for we never know what sorrows tomorrow may bring. It would be nice for you too, Maryse,' she added, generously, 'for we may be old, married ladies, but you are still free!'

'It's a wonderful idea!' Maria said, adding, 'It will just be a *small* crowd, though? I am not presently light of heart enough for anything too grand.'

'What ails you, sister?' asked Aénor.

'It is only that I miss my boy,' Maria replied.

'Just us and our ladies and courtiers,' Angelique assured. 'Aénor will stay for two weeks, which gives us ample time for preparation. We could arrange the dance for the eve before her departure. Guillaume can come that day and be her dancing partner, and Richard, of course, shall be mine! Perhaps you could ask Eble to attend, Maria, or would the journey from Ventadorn be too long for such an entertainment?'

She did not wait for a reply, just chattered on excitedly. She *did* seem much improved and more like her old self, and I wondered if woman in the woods had done her some good after all. Soon she had infected her sisters and myself with enthusiasm for the dance, and a variety of gowns had been pulled out and tried on before breakfast.

I was surprised when Maria ushered me into our shared chamber. When her sisters were by, I was used to being ignored. At first I was afraid she would chastise me for spying so I stood up tall, preparing to defend myself.

'You must miss little Eble dreadfully,' I began, stoutly.

'Oh, I do! Oh yes, I do,' she said with feeling. To my surprise, she took my hand in hers. 'Thank you, Maryse, for thinking on it. In fact, that's why I called you here... You've finished eating, I trust? Do sit, please. I cannot really broach the subject with my sisters ... but you know my plight and give such sound advice.'

I was intrigued.

'I *had* hoped to stay here at Turenne a good ten weeks and put some distance between myself and ... *Gui* —' the name was whispered — 'but in truth, my mind has been so entirely occupied with little Eble...' She paused.

I sensed there was something else.

'You, Maryse, are the only one alive I can admit this to.' She lowered her voice to the lightest whisper. 'The idea of Gui with *her* is more than I can bear. I know it is most likely... I know it is probably for the best... But still I cannot bear it. However, the torment I feel at not knowing what has passed between them is *worse* than knowing for sure they are together. Now that Angelique seems well, I thought I might return to

Ventadorn. What think you, Maryse, are you ready to return with me so soon?'

In fact the plan suited me well, for I was anxious to try the love potion out on Lord Merle-Beaumont.

'Maria,' I said, 'your word is my command. You know I am happy to follow you back to Ventadorn, if that is what you wish.'

'But do you think it *right* I should return so soon?' she asked. 'Have I given enough time to Angelique?' She lowered her voice again. 'Do you think I've allowed them enough time... Gui and the girl, to truly fall in love?'

I shrugged; how should I know?

'If they are betrothed, we will send them from Ventadorn,' she said. 'Not to be cruel, of course, but it will be better for all of us that way. I could not bear to see them carry on in love. It's safer if the love-birds take flight and discover their own land, free from those who'd wish them ill. For I suppose *she* has many admirers too who would be glad to put an end to Gui because he is her choice.'

On the evening of the dance, all three sisters were dazzling, but it was Angelique who really drew the eye. She wore only a simple gown of white linen, embroidered with bluebells and angels, but her skin was both pale and pink like the first blush of spring through winter's snow, and her eyes were as clear and sparkling as a mountain spring. Her lips were stained as red as holly berries and her white-gold hair shone like a halo over her head. Her movements were lively as a bee's moving from flower to flower, and all the men lined up to dance with her. Even my uncle Raoul took his turn with her, though he danced as seriously as a bishop and as stiffly as a corpse. Still, his long and elaborately attired feet made the steps with surprising grace and precision.

Surrounded by Turenne's most famous beauties, it was little wonder I spent the eve alone upon a bench without a dancing partner. I occupied myself with thoughts on how I would minister the love-potion to Lord Merle-Beaumont. Once or twice the squire with yellow hair came stubbornly to mind, but I forced myself to think again on the lord.

CHAPTER SIXTEEN

Apart from our horses' clattering hooves, the journey back to Ventadorn next day was passed mainly in silence. Viscount Eble travelled on horseback before our carriage, accompanied by his men. Occupied with her troubles, Maria spoke only once to make comment on Angelique's improvement.

'Was not she as light of foot as a young doe?' she said.

I said I'd hardly seen a doe as I was so rarely out of doors.

We arrived at Ventadorn in good time for the midday banquet which had been prepared for our homecoming. The food was rich and plentiful and in my heart I was glad to be home. Just as we were starting on dessert, Ventadorn played some notes on his crystal glass and rose to make a speech.

'We are *so* glad you have returned, my love,' he said to Maria, 'We missed you *most* profoundly.'

The doors of the hall flung open and a single trumpet sounded. Everyone looked towards Maria, who rose, bewildered, with the rest at table. It seemed that Eble had planned one of his surprises. I laid my dessert spoon down reluctantly.

A tall and heavy stranger then approached, wearing a fashionably cut suit of light chainmail and red feathers in his broad, navy cap. He bowed low before Maria.

'Forgive me, Lady, for my bold entrance. I am the troubadour Gaucelm Faidit returned from the Holy Land. I am at your service, most esteemed Lady.'

Maria glanced at her husband, pleased. 'And we are honoured, sir, to receive you,' she said to Gaucelm Faidit.

After a small discussion, it was decided the troubadours would give an impromptu performance that night in the great hall to celebrate our homecoming and to give Gaucelm Faidit occasion to sing of his adventures overseas. Such gatherings were commonplace at Ventadorn, and soon the posts went up and all the courtiers went rushing off to prepare themselves.

Unlike Gui d'Ussel — whose voice was like ripe figs in summertime — Gaucelm Faidit's voice was as harsh-sounding as a puck goat's and could not be used publicly. A sweeter-voiced minstrel therefore accompanied the troubadour and sang his compositions.

Although his verse was filled with descriptions of the hardships he had endured at sea; the strange and hostile lands he had visited and the loneliness he had felt for his homeland, Gaucelm Faidit looked well-fed and content enough to me as he languished on many cushions. Images of the comely wife who had shared his bed before he went away and to whom he yearned to return were contrasted, I thought, by the bevy of fresh-faced maidens he pulled around him now. His lyrics spoke of months of deprivation and starvation, yet he had many chins and a great belly.

It seemed the Monge had thought the same, for he made some witty comments about Faidit's comfortable appearance, to the great amusement of the court.

'How is it, Gaucelm Faidit,' cried the Monge, 'you speak of giving up all worldly goods to serve God's army, yet your purse and — indeed — your belly seems full enough to me?'

Only Gui d'Ussel remained apart and silent as he always did, while the guests grew more and more rowdy. I did not see the girl Rosamund among the gathering. Maria and her husband were seated in a special box, perched above the podium. This way, the audience could gauge its own reaction by theirs; if the

Monge said something funny or mocking to which Gaucelm Faidit gave a serious reply, all would look first to the viscountess to learn how the remark should be received.

Only once did I note Maria and Gui d'Ussel lock eyes. In one of his verses, Gaucelm Faidit had written about a brave soldier who'd fought alongside him, bearing the nickname 'Emerald.' He was, of course, referring to Hugh La Marche.

'A strange nickname,' the Monge remarked, glancing towards the noble box, 'but I suppose there is an interesting tale to be told of *emeralds.*'

The crowd cheered, knowingly.

It was then that Maria and Gui's eyes seemed to lock, but only for a moment. The girl Rosamund entered then with a few others of her age — both male and female — as was customary at Ventadorn. She was the perfect picture of youth and beauty. Her sunbeam locks were falling loosely to her waist and her deep-set eyes lent to her an air of mystery that set her apart from her peers like a rich jewel against a plain setting.

Gaucelm Faidit spotted her at once and called her to sit by him, but she ignored the request. Neither did she sit with Gui d'Ussel but moved instead, with her own group, to another corner.

Busy pouring the mead wine, I was followed about — most annoyingly — by the squire with yellow hair. As soon as he'd seen me, he'd made directly for me and I had not been able to shake him off. Even when I called him a nuisance, he would not leave my side. I knew that Lord Merle-Beaumont would not be in attendance tonight for it was too wild for him, so I decided to tolerate the squire and, again, found that I enjoyed his company. Once, when he made a comment on my figure, I rounded on him. 'Go down to the Rooks' Rest and find some painted girl there who will satisfy you, for I am a respectable lady and will have none of that!' I said.

'A lusty dame such as yourself not being used to purpose makes me hotter than any working wench could,' he replied.

I told him that, as I was mindful of my reputation, he would not be able to enjoy me out of wedlock. Nor could he have me as his wife, for he was not rich enough.

He caught my meaning well and did not try to lay his hands on me but only helped me pour the wine. In truth, I'd have loved to have had a go with him in the mead closet as I had done before with La Marche's man, but there were too many spies about at Ventadorn and I could not risk it.

Gaucelm Faidit called his minstrel to him and, staring at Rosamund the Fair, cried out: 'Enough of war and of suffering, let's sing of love and beauty!'

'You waste your time on *her. Her* heart belongs to another! Sing, young Gui d'Ussel!' the Monge called out. 'Sing of whatever lies hidden in your shady heart. For I am sure all who are present here would like to hear that song!'

The place was silent as a church and all eyes turned towards Gui, whose orbs of liquid gold seemed to pierce through all the grandeur of the courtiers, through to their very souls. They shifted uncomfortably on their cushioned seats.

Strolling up from the back, Gui stopped before the viscountess, lowering himself slowly and gracefully down on one knee. 'My lady,' he said to Maria, 'do *you* wish me to disclose the secrets of my heart?'

I held my breath, afraid the foolish troubadour would go too far.

'You may do as you please, Gui d'Ussel,' Maria replied, as lightly as possible. 'You are a free man.'

'Lady,' Gui replied, 'I am *your servant.*'

A trickle of appreciative laughter ran round.

'I ask you again,' said Gui, 'do you wish me to disclose what's in my heart?'

Bemused, the guests looked towards the viscount. Delighted with the chivalrous attentions to his wife and entering into the spirit of the game, Ventadorn beamed broadly, dictating a generous applause.

'The viscountess must concede,' he declared, addressing his guests, 'that the troubadour is right. He is, indeed, her servant, as all would-be courtly lovers at Ventadorn are. Therefore —' he turned to Maria — '*you* must dictate whether or not Gui d'Ussel will disclose the secrets of his heart!'

Maria did not speak but only lowered her gaze, which could be broadly read as modesty. Gui d'Ussel then went to speak again. I was most alarmed now, for I was afraid he would say something that might betray their history.

He turned to address the gathering. 'Maria de Turenne once argued that a lady should never allow her lover to be her equal but must always retain *suzerainty* over him. *I* argued that once a lady has accepted the man as her sworn lover, the two should then be equal, for love knows no divide between the sexes, religion, colour, age or class. The lady has power *at first*, to accept or reject the lover but afterwards, once she has accepted him, I say the lovers should be equal. What say you now, Lady, do you hold still by the same argument?'

Maria's reply was faint. 'I do,' she said.

'My lady refuses to accept me as her lover,' Gui went on, 'so I must remain her lowly servant, even though I wish with all my heart to be her equal. Why should I toss alone, tormented, on the stormy seas of unrequited love when the lady I love sleeps peacefully in her feather bed? What say you, Viscountess? What advice do you offer your humble servant?'

The atmosphere was strained now like a harp string pulled too tight. I hoped it would soon be over. Gui's words could be read as a mere trope of courtly love or they could be taken not as game but truth. Also, it was unclear whether the reference to his lady was to Maria or Rosamund.

Ventadorn spoke up then to clear the air. 'Do not forget your place, Gui d'Ussel.' His voice was light-hearted enough. 'Maria de Turenne is now the viscountess of Ventadorn and answers to none other than her husband.'

'With due respect, Viscount,' the Monge put forth, 'you know as well as I that *fin amor* has always reigned freely outside the binds of matrimony. Courtly lovers answer to no other authority but to the God of Love!'

'Therefore it follows,' cried Gaucelm Faidit, 'that while a lady should answer to her husband, for she is bound to him (as I hope my wife will always do *my* bidding); the lady is her courtly lover's *domina*, for *he* must please her where her husband cannot!'

The bawdy remark won some applause.

'I argue, simply,' said Gui d'Ussel, 'that the lady's love should be equal to her lover's, no more nor less, for true love *knows no divide.*' He turned back to Maria. 'I have been asked to speak of the love that's in my heart, but I find that I cannot. I will therefore sing of it.'

The song he sang then filled our hearts with such a melancholy longing that all who had been merry before were suddenly teary-eyed.

Afterwards, the Monge and Gaucelm's minstrel joined Gui d'Ussel in another song about their great patroness and how she was the fairest in the land.

I breathed easily again, for I had been afraid that Gui d'Ussel would do something bold and brave that would get us all in trouble. I was myself confused. It was not clear to me if Gui d'Ussel and Rosamund were indeed betrothed, for when the troubadours paused and the musicians played a courtly tune, Gui stepped towards Rosamund, inviting her to dance. Perhaps it was the upright nature of the dance, but there seemed to be a lot of distance between them.

When the dance was over, he kissed her hand, formally, and she returned to her place. He disappeared behind the curtains, and I noted Maria making her excuses to her husband and slipping away as well.

Looking about me, to make sure no one was watching, I followed them out.

Soon, I heard their urgent whisperings coming from close by and I hid beneath a staircase to listen and watch.

'I don't understand,' Maria was saying, 'do you not love the girl? What do you mean by putting me on the spot so publicly? Was it your intention to humiliate me?'

Eyes aflame with passion, Gui caught hold of her arms. 'How can you believe my heart to be so fickle as to turn from *you* to *her*?'

'But she is so young and fair,' replied Maria, 'and she loves you truly.'

'Loves me?' said Gui. 'How can she love me when she does not know me? How could I love *her* just for her appearance? Close your eyes, Maria, and maybe you will see things clearly. Here, I shall close them for you.' He drew his hands over her eyes, placing her hand on his heart.

'It is the eternal spark in you I love,' he said, 'the part that will live on in memory long after both our lives have been extinguished. How can you believe that I could fall for another when your heart is in my heart? If your heart flies from mine, I am as good as dead.'

'Gui, you must not speak like that.' Maria's eyes flew open. 'But is there really nothing between you and the girl? How could I have been so deluded...? Did you not accept her ring? Did you not dance with her tonight? I do not understand... Why did you accept her ring if you do not love her?'

'I accepted her ring,' Gui replied, sharply, 'because I had no desire to humiliate her in public or ruin her future chances of finding a suitable mate.'

'But then there must be some misunderstanding on *her* part,' said Maria, 'for I am sure she thinks you are in love with her. It was wrong of you, Gui, to lead her on so when you did not mean it.'

He drew her to him, holding her tight. 'I sent the ring back to her directly afterwards,' he spoke into her ear, 'so there would be no mistake. I told her I loved another. She was grateful for my honesty and asked that we wait awhile before announcing we are *not* betrothed.'

'So you ... do not love her?' Maria said, slowly. She started crying, perhaps with relief.

'I do not,' said Gui. 'I love only you. You have the power, Maria, to accept or reject my love. What is it to be?'

'Gui, this is too much, I cannot... You *know* it's not that simple.'

'By the rules of *fin amor*,' said Gui, 'the lady may *choose* her lover, even if she is married!'

'It is a *game*, Gui, it is only a *game*!' Maria said in anguish.

'It is not only a game to me,' Gui replied.

'No, it is not a game to you,' Maria repeated, as in a trance. 'I know it has never been a game to you. It is your reality.'

'Do you not love me as I love you?' he asked. 'If you do not, all is darkness for me. My life would be a long night, without promise of day.'

His frank words, so charged with feeling, were accompanied by an aspect of such uncorrupted beauty I could not help but stare at him as though he were some illuminated artwork.

They found each other's lips and kissed passionately. I withdrew quietly, back to the hall.

CHAPTER SEVENTEEN

The first snow came early that year to Ventadorn. Sensing the chilly air, I pushed back the bedclothes with some reluctance. The dark earth was sprinkled thinly, like sugar on a chocolate cake, not falling thickly enough yet to coat it. Servants were beating the closet dust out of the winter fleeces before taking them indoors to spread on the courtiers' beds. Some others were going with sacks and axes towards the forest.

I dressed quickly in a simple woollen dress and exited the chamber with a spring in my step. There was to be a gathering of courtiers in the great hall that evening to celebrate the viscount's birthday, and I would be employed pouring the mead wine.

Lord Merle-Beaumont would be there — of course — and I had fixed on the occasion as the best time to administer the love potion. I hoped the event would provide the opportunity for me to exercise my plan without interruption. I thought on how the viscount would be surprised to find his grand friend suddenly head over heels in love with me. The thought made me smile and gloat inwardly, for Ventadorn was no friend of *mine*.

When I entered Maria's chamber I was startled to find Ventadorn by her side. One half of his body was bathed in morning light; he was offering a hot beverage to Maria. The viscount was a strong and handsome man yet. There were many ladies who would gladly trade places with Maria in his bed, if he were to encourage it. No such invitations were forthcoming, though, as he was so devoted to his wife. Ventadorn was renowned not only for his magnanimity, but for his integrity as well. Perhaps it was this purity of heart that made him so attractive despite his advancing years. Certainly his smile was radiant enough now to set the chamber aglow with light and warmth.

'Maryse, come in and close the door at once,' he said.

'I do not wish to disturb,' I began, but he hastened to silence me.

'It is good you are come,' he said. 'Maria must not stir before the house is warmed. I've given orders to the servants.' He looked at her lovingly. 'She is not as strong as she likes to think. See to it she does not rise, Maryse. I shall be most grateful!' He turned his sun-ray smile on me.

I cast my eyes downwards, curtsying my assent. Such intimate proximity to the noble couple embarrassed me.

When Ventadorn departed, Maria ushered me in, saying, 'He does not bite, you know. I don't know why you dislike him, Maryse. He is the kindest of men.'

Irked, I murmured that while he and I had a sound relationship, he did not exactly have *her* undivided attention at all times.

'Very well,' she said, quickly, 'I do not wish us to quarrel, Maryse.' She threw back the covers. 'Do please help me find my scarlet cloak. I think it is the warmest.'

'Maria, your husband gave orders you were not to stir.' My voice was stern. 'Now *I* will be in trouble if you disobey him. Please stay where you are, even for just a while.'

'Oh, very well.' She gave a defeated shrug. 'Only you *must* keep me company, or I swear I'll run around the yard in my nightdress for all the court to see. Then you really will have to answer to the viscount. Though I'm sure you would not mind, since you and he are such good friends.'

I saw there was a twinkle in her eye and allowed myself to smile.

'So,' she whispered excitedly, 'are you prepared for this evening?' She was referring, of course, to the love potion.

'Oh yes,' I said, 'but fearful too, for we do not really know if it will work. Or if it does, and the lord behaves strangely or wildly, it may arouse suspicion, and what then if I am discovered? The viscount would be angry and my reputation damaged... What of the other ladies who have set their sights on him? Jealousy might excite their tongues to slanderous remarks once they see he favours me. Do you really think it wise to go through with it?'

'I think you may as well try,' she said. 'Do not think of it as a trick, but rather as an encouragement to love. It is a noble act rather than a ruse, for you are in love with him and he is alone. You will both therefore benefit if the charm is successful. On the other hand, if it does not work you will have lost nothing. You see it is for the best that you try it out, Maryse. Now, you are not planning to wear *this*, I trust? Let us look for something more ... appealing.'

She dressed me in a tight gown of velvet burgundy fringed all about with ermine fur. My mink-coloured hair was piled high on my head and secured with pearl pins and my eyelids were shadowed with glittering gold powder to set off well my sapphire eyes.

The alluring attire won me a few appreciative glances as I entered the candlelit hall that night.

Towering over his companions, I noted Lord Merle-Beaumont's head turning in my direction. Escaping to the mead closet at first opportunity, I had not been alone for more than a few minutes when a loud rapping began at the door. Unbolting it quickly, I was dismayed to find the squire with yellow hair standing there. He must have registered the displeasure on my face, for he said at once, 'I only came to see if you needed assistance. I will go away again directly if you do not.'

I assured him I needed no help. 'Thank you for the thought,' I added, hastily. 'I do not wish to be unkind, but I must ask you to leave lest we be discovered here alone together. I have heard rumours of maids who meet alone with men in mead closets. You know how tongues will wag.'

'What rumours have you heard?' he asked, teasingly.

'I have heard that, while they enter the closet a maid, when they exit after the encounter they are a maid no more!'

Left again to my own devices, I poured the potion into a painted goblet and mixed it well with mead. Filling many other goblets and placing them on a gold tray, I placed Lord Merle-Beaumont's drink at the front, where I could distinguish it from the rest by its particular markings.

Thankfully, when I re-entered, the viscount was speaking with Merle-Beaumont and so I went straight to them. I handed the viscount a cup first before offering the potion to Lord Merle-Beaumont. Ventadorn urged me then to circulate, so I could not hang about to see whether or not the lord drank fully of the potion.

PART THREE

CHAPTER NINETEEN

Château de Ventadorn, 1207

Three summers had changed the little heir of Ventadorn from infant to sturdy toddler, and everyone doted on him. With his mother's clear, slate eyes and impassioned spirits and his father's keen perception, he seemed a promising prospect as future Viscount of Ventadorn.

His boundless energy exhausted fast my own reserves and, as there were no other young children at court, he often went to Aénor's estate to play with his small cousins. I was entrusted with the task of carting him to and fro, and as it was a mere half hour's journey (with a shortcut through the forest) we normally departed late in the morning. The practice had begun in early spring but now that the temperatures had risen to summer heights, I decided we would leave at first light, when all was cool and still. Little Eble had therefore spent the night in a cot at the foot of my bed, so we would not disturb anyone by our early rising.

We set out just as the first slivers of dawn were streaking the horizon. Securing the child in front of me with a leather strap, I breathed the dewy freshness of the air in gratefully. Trotting to the forest's edge, I paused a moment to admire the mystical haze hovering over the ground. Some slight movement drew my attention to a shaded grove within. As I was in no hurry, I decided to go and investigate further; the forest being a lovers' meeting place, I thought I might spy something intriguing.

Tying the horse to a tree, I took the sleeping child in my arms and snuck towards the spot. I picked my way gently, careful to make no noise. I saw something then that made me stop in my tracks. Two lovers were entwined on the dark, damp grass. They were panting heavily and their naked bodies were glistening with damp, like figures freshly moulded out of river clay. The woman's dark hair was strewn about her, and the man was covering her face with slow kisses.

I watched as he began kissing down her neck, lingering awhile around her full breasts. The lady lifted up her head and I saw her face clearly. The lovers were Maria and Gui d'Ussel!

Although I'd long suspected it, I still received a shock to see the adultery so blatantly before my eyes. My first thought was for the innocent, sleeping child in my arms and I was ashamed for Maria.

The very air seemed charged with blind Eros's dangerous spell. Afraid the sleeping child would wake, I left as stealthily as I had come and delivered the young heir to his aunt.

On my return, I followed the forest path back to the same grove where the lovers had lain but an hour earlier. Dismounting, I examined the place for signs of what had passed. All was deserted; the grass which they had coupled on bore no trace of lovemaking but looked like normal grass. Eros's poison-tipped arrow was nowhere to be found. Yet I did not question what I had seen, for I saw them still clearly in my mind's eye — two lovers hopeful that night's sumptuous raiment would cover up their sin, for adultery *was* a sin.

Funny, I'd always thought of myself as the sinner and Maria as the saint, but now I found that the reverse was true. I wondered if there were other witnesses or if only I had seen them. I would never tell, but others would and then Maria and I would both be in trouble. What if Gui d'Ussel had planted his seed in her and she grew big with his child? Would the viscount know he had been cuckolded?

Such variety of thought rushed through my head I started to feel dizzy. I sat a moment on the grass; it struck me that if Maria could have fun with Gui d'Ussel, then I too could have fun. For though I was set to marry Lord Merle-Beaumont this coming spring, I was not yet his lover. I was as hot for the squire with yellow hair as he was for me, but I was so afraid for my reputation I had not lain with him. The thought that I could have him sent pleasurable sensations cascading through me and I felt the heat rising to my cheeks. It did not help that the days were long and hot and sounds of lovemaking could be heard regularly about the château and its grounds.

My courtship with Lord Merle-Beaumont had been long and tedious, for he believed me to be a pious virgin and would not dream of touching me. The squire, on the other hand, hung around me constantly and never failed to think of some new innuendo that would madden me with desire. I could not help but flirt back, and our talk had reached a point where I felt I must have him or go mad.

My dallying caused me to be late for lunch with Lord Merle-Beaumont, and I arrived quite breathless and unusually dishevelled.

'Maryse,' he said, eyeing my dull hair, 'I wondered if you had forgotten our arrangement.'

We sat stiffly apart, him at one end, myself at the other.

'You must forgive me, my lord,' I smiled falsely. 'I intended to be up at cock's crow to drop young Eble off at his aunt's, but I slept late and have been behind the clock ever since!'

He relaxed back in his chair. 'I forgive you, Maryse,' he said. 'You are in fact only a quart hour late. It is not much. I took the time to say my prayers, so it has not been wasted.'

I suppressed a smile. The lord was fonder of saying his prayers than of any other occupation. He also preferred water to any other beverage and ate red meat only on feast days. I was shortly to marry a monk!

'Very good,' I said. 'Shall we say grace together now?'

It was our custom to pray together before every meal, and I had impressed him much with the Latin creeds I'd learnt at Turenne. I suspected that this, rather than any love potion, was what had won him over.

I poured the water and broke some bread for him.

'You are a good woman, Maryse,' he said, after a thought. 'You will make a fine, industrious wife.'

Industrious! I sometimes wondered if the man had any blood in him at all; I'd try to slip more red meat into his diet once we were married.

Over the next few days, I watched Maria closely. Though she seemed in good spirits, I did not think her behaviour in any way betrayed her heart. She was as dutiful a mother and wife as she had ever been. In fact, her relationship with the viscount appeared perfectly harmonious as they dined and laughed together. She rarely spoke to Gui d'Ussel and did not show him any special favour.

It was rumoured that Rosamund the Fair had broken Gui's heart by breaking their engagement, and so none questioned why the beautiful troubadour had no mate. I listened closely for any rumours circulating about Maria and Gui but heard none. Still, next time I was alone with Maria, I dropped some hints that I hoped would warn her off future rendezvous with him.

'I am quite afraid to walk into the forest this time of year for all the obscene sounds that can be heard about the place,' I began. 'This summer's heat has turned our nice court maidens into harlots, has it not? And as for our genteel knights and gallants, they are no better than rutting stags! What think you, Maria, have you ventured into the groves at dusk or dawn yourself of late? I mean for a stroll, of course, not as a participant in these wanton games of love.'

I laughed as I spoke, but I turned quickly and looked her squarely in the eye. She flinched, answering too quickly that she preferred to take her walks down by the sea and avoided the forest completely. Wanting to make certain she caught my meaning well, I carried on, 'Are you not curious to know who is making the love sport with whom?'

'Have you *seen* something, Maryse?' she asked then, sharply.

'Not I,' I said firmly, standing my ground. 'I do not indulge in vulgar spying. But it is impossible to close one's ears to rumours, is it not? And sometimes I hear things. Rumours of adultery would shock you to the very marrow.'

We were interrupted then by a servant, but I was satisfied that I had made my point well. I hoped Maria would be too frightened to return again to the forest with Gui, for it really was too risky. Still, I supposed their passion would find an outlet somewhere and I wondered where it would be, for certainly none of the château's chambers would be safe from spies. I determined to watch their movements closely so I could warn them when the time came.

CHAPTER TWENTY

I started accompanying Maria on her long walks by the sea. At first, she seemed amused by my latent interest in the outdoors but after a time she found my constant companionship irksome, and I knew why. She could not meet so easily with her lover.

'I do not understand why you suddenly must be always by my side,' she complained, as I panted heavily behind her.

'Why should I not be as enchanted as you are by the out of doors; do you think me so incapable of admiring the ocean?'

'This is a sudden change of heart,' she said, eyeing me suspiciously.

We had just climbed the sharp path down to the sea's edge and were walking towards an attractive ruin some distance away. I was, in fact, greatly fatigued for I had much more weight to carry around than she.

'Very well,' I said, 'you go on alone and I'll rest here awhile.' I sat down heavily.

'I'll pick you up on my way back!' she called back, already ten paces away.

I was so busy catching my breath and wiping the perspiration from my brow, I did not note the figure climbing down the path until he was almost upon me; it was the squire with yellow hair. I was so happy and surprised to see him I let out a little cry and held my arms out to him. Before I had a chance to think, we were locked in an embrace and I felt his lips on mine. I drank in his embrace like sweet, refreshing wine. I let him lead me into a narrow cave and I was so maddened with desire that I did not think or care about my reputation. I made the love sport with him as if it were the single thing on earth I had been made for.

It became our habit to meet in this same spot close to the water's edge, where we would make love and talk during the period of time it took Maria to walk to the promontory and back. Maria seemed to stay away longer and longer, so sometimes we would be left in peace the whole afternoon before we'd spot her diminutive silhouette returning towards us and he would hide back in the gorse while I would venture out to her as if I had been napping.

From our hiding place, we had a clear view of anybody who would descend the cliff and so we fooled ourselves into believing we were safe. Never had I fancied it was possible to feel as light of spirit as when I was with him.

I discovered that the squire's name was Gerard and he was the youngest of a large family, four of whom were boys, all aspiring to be knights after their father. The family, though well respected, was not well off enough to afford horses and armour for all the brothers, and so their father decided that only two of them would go into the profession.

Gerard was the most athletic of the siblings as well as his father's favourite; his father therefore chose him over two of his brothers to train as a knight. Tragically, his father had passed away before he could oversee the plan, and any funds which had been meant to endorse Gerard's future were needed for the upkeep of the family.

Gerard had found a job and worked hard to support his mother, but he had taken riding and fighting lessons at the court under Sir Walter's supervision. His talent had eventually earned him a place as squire at court, but he still had not sufficient funds to pay for the horse or armour required for knighthood.

After listening to his tale, I admired Gerard much, for I could see he was a self-made man in much the same way I was a self-made woman. It seemed an awful pity that his obvious qualities and ability, the strength and chivalry which would make such a great knight, would be squandered for want of funds. I felt a great accord with him, for I had always thought I would have made as powerful a lady and as pleasing and useful a wife and mother as any high-born woman, had I been given the chance.

I liked him more and more, for he was always courteous and never treated me roughly or made demands of me. As well as that he admired my obvious mettle and independence and loved my soft, plump body and my expansive bosom. Sometimes we would not make love at all but would merely lie there talking. It was this I came to value above all else, for I had never before had someone who cared for only me. Sometimes, when we talked, we'd fancy what our lives would be like if he had gold enough to become a knight and I became his wife. But we both knew that it was only fantasy, as he did not have the means to keep me and I was already engaged to a rich lord who would keep me in the luxury I desired above all else.

At first he begged me to break my promise to the lord and pledge myself to him instead. I said I would not hear of it, for I had worked so hard to get myself engaged to the lord.

'Do you love Lord Merle-Beaumont?' he asked, foolishly.

'Of course I do not love him,' I replied, impatiently.

But I did not tell Gerard I loved *him* either. He understood me better when I told him of the hardship and loneliness I'd endured in my early life and how I'd always sworn I'd find a way out of the poverty and servitude that had made my life so miserable. I told him how I'd learnt the hard way that love had no lasting value — it was as puffs of smoke — while gold had much more lasting worth. I told him how I'd thought my mother loved me but then she had let them take me, and how I'd loved a man (I did not name him) who'd gone away and I was left with nought but sorrow.

He thought on it awhile and then said, 'Still, I suppose when you are dead and gone, you will have little use either for gold or love!'

'Not true,' said I, 'for you can leave your gold behind as a legacy for your children, so they will have a better chance in life than we have had.'

He could not argue with that.

Gerard was watchful over me and if I chanced to stand with Lord Merle-Beaumont in a public place, I'd feel his eyes on me. My manners with the lord were always reserved but if I knew Gerard was watching, my cheeks would burn with shame. Once or twice the situation grew most awkward; on one occasion the lord mistook Gerard for a servant and ordered him to bring me fresh water! I quickly pointed out the mistake and the lord then insisted on an elaborate apology. Gerard stepped forward to receive the apology, offering to fetch the water anyway.

'It would be a great pleasure for me to satisfy the lady,' he said, cheekily. 'I could not call myself chivalrous if I did not attend to her needs.'

The innuendo filled me with trepidation and, afterwards, made me cross. He succeeded in making the lord appear like a foolish, old cuckold, particularly when he asked Gerard to join us at table. Thankfully, he declined, but frightened me with even more pointed innuendo. 'Though I am sorely tempted,' he said, looking straight at me, 'as it looks most succulent, I am, at present, fasting.'

When next I spoke with Gerard alone, I told him that I would never see him again if he continued to behave in such a flippant and dangerous manner. He retorted that he was so maddened with jealousy he couldn't help himself. I told him, with practised coldness, to stay out of our way, then, if he did not care to see me with Lord Merle-Beaumont.

We each sulked for a week or so but, as we could not bear to be apart for long, we fell back naturally into our old ways. So caught up was I with my own affairs, I failed to keep a watchful eye on Maria and Gui d'Ussel. It came, therefore, as a terrible shock when Ventadorn summoned me to a private interview one awfully hot afternoon in late August.

When I entered the chamber and saw his grave, troubled aspect, I was sure the game was up.

'Maryse, please sit,' he said, remaining standing himself. 'You and I have not always seen eye to eye, have we?' It was not a question but a statement. 'And I understand that, of course, your first loyalty is to the viscountess. You are not, of course, my servant and I know you have a special arrangement with Maria regarding your earnings.'

He paused, sucking some stifling air in deeply. I could tell he was agitated.

'However,' he said, 'whatever money Maria gives you, you must know comes from our treasury and is as much mine as hers.'

He must have noted my surprise. Why would he mention my financial arrangement now after all these years?

'I do not accuse you of anything, Maryse. You are not under trial and, since you must wonder why I've called you here today, I'll quickly arrive at the point. Though you have been given much independence at court, I should remind you that you still live under my protection. As viscount and head of this estate, I have the power to turn you out if you lie to me or betray my trust.'

He paused again, wiping beads of perspiration from his brow.

My heart was pounding as I mentally tried to forge excuses for whatever he was about to throw at me.

'Maryse,' he said, more calmly, 'I only ask you for the truth. Please think carefully before you reply. Is it true that you and Maria held a secret meeting with a … a cunning woman when you were last at Turenne?'

I could have cried with relief, for I was sure he had been about to speak of illicit love. 'It is true,' I said, directly, for I did not think it was a matter of great importance. 'We met one evening with a wise woman to discuss natural medicines that could be used to cure Angelique. The physicians' remedies were proving ineffective and Maria — the viscountess — understands something of these things…'

'Foolish women,' he barked, 'to think they know more than the physicians! To think of the damage caused by their ignorance!'

'What of the physicians' ignorance?' I protested.

He raised a hand, halting my speech.

'How were we found out?' I asked. 'We were certain no one was watching.'

'Someone is *always* watching,' he frowned. I nodded sagely, knowing this to be true. 'However, in this case, the woman came forward herself and admitted to the meeting. It seems that Angelique has fallen ill again, more gravely this time. Confounded by some unsolicited potions they found hidden, which she admitted to ingesting, the physicians conducted a rather brutal investigation which has left one young townswoman maimed for life. How could you have been so naïve? Surely you knew there would be consequences.'

I did not reply but stood there looking sorry.

He let out a long, tired sigh. 'It seems the woman then came forth and admitted all. I do not wish to alarm Maria unduly on her sister's account, nor do I want her running off to Turenne and facing an unhappy mob herself. You will be lucky — all of you — if you are not accused of sorcery. No, she must not be told of it before we have more information. I order you not to speak of it to her. I will go myself to Turenne and clear the matter up, if I can. Maria must not know where I have gone. Do not speak to her of it, Maryse, until further notice.'

I promised I would not.

Later that evening, when I told a much surprised Maria that Ventadorn had taken leave at short notice to attend to urgent business, she suggested that I take some time for myself to do as I pleased while he was away.

'For what reason?' I asked, innocently. 'I am as content in your company as I am in my own — in fact, it is almost the same thing!' I could tell she was itching to run to Gui d'Ussel, but I would not allow it.

'But surely, Maryse,' Maria stated, firmly, 'you would like to spend more time with your betrothed?'

Something in her tone warned me this was a trick question.

'There is no need,' I replied, lightly. 'Soon we will have all the time in this world to be together.'

'Or perhaps you would like to spend more time with the blond squire I see you with sometimes?'

I had not thought we'd been observed. 'He is nobody,' I replied, quickly, 'just a friend.'

'A pretty friend,' she said, but there was no judgement in her tone. 'Perhaps you would like more time to spend with him?'

I blushed under her clear-eyed gaze; I knew not what to say.

'So,' she said as she drew her eyes away, 'you do as you wish and I — likewise — will do as *I* wish. We neither of us shall judge the other. But more importantly, we should not follow each other about, or attempt to curtail the other's freedom in the same way our menfolk do. Let us each be free for a short time.' As I was thinking on this, she repeated, softly, 'Let us each be free.'

There was such a wistful, dreamlike appeal in her tone, I was wholly convinced her proposal was the only course of action, whether or not it was the 'proper' course.

But the château's very walls were covered in eyes and ears and so, although I did not follow her about as I had done before, I followed Gui d'Ussel.

I had never been inside the troubadours' living quarters, for they shared their own small apartment in one of the out-houses at the château's edge. Once I'd set my mind to it, I gained access easily under false pretences. I spun a credible tale to the guards about how Maria was planning a surprise performance for her husband's return. I was to meet with the troubadours regularly to make the arrangements and the guards would be paid to keep their lips sealed. I promptly procured a key to come and go as I wished.

'When I say speak of it to no one, I *mean* no one,' I stressed, 'not even to the poets themselves, for there is always someone listening. If word leaks out, you will not be paid.'

Such plots were commonplace at Ventadorn and no one suspected a thing. I was sure that my status as Maria's right-hand lady, coupled with the fact I was soon to be married to a rich lord, inspired fear and respect in these men and made them doubly willing to do my bidding. The knowledge made me glow with pride.

Of course, I made sure the troubadours were out before I went snooping. At a glance, I could tell which cot belonged to Gui d'Ussel. His was the most austere-looking, placed furthest away from the others. I knew it was his from the familiar parchment and from his quill and ink, the same Maria had bestowed on him at Turenne all those years ago.

Knowing that I had a few hours' grace, I strolled about awhile. I noted the Monge's untidy heap of bedclothes, but noted too his neatly rolled parchments and his orderly writing desk. The parchments were sealed — I supposed to stop anyone from reading them. It was true his works were considered as valuable as gold. Perhaps he was afraid that one of Gaucelm Faidit's lady visitors would steal a glance. Or it could be the Monge was afraid that Gaucelm himself would sneak a peek. I was sorry, for out of all the troubadours, I liked the Monge's verse best.

Gaucelm Faidit had curtains hanging about his cot to be private from the others when he was 'entertaining'. A luxurious shade of red with bright gold fringing, the curtains were nonetheless made of a cheap, shiny fabric, itchy to the touch. Unlike the Monge's mess, however, his bed was immaculately dressed, but his verses were scattered about the place on rough parchment.

I examined their sparkly costumes, but they did not look as elegant or mysterious by day as they were in the evening when they were animated. Gui d'Ussel's costumes were the most modest, for he wore only the plainest colours in contrast to the dazzling ones worn by Gaucelm Faidit. But Gui's were composed of beautiful, natural stuff which it was rumoured he'd learnt to make himself; there were bone needles and spools of silk lying next his things. I could not help but stroke the soft, muted leathers and furs and inhale their pleasant aromas.

I wondered what it was that made Gui d'Ussel so intriguing. I'd known him since he was a boy and yet I knew so little of him really. I hoped to gain some insight now, some clue, that might help decipher his unsettling nature. Though I'd vowed to hate him after the disgrace he had brought on Hugh La Marche, I'd grown to find him tolerable. Still, I was afraid of him and avoided meeting his gaze, for his eyes burnt with an unfettered passion.

I was not the only one who was afraid of him, and many whispered that he was either a miscreant or an alchemist. He had a certain loftiness I did not like; it was as though he considered himself above the other courtiers by the way he stayed apart and did not care to mix or even take a drink with them. Many said that, despite his claim to despise the class division, Gui was as haughty as any other. For myself, I noted that while he sometimes treated me kindly, at other times he did not hesitate to order me about like a common servant.

I was glad to see he did not share the Monge's fears and a manuscript of his verse lay open on his desk for any person to read. I checked, too, his drawers, one of which was locked. I was content, for now, to study his verse. It was such an intrinsic part of him, I was certain I would find some answers there.

Leafing through it, I saw at once the recurring theme of Melancholy. 'Birds of Melancholy', one was titled. It was dated to February, 1207, just six months past:

Skin peeling down my body
Horror shivers through me

Nauseating
Mocking my feeble mortality
Shrivelling me up alive
Marrow freezes in my bones then runs a pale bile
Poison seeps to the brain
Birds of Melancholy: you have not forgot
Birds of Melancholy: you have come again.

What a horrible, savage verse! No wonder he had never read it out at court. He was considered a master craftsman, despite his youth, but some complained his verses were too raw. Ventadorn, Maria and other knowledgeable persons were certain he would be the greatest troubadour who had ever lived once his verse matured.

Turning the pages, I saw more of the same. I noted, too, some comments scribbled in Maria's hand. There was nothing remarkable in that; Maria was herself a worthy poet and often revised the troubadours' compositions.

I remembered then how all those years ago at the Twelfth Night celebrations when Gui was a prisoner at Turenne, I had overheard Maria speaking with the troubadour Arnaut de Marveill about Gui's melancholic disposition. Arnaut had reported that Gui had become sick when he had tried — and failed — to write verse. It struck me that his verse and his love for Maria — which was bound up with his verse — were the sole purpose of his existence. Without these he had little else; he did not care for wealth or status as I did.

I wondered why a nobleman like Gui d'Ussel, with the chance to marry well, would have thrown it all away to become a struggling poet. Like the Monge and Gaucelm — both top of their game — Gui would never earn enough to support himself independently without the patronage offered by a court such as Maria's, a patronage that was never fully secure and which could not last forever. Still, as I looked about his modest dwelling, it struck me Gui was living as freely as he could, unrestrained by the social hypocrisies he would have had to endure if he'd married the rich duchess. I was reminded of the yeoman from whom I had fled, never having once looked back in regret!

Gui and I were not so very different after all. Maria's words echoed in my head, *let us each be free*. We were each — Gerard included — struggling to live our lives according to our own rules despite the rules imposed on us. But I did not understand Gui d'Ussel's self-professed melancholy and had no patience with it. For he had led a much more privileged life than most, and why should he have written fancied complaints about fancied afflictions when there was much real pain and suffering about? I could not help but see it as self-indulgent nonsense which could be cured, most likely, with a good dose of manual work. I was too busy to be melancholic, and none of the servants had the luxury of such complaints.

Leafing again through the book, I lingered at a much earlier entry, dating to May, 1199, almost nine years past: 'Lady in the Indigo Cloak'. I read it through and then I read again the last few lines:

Dark circle stains the indigo to purple
Juno banishes our fears
It is done: we are one
Her hand cupped in mine
Our faces wet with tears.

An image blew with force into my mind: a mysterious outline of silver birches, accompanied by the haunting song of the night throstle. A fluttering cloak of indigo moving between the trees as a shadowy figure recedes in the background. Her face, tears on her cheeks, as she runs back towards the château. It happened just before we left Turenne, when I was ill with fever. I'd somehow buried the memory or it was only half-remembered, like a dream that flees upon waking. His words had turned it into truth.

I was shocked, for I had not thought their affair was consummated all those years ago at Turenne. In a strange way, this made Gui d'Ussel Maria's true husband, if she *had* lain with him first. And I had often wondered why Maria had locked away her favourite cloak and refused to let her sisters wear it! Perhaps she had not been able to remove the blood of her maidenhood, or maybe she wanted to preserve the memory, hidden away like a rich jewel in a treasure trove.

Aware that time was pressing on, I searched for the key to the locked drawer and located it easily under his head mat. The first object I spied in there was Maria's crystal pendant, the one she had always worn as a maiden. Two locks of hair were entwined inside, his honey-gold blending well with her deep chocolate.

I quickly fingered through some scraps of parchment which, when examined, seemed to suggest dates and meeting places. As the venues were all taverns hereabouts, I knew the meetings did not concern Maria. I wondered then if Gui d'Ussel had another lover besides Maria. Or perhaps they were simply appointments made with other poets and musicians, but then I did not see why he should have to keep them locked away. I determined to follow him closely to find out exactly who he was meeting with and why.

Twilight's delicate beams were entering the cross-panelled window and the light in the chamber was growing too dim to read, so I decided to return to the château where the troubadours would soon be finishing their entertainments. I had no doubt Maria would be hoping to spend some time alone with Gui d'Ussel afterwards.

As I entered the great hall, I almost bumped headfirst into Lord Merle-Beaumont. I was as much surprised as vexed, for he never normally attended the evening banquet; he did not like the 'excessive frivolities' and the heavy meats and potent wines. And yet, here he was before me, looking both bashful and pleased.

'Maryse,' he said, 'I was just looking for you.'

I had no recourse but to go and sit with him. Colourful bowls of fruit were being passed around the hall as the troubadours changed out of costume behind the stage curtains, preparing their final verses.

'You must be surprised to see me,' said Lord Merle-Beaumont. 'The viscountess suggested I take some time for myself while our lord is away. She herself invited me to attend this evening. I am following your advice also,' he smiled, 'for you tell me I work too hard and should relax more.'

Much distracted, I smiled vaguely, scanning the hall to try and locate Maria. She was not seated in her chair but — as many of the guests were wandering about at this time — she could have been anyplace nearby. 'Have you seen the viscountess?' I asked, abruptly.

'The viscountess? Yes, of course.' He looked to her empty place. 'She was there but a moment ago…'

There was some applause as the curtains pulled apart and the troubadours stepped out. Gui d'Ussel was not among them. I could not escape to investigate but was forced to suffer the rest of the long evening in company with Lord Merle-Beaumont.

CHAPTER TWENTY-ONE

I was glad to see Maria had, at least, slept in her own bed. Still, she had a certain glow about her that made me suspect she had been meeting with Gui d'Ussel. We went through her ablutions, and I quickly took my leave, going again in search of Gui.

Tracking the troubadour was not an easy task, for he was as solitary and furtive as an owl. However, after a time I began to learn his routine. He spent the mornings writing in his apartment, sometimes conversing with the Monge. After lunch in the château, he would either return to his writing or go walking alone in the forest. His lips would move as he walked, as though he was reciting under his breath. Sometimes he would stop and fixate on an object, staring at it, but I could see nothing of interest there.

Whenever he encountered other courtiers he would often pass by without a word of greeting. But now and then he would stop and speak with a poorer-looking servant or peasant. I was surprised at how warmly these people greeted him, as though he was beloved by them.

These small discoveries aside, I learnt little of his character. His behaviour was erratic, his moods extreme, but in one thing he *was* consistent: he was always beautiful to look upon. I could not take my eyes from him. He spoke with an economy and integrity unusual amongst his peers. I could tell that many of the courtiers did not like him; the men were envious of him and the women felt slighted by his indifference to them. Gui had many potential enemies at court.

One night I followed him as he slipped into the forest. A rotund moon was casting its generous white light and Maria's light figure appeared out of nowhere like a ghostly apparition. They did not speak, but went directly to a massive, uprooted tree and sank into its cavernous enclave until they were out of sight; a clever hiding place. Just when I was starting to pace around with boredom, the sweetest sounding words I'd ever heard transfixed me to the spot. Afterwards, I could not recall one of those words. I knew that as my ears filled, my heart expanded with such gladness and sorrow, I had to stop myself from singing out like a joyful songbird.

Their voices melted together so delicately and their lyrics were so sad and true that tears came to my eyes and laughter to my lips at the same time. No croaking toad, no hoarse cricket dared disturb the poetry that was wafting through the air like heavily perfumed jasmine. I recalled the night in the attic at Turenne when they had first cast their spell over me. They had clearly practised much at it since then, and it was as though pure love was pouring from their lips as certainly as blood streams out from the wounded heart.

The spell was broken only when Maria emerged from the raggedy chamber. I noted she was clutching a parchment to her breast. Moments later, Gui came out and went off in a different direction. Keeping as still and silent as death, I followed him out of the forest and onto the dusty road. I had no idea where I was but I was determined to follow him. I moved behind him in the shadows until he stopped at an inn on the outskirts of a village.

My first thought was that Gui must be meeting with a lover. Perhaps Gui — now in his prime — was happy to satisfy his unhappily married patroness while satisfying himself on the sly with some fresh village rose. If it was true — and Gui really did have another lover — I wondered how I would tell Maria. Of course she would have to be told if he had been unfaithful, but Maria's constitution was frailer now than ever before and I was afraid such news would hurt her health.

Maria would surely banish Gui from Ventadorn and her reputation would not be in danger anymore; my own position, too, would be safer. I wished for the bold, brilliant Gui to take flight back to his own land before bringing trouble on our heads. I was sure that, if he was no longer present, Maria's memories of him would fade and she would be content with Ventadorn.

I watched through the tavern window as Gui stood up to greet a woman. So I was right! The troubadour had a secret lover! I strained to get a good look at her, for she must have been a creature of great beauty to have captured his interest. As she was turned to the side, I could not see her face, but only took note of the tight scarf she had shrouding her hair and the long, loose clothes which were hiding her willowy figure. I supposed it was a disguise so she would not be recognised.

I barely had time to wonder at the discovery when another woman joined them. Soon they were joined by more people, and there were both men and women amongst the group. I was much confused, but still I watched to see the face of the woman next to Gui, for I was certain she must be his lover.

When I did finally get a view of her face, I nearly cried out in shock. She was as old as the trees with no teeth and had a horrible, sour aspect. In fact, all the women present were such plain-looking creatures I could not imagine him liking any one of them.

I watched and waited for a fancy lady to arrive, but no one came. I could not hear what they were discussing, but I noted that their garb was drab and poor. They did not drink ale but took only bread and water, and spoke in serious, hushed tones; a morbid party indeed.

The man who served them seemed cross and impatient and, finally, he demanded that they leave. His voice was so loud I could hear him through the glass as he branded them 'penny-pinching heretics'. The term 'heretic' was a popular insult now amongst the courtiers, but I did not know why.

Before breaking up, the group performed a strange ritual. All parties knelt before the tall, old woman next to Gui, who moved about touching their heads and muttering some mantra. It struck me then that Gui was part of some religious sect. I recalled how warmly the peasants greeted him and it occurred to me they might all be members of it too. The others saluted him respectfully as he walked out past them. I followed him back to the château, satisfied he was not having an affair.

It was not surprising, for Gui had always liked to subvert authority. I thought of the great risk he had taken as a boy when he had thrown the toad at Hugh La Marche and for the first time, the memory made me smile.

A few short hours later, I was pulled out of my sleep by the sound of Ventadorn and his men returning from Turenne. Arriving unannounced, orders were being shouted loudly to the guards to draw the bridge down and servants were running about in confusion. I wondered why they had not sent a messenger before them so we could have been prepared.

To my alarm, I was summoned by Ventadorn, who commanded I go wake Maria and bring her to the inner chambers. So gravely was the order delivered I did not dare argue but went about calling her directly.

Maria was already sitting up alert in bed and responded with trepidation to my instructions. The early hour and unexpected event put us both in mind of her forced and untimely marriage.

'Do not fear,' I told her, 'I am sure he wants only to give you tidings of his trip while it is still fresh in his mind.'

'It could have waited until breakfast,' she rightly observed. 'He could have come to wake me himself in our bedchamber; why the strange formality?'

'How should I know?' I shrugged, irked by the trouble and the lack of sleep.

In fact, I suspected Ventadorn was going to tell Maria of the real reason he had gone: to deal with the medicine woman at Turenne who had ministered the flawed potions to Angelique. Still, his troubled aspect had made me uneasy and I too was afraid he had bad tidings.

After helping Maria into one of her more formal gowns, we descended the stairs together. We stepped over her delightful bath regretfully; normally she would be lowering herself into it now. I noted she looked pale and swamped in her gown and I was sorry I had not chosen something brighter for her to wear. I too was dressed unbecomingly in a frumpy, dark dress, the closest at hand this morning. At times like this there was little difference between us, for we were just two weak women trying to survive in a world of men. What had we for defence but our little artifices like silly cat claws against bears' maws?

Ventadorn came forward to kiss her, gravely, on both cheeks. It was clear that something was wrong.

'I'm afraid I have some terrible tidings from Turenne,' he said. He looked down at his feet. 'Your sister, Angelique, is dead.'

Poor Maria cried out, 'No! It cannot be. She is not! You are mistaken, Eble, you are mistaken.'

I surprised myself by bursting into tears.

What followed over the coming days was like the worst of nightmares. I myself was stricken with such awful, ugly sensations in both body and brain that I could be of little help or comfort to Maria. Maria was lost, as though she had fallen out of our world of light and into a dark, unreachable place within herself. The only sentence she uttered, repeatedly, was that it was not true. Her eyes, normally so full of defiant spirit, were grown dull and distant.

I could not recall how we ate, dressed or carried on. It was as though all the air had been sucked out of the world and we'd been flung into some hostile place where all was distorted and all comfort was lost. I vaguely recalled passing by Maria's still-hot bath on our return and wondering how steam could rise in such a crumbling world. The fragrance which had seemed so pleasant before now made me sick to my stomach.

Over the next few weeks I was so nauseous I had trouble keeping any food down. Maria faded away like a flower withering before our eyes.

Three days later, we attended Angelique's funeral mass at Turenne. Flaming torches lit the way from chapel to graveyard. The last time I'd seen her, she'd been dancing with the courtiers as lightly as some enchanting winter fairy; now six of them were lowering her small coffin into the earth. I could not believe it. Horror rushed through me, and my stomach lurched again in violent sickness.

Later, when the mourners had departed and the family was left alone, Aénor flew at Maria. 'You know it was your friend's potions that they say poisoned her in the end!' She wailed, like a wounded animal.

The shock made Aénor lose the child she was carrying. Though Maria had defended herself with Aénor, in time she came to believe she was indeed responsible for her beloved sister's death.

It had emerged that Maria had helped the medicine woman's sister gain her freedom after she had been imprisoned at Turenne for murdering babes in their mother's wombs. I recalled having seen her there when we had gone to question Gui d'Ussel. The woman and her sister were burnt not long after Angelique's funeral; Maria was powerless to stop it.

Raymond and Élise did not attempt to defend Maria, for they had been turned all to stone with shock. They had been cruelly robbed of their youngest — and sweetest — child. Élise turned to her strong faith for comfort, locking herself away to pray and cry, cry and pray. But Raymond crumbled before our eyes like some magnificent old monument struck tragically by war.

Aénor returned to her husband and children not long after the funeral, but Maria and myself stayed on at Turenne until Christmas. After a time, Maria started eating small amounts and began accompanying Élise to the chapel. She too found solace in religion.

'I have been wayward and foolish all my life,' Maria said to me one day. 'I always feared my nature would lead me to do terrible things. Now I must make amends for the life that I have lived.'

I did not ask her what she meant, for her nerves were already so frayed. Before Aénor departed for Montvert, Élise insisted she take her share of their inheritance as Raymond was not of sound mind and she wanted to ensure her daughters' legacy. The contents of the treasure chest I had coveted for so long — which should have been divided between the three sisters —

was split between the two. Maria did not note it or care, but I observed with rage that Aénor got the richer half.

In time I stopped thinking on Angelique and my appetite returned with renewed vigour. To make up for lost sustenance, I ate twice as much as before until I grew quite fat. Now that she was so often at prayer, Élise was not so watchful over expenditures and I had better access to the kitchen. I benefited from her sorrows by eating heartily of the cook's fine pies and puddings. When no one was watching, I'd stow them away to the attic where I could enjoy them covertly.

One evening as I was returning from the pantry, I had a nasty shock. I opened the door to see my uncle Raoul in my chamber. He had not been in attendance at the funeral and I'd not seen him at all during our stay, so I was most upset to suddenly find him sitting in my armchair.

'Uncle,' I said, my voice sounding high of pitch, 'what are you doing here?'

'What am I doing here?' he said, drawing his eyebrows high. 'I *live* here! One would think you were not pleased to see your uncle; the only relative who has shown you any kindness.'

'I did not mean I am not pleased to see you, Uncle, I am most pleased,' I said, weakly.

I was wondering how to keep the pie concealed. It would be better if I could sit, but the chamber only had one armchair and Raoul was in that. Perhaps I could perch myself on the bed, but that might appear rude... I'd have to keep standing and hold the pie under my cloak until he left.

'I am pleased to see you, Uncle,' I repeated, 'only it is a surprise.'

'I was away on business,' he said, puffing out his chest in self-importance, 'the business of stamping out the heresy which is spreading like a plague across our land.'

'Indeed?' I shifted the pie.

'I have been commissioned by the abbot of Citeaux to ferret out these heretics and make them renounce.'

'Heretics?'

He looked at me closely. 'You have heard the term used, perhaps, Maryse? I see you have heard the term before. Of whom have you heard this term being used?'

I recounted how the innkeeper had thrown the same term of insult at Gui d'Ussel's company. I'd never have mentioned Gui had I known it would get him into trouble. I'd never have betrayed him, for I had almost grown to like him, despite his loftiness, but when Raoul confronted me I was ill-prepared and distracted by the stolen pie. I therefore spoke without caution of Gui and the strange ritual I'd witnessed in the village tavern.

CHAPTER TWENTY-TWO

Not only did Maria spend long hours in the chapel by day, she also knelt by her bed and prayed by night. Sometimes I would kneel alongside her until it grew too late, then I would urge her to retire, but she rarely did. Her praying frightened me; the weather being too inclement to take long walks, I suggested that she write some verse to ease her troubled soul. She looked at me with scorn, asking how she could indulge in such a practice with her sister freshly buried in the cold, dark earth.

'Suit yourself,' I said, irked by her contempt.

Turenne had become as grey and lifeless as a stagnant pool, and I was eager to return to Ventadorn. I longed for Gerard's company and wished I could speak to him of all that had passed. I even pined for the toddler, little Eble, wondering how Maria could bear to be without him.

'Maria,' I said one day, 'are you not longing to return to your son?' I wondered if she thought on Gui d'Ussel as well.

Casting her gaze over me, as if trying to place me, place her son, her eyes at last flickered with recognition. 'I miss him dreadfully,' she said.

This, at least, was something. Heartened, I ventured, 'Don't you think it is time we returned to Ventadorn?'

'Returning to my son is not a luxury I can afford. I am comforted that little Eble is well cared for by his aunt and cousins,' she said, briskly.

'Forgive me,' I said, carefully, 'but I do not understand. Is not your first duty to your son and husband? Should you not return to them?'

'How could I leave my father, my mother, in this state, my father having lost his reason? What would *you* do? How can I forget them and return to my old life? I am not like Aénor, I cannot just move on. I must help them with their suffering. I must pray to ease my own suffering. Do you ask that I leave my sister all alone here in the dark earth?'

Her face convulsed with passion; a lump had formed in my throat so I could not reply.

'Leave me please, Maryse,' she said. 'I must pray now.'

But she could not stay in Turenne forever and a little under a week before Christmas, I was overjoyed at the arrival of Ventadorn and his men, come to take us home.

On the morning of our departure, I went with Maria to Angelique's grave. Laying bunches of fragrant lavender on the damp, earthy bed, she whispered that she hoped the scent would reach her where she was. She hoped she was dancing there, wearing her dress of bluebells, wearing her angels' wings. She had always known that Angelique had only been lent to them awhile, for she was such a pure and joyous spirit, not meant for the sorrows of this world. She was sorry that she had not conceived the child she had so longed for, but now she could be mother to all the little children in heaven. Though the gain was all theirs, she said, the loss was all hers. She was sorry she had not spent every waking minute of her life with her. She was sorry they had ever grown up and got married and gone away from each other.

I led Maria away, my own cheeks bathed in tears.

Night was falling as fast as a hawk descending on its prey as we approached Ventadorn. The château loomed ahead like a huge, shapeless tree sprung out of rock. I'd been dreaming of gold and of a bairn with golden hair who called me 'Mama'. The dream was as sweet to me as mead drunk from a golden chalice and I was loath to wake from it. I was conscious of an aching below my navel which only a man could ease.

Ventadorn ordered me to help Maria undress and promised to join us presently. I was glad to find the fires had been lit some time before and were crackling and spitting with hearty appetite. True to his word, Ventadorn had soon rejoined us but when I stood to go, he stopped me.

'I spoke with your uncle Raoul at dinner yesterday, Maryse,' he began. Fear rushed through me. 'He had some intelligence concerning one of our troubadours he claimed had come from you. Is it true that Gui d'Ussel has turned to heresy?'

'I do not understand,' Maria said, alarmed. 'Is Gui d'Ussel accused of something?'

My heart stopped a second then galloped a beat or two ahead.

'No, he is not accused as such,' said Ventadorn. 'He is currently only suspected of fraternizing with heretics, based on evidence given to Raoul by Maryse. It is also known that he does not attend at Mass, abstains from meat and wears poor clothing, which could be signs of heresy.'

They turned and stared at me.

'Maryse, you must tell us what you told your uncle,' said Ventadorn. 'Is it true you witnessed Gui d'Ussel attending an Albigenses gathering?'

'Not the heretical sect?' Maria said. 'Maryse,' she added, sternly, 'how have you come to suspect such a thing? I am sure there is some misunderstanding. It cannot be true.'

I told them I had stumbled — by chance — on a secret gathering at which Gui d'Ussel was present. I said it was my uncle, not I, who suspected it was a heretical gathering. 'It could just as easily have been a poetic gathering,' I said, 'though no one was speaking verse…'

'There!' Maria turned to Ventadorn. 'I told you it was not true. Maryse, you should not go around telling stories, even to your uncle.'

I ignored the reprimand; her voice sounded light and non-accusing, more for her husband's ears than for mine.

'It is just like the two of you to make light of such a grave situation,' Ventadorn said.

Maria hung her head, but I met his eye squarely.

'I must ask you, Maria, *not* to interfere in this affair. It is better to leave matters of religion and court affairs to men while you women deal with the finer arts,' he said, in gentler tone. 'I will question Gui d'Ussel, though I have always found him to be honest and direct and am surprised to learn of this covert activity. It is likely he is innocent and not a member of the sect at all. Maryse, you shall accompany me when I question him. If it *is* true, then he will either have to renounce the heresy or be turned from Ventadorn. It would be a terrible pity, for he will be throwing away a brilliant future.'

I did not sleep a wink that night. In the morning I accompanied Ventadorn to the great, empty hall.

When Gui d'Ussel entered, I shrank into the shadows.

'Sit where you please.' Ventadorn gestured to him, broadly. 'You too, Maryse,' he said, drawing me from my hiding place.

When I went to sit a good distance away, he pointed authoritatively to the bench opposite Gui. I placed myself, miserably, between the two of them.

'Now, I shall not keep you long,' Ventadorn said. 'Gui, I wish to be as frank with you as you have been with me, so I will arrive directly at the point. You have been seen outside the château grounds at night. Is it true you have been meeting with heretics in the taverns hereabouts?'

Gui fixed his fascinating orbs on Ventadorn, gazing at him fearlessly. I fretted inwardly, like a trapped bird, raging at myself for bringing trouble on my own head. Gui delayed his reply and the minutes ticked away with agonizing slowness. It all seemed vaguely familiar, as if it had happened before.

'Come, Gui, we are friends, are we not?' said Ventadorn, breaking the silence. Still he made no reply, just gazed calmly, loftily, at Ventadorn, as if to say, *I am above all this.*

Ventadorn shifted in his seat, as if *he* were the guilty one. 'I am asking you as a friend, not as your lord and master. It has been brought to my attention… It is for your own protection… It would be better if you gave me some reply. Is it true you have been meeting with heretics, or is it just a rumour which you'll not grace with an answer? Come, Gui, I must know one way or the other.'

The troubadour finally spoke. 'How can I speak in my own defence?' he said. 'If I say it is *not* true, it is only *I* who says it, and for all you know I may be lying. So there is only one acceptable reply.'

'Are you saying it *is* true?' asked Ventadorn. 'Or are you saying it is *not* true but you are afraid you will not be believed if you say so? I am a reasonable man, Gui; if you say it is not true, I swear you will be believed. So tell me, is it true or not? Maryse here says she saw you with her own eyes. We know you met with some group in a tavern; we only wish to know with whom you were meeting. Perhaps it was merely an artists' gathering?'

The dreadful moment had arrived. Gui turned his eyes on me with fierce intensity. I felt myself grow weak.

'What has Maryse seen?' Gui said, in a mocking tone.

I was too mortified to speak; fear had frozen my tongue.

'She says she saw you at a gathering in a tavern with some poorly dressed — heretical-looking — folk.'

'Heretical-looking?' Gui smiled again, this time with real amusement.

'I am sure,' said Ventadorn, smiling too, 'this sounds like nonsense to you, Gui, and I must admit it *does* seem petty. Let me assure you that no one, Maryse included, is attempting to persecute you. We are merely seeking the truth.'

'Persecute?' said Gui. 'We are all guilty of some form of persecution, are we not? We each persecute those we deem below ourselves in class or station or character or morality... We do it every time we make a judgement against our neighbour. Why should one religion be called the "true Church" and the other named a heresy? Is it not persecution *en masse*?' He turned his gaze on me. 'They say,' he continued, 'those who have themselves been persecuted are likeliest to persecute others. I am guilty myself of persecution each time I look down on someone who is my social inferior.'

My eyes and cheeks were burning and my throat was parched. I was sure that Ventadorn was enjoying my discomfort.

'Come, Gui,' said Ventadorn, 'tell us if it is true or not.'

'The people I meet with are not heretics,' said Gui, 'though some ignorant folk may call them that.'

It was as clear a confession as Ventadorn could hope to get from the elusive troubadour. For the first time, he looked concerned. 'We must deal with this as quietly as possible,' he said. 'I do not want word to get out. Gui, I have been informed that great pains are being made — and more are to come — to stamp out heresy. Many important personages are grouping together to make a stand against it. Raoul told me of the protocol that must be observed if you were to confess. You must either renounce the heresy at once, in front of witnesses, or you must leave the protection of Ventadorn. I dearly hope you will choose the first course and deny the heresy, for it would be a great loss to all if you do not.'

'I shall not deny it,' Gui said.

'You won't deny it?' asked Ventadorn, dismayed. 'Then you will have to leave us. Please consider it more carefully, Gui. If you choose the heresy, you will be choosing to sign away your freedom; you will not be allowed to write verse. Are you willing to sacrifice your art for this? Think on your viscountess, if not on me, of the faith she has invested in you. She is in mourning now, and I am sure you would not wish to upset her even further.'

Gui blinked, for the first time looking troubled. 'Perhaps,' he said then, 'it would be better if I spoke to the viscountess first before making any decision. It is only a matter of different ideology, and I just do not see why we should be persecuted for religious difference.'

'That's the spirit,' said Ventadorn, 'only Raoul did speak of a movement against heresy. He spoke of it with urgency as though ... I can hardly say ... as though the powers that be were in great haste to stamp it out. I do not care about religious difference, only I do have to adhere to the laws of land and Church and ensure the protection of my people. However, I do not wish to be unfair to you, Gui; you have served us well. I will request further advice on the matter, but be warned; you will be placed under surveillance and asked to curtail your activity until the storm clouds have blown over. If you are caught leaving the grounds, you will be arrested.'

'No matter,' said Gui, light-heartedly. 'I have been a prisoner before. I can continue to practice my faith here —' he tapped his head — 'and here —' he touched his heart. 'No walls can make a prisoner out of me.'

'Very well,' Ventadorn said, vaguely, 'as long as you keep your opinions to yourself.'

'What troubadour *ever* keeps their opinions to themselves?' Gui said, smiling.

They shook hands then and parted amicably; neither of them even looked my way.

Maria was agitated when I reported to her what had passed.

'You are not telling me that Gui is party to heresy?' she said.

'He confessed as much,' said I.

'But how could he? It is *blasphemy*; it is against the true Church.'

'They may force him to leave if he does not renounce it,' I warned, 'for they take it most seriously.'

'Of course he will renounce it,' she said. 'There is no question. He *must* renounce it.'

'But he says that he will not,' I said. 'You will defend him, if it comes to it?'

'Defend him?' she asked. 'Ah yes, if they force him to leave... But there won't be any need. He will renounce it, Maryse, he must.'

I was not so sure. Gui d'Ussel was servant to no one but his own stubborn will.

'Bring him to me, Maryse,' Maria said. 'Bring him to me so I can persuade him.'

She had taken out her crucifix and was down on her knees praying before I'd exited the chamber.

As soon as he entered, Gui rushed to embrace her, despite my presence. Glancing at me, alarmed, she only shook his hand.

He stepped back apace.

'Forgive me, I forget myself,' he stammered. 'It is only... I wish to tell you how terribly sorry I am for your great loss. I was most aggrieved to hear of your beloved sister's death. You must suffer unendurably. I can only guess at the depth of your sorrow, Maria.'

Her eyes filled with tears which she had to keep from overflowing. Tenderly, he took her hands in his. 'If I could ki...' He stopped. 'If I could only take away even a part of your pain, believe me, I'd gladly take it to my own heart.'

Her tears were falling freely now. 'It is impossible...' she said, in a choked voice. Pausing to compose herself, she said, 'Gui, I thank you for the sentiments you have expressed and I am grateful.' Her tone was formal. 'Though you cannot take away the pain, there *is* something you can do for us. I have been told of your involvement with the Albigenses heresy.

'I must confess I was surprised to hear of it, as you have never mentioned it to me and I thought we were the kind of friends who would tell each other everything. I did not think you would keep a secret like this from me. Is it true, Gui, that you have been practising heresy?'

'Yes, it's true,' he admitted, 'but I was not withholding it from you, Maria. It is advised not to speak of it to anyone. It is done not for secrecy, but for safety reasons, for we are not well thought of by everyone, as you know.' He smiled.

'It is *heresy*, Gui, *blasphemy*. How can you practise it?'

'It is only termed heresy by those who do not understand it. All people should be free to practise their faith as they choose. No one church should be allowed to impose its authority over another.'

'Don't speak to me of equality, Gui. There's no such thing,' she said. 'Why do you *insist* on speaking of equality when it does not exist? I just stood by and watched two innocent women brutally burnt at Turenne. You know what their crime was: attempting to help other women! Don't speak to me of equality... This heresy is dangerous; you could get hurt. You could hurt others...'

'You are right, Maria, there *is* no equality, but there should be. If we do not strive for it, it never will exist. It is up to us, the artists, to strive for it. If we do not, who will?'

'I cannot argue with you now in this vein, Gui. I am too tired; grief is exhausting. I only know that it is wrong of you to practise the Albigenses heresy and — as your Lady — I command you give it up.'

'Do not speak to me as though I must do your bidding,' he said, sharply. 'I answer to no one's conscience but my own.'

'You must renounce the heresy, Gui,' she insisted. 'You put all of us in danger if you do not!'

'Then I will leave,' he said. 'I do not wish to place anyone in danger.'

'I do not mean for you to leave...' Maria started.

He interrupted her, 'It is for the best.' He turned the palms of her hands upwards, examining them abstractly, as if deep in thought. 'I shall leave Ventadorn for a while, Maria, until things have calmed down. I'll not stay away for long.'

'Perhaps it would be for the best,' she sighed, 'until things have calmed down. But Gui, you must promise you will not practise heresy, though you do not renounce it. I shall have no peace until you promise. Think on the loss I have had; I could not bear another. Do it for me.'

'I promise not to practise it for your sake,' he agreed, 'but I cannot give it up at your request.'

'I know I cannot command you to give it up,' she said, 'but as a friend, I entreat you to give it up, Gui.'

'I'm sorry,' he said, firmly, 'I cannot do your bidding; I am a free man. As your friend, I agree to cease practising until it is safe to do so, but I say to you again, I cannot give it up.'

'Always the old argument between us,' Maria smiled, sadly. 'You will not do my bidding but insist on going your own way, despite the pain it causes. It is understandable. I shall miss you greatly, but I shall rejoice again on your return.'

CHAPTER TWENTY-THREE

Maria settled into a mundane — but peaceful — existence. After rising and bathing, she'd go to the chapel and pray all morning. She did not walk out in all weathers now but spent the afternoons indoors. I noted she preferred to be in company at all times — but only with those she knew of old — she would not suffer new acquaintances for long. During her leisure time she went about either with her ladies or with her son. Ventadorn was jubilant when she returned to his bedchamber, but I suspected from her resigned aspect she did so out of duty and not pleasure.

Sometimes I accompanied her to the chapel to pass away the long, dark winter evenings. A fire crackled cheerfully in the chapel grate at all times and the melting, beeswax candles lining the crooked walls lent a comforting appeal. I met there often with Lord Merle-Beaumont, who was — as usual — pleased by my piousness. He even ventured to whisper to me that my piety made him long for the day we would be man and wife! I wondered if I would have to dress up like a nun to please him in the bedchamber. Perhaps there was some life to draw out of the old monk yet.

Gerard had returned to his mother's house for Christmas and I'd not seen him since. Perhaps he stayed away on purpose lest the preparations for my wedding cause him too much pain. I thought it best he stayed away, for only then could I truly put him out of mind. Lord Merle-Beaumont and I were set to marry in spring, and I was eager for the largest and most extravagant wedding feast that gold could buy. I had spoken to the dressmaker of my wishes for a dress as regal as any queen's and for a train so long, twelve pages would be needed to carry it.

'That is not the usual custom for a waiting lady,' the dressmaker had observed.

'It is *my* custom,' I retorted, stoutly. 'If you do not carry out my orders, you'll answer to the viscountess.'

She uttered not another word in protest.

I was eager for the marriage to reflect both the lord's wealth and my new status as his wife. I hoped that no one would appear before the wedding to inform him of my lowly birth and tell him that I'd come to be Maria's waiting lady only through cleverness and hard work and not by birthright.

When I showed Maria drawings of my lavish costume, she asked if I did not think a modest gown would be more fitting.

'I cannot say I share your taste, Maryse,' she said. 'It will be expensive, I daresay.'

I told her stoutly that she need not fear, my husband would pay the cost and rightly so. She smiled. 'You are your own boss, Maryse,' she said, adding, 'He is a good man, Maryse, a pious man.'

'Yes, yes,' I agreed, impatiently, 'he is both good and pious, but he is also rich!' I had forgotten myself, so I added formally, 'I hope that I will make him an excellent and virtuous wife.'

She looked sideways at me.

'Do you miss the troubadour, Gui d'Ussel?' I asked to change the subject.

Blushing, she replied, 'I think on him always, Maryse, but I believe it is better he is away at this time. It will give us a chance ... Eble and I ... our family ... to grow closer.'

It struck me again how similar our fates were, for I was also able to tolerate Lord Merle-Beaumont much better when Gerard was away.

'Are you going to invite another troubadour to take his place soon?' I asked. 'I would like to have as many troubadours as possible for my wedding banquet.'

She was irked by the question, I did not know why. She answered that she did not have any plans to invite another troubadour to take Gui's place as he would be returning himself shortly.

'Very well,' I replied, crossly. 'Only I would not *count* on his return. He has not been honest about his whereabouts in the past and he has always been as untamed and unruly as a March hare. He answers to no authority but his own.'

'That will be all, Maryse,' she said, dismissing me with a wave.

I had not eaten any breakfast in preparation for my costume fitting and was as bad-tempered as a vixen. I had, in fact, been starving myself these past three months to fit into the dress.

Gazing at myself in the glass, I was glad to see my hard work had been well rewarded. The pale green and blue diamond bodice showed off well my newly carved waistline, while the warm gold edging round collar and sleeves was a perfect match with my artfully lightened hair. Primrose paste had turned my hair from its usual mousy brown colour to a glowing yellow.

The dressmaker surveyed her work proudly. 'It suits you well, this colour,' she said, 'draws out the light in your eyes.'

It was true the rich, blue silk of the dress matched well my sapphire eyes, but I was gazing not on that but on the huge pearl dropping from the braid around my middle, gifted to me by Maria, from the sisters' treasure trove. The gift had meant more to me than any words of love, and I'd even shed a tear on receipt of it.

The dressmaker placed a sumptuous headdress of royal blue on my head. Its tiny gold fringe was dripping with delicate water-pearls which fell just over my eyes.

'It's perfect!' I exclaimed. 'I look most beautiful.'

'Well!' she said. 'You cannot be accused of false modesty, that's for sure. But you *do* make a lovely bride.'

'I know it,' said I, with satisfaction. 'It's all I've ever wanted, a costly wedding to a man of standing and to live in a grand house with children of my own...'

'Well then,' she said, 'you will have your heart's desire soon, please God.'

My mood much lightened, I stepped out of the dress and went outside to inspect the newly blossomed roses and lilies that would be strewn along the path for guests to walk on, releasing their fragrance into the air like heavenly perfume. So fixated was I on the flowers, I failed to note the approach of two court ladies from behind.

One of them I recognised as Lady Adel, who'd set her sights on Lord Merle-Beaumont as well in the early days. It was no great surprise he'd chosen me instead, for she was as shapeless and wart-ridden as an old sow. Normally I met her sour look squarely with a gloating smirk, but today I sensed an aggression in her that made me want to exit quickly. Her companion was heftier and uglier even than she and, compared to them, I seemed almost a delicate lass.

They stood so in my path that I could not get by and when I went to pass around them, they shoved me back roughly. Lady Adel was leering in my face, and I was so frightened by her massive companion, whose eyes were as dead as a strangled hen's, I could not even speak.

'My, my,' said Lady Adel, 'will you not stop to speak with us, *Lady* Maryse, or are you too high and mighty for us now? My friend has come twenty miles to see you. Will you not shake hands with her?'

My heart beat wildly in my chest; I could not hide my fear. 'Get out of my way and let me pass.' My voice was weak.

'I would not shake this whore's hand for all the world,' her companion snarled.

They lunged at me then. Lady Adel held my arms while her friend bit into my shoulder. I screamed, fell backwards and landed on the ground. When I moved to stand, Lady Adel sat on my chest so I could hardly breathe.

'Are you mad?' I gasped. 'The viscountess will have you hanged for this!'

'I think not.' Adel spoke in a menacing tone. 'Now, you listen to me, Maryse, and listen well. You will do exactly as we say, for you are no lady but only a dirty, common whore. You see, we know about you, Maryse; your antics have not gone unnoted. We know you have the devil's itch in your privy parts. We know you've had it scratched again and again by men who are not your betrothed. We've seen — and heard — your screams of pleasure when copulating with the blond squire — and Lord knows how many others.

'We've seen you perform unspeakable acts on him as well … acts no lady would perform, acts of a depraved whore. It is no wonder, for you were born a common serving girl and thought to trick us all into believing you were a lady. You see, we had you followed, Maryse. We hoped to invite your betrothed along to surprise you in the act of which you are so fond, but you've been good these past few months — in preparation for your wedding, I suppose — so we have not been able to catch you at it.'

I thanked God in heaven at least for that one mercy.

'Since we could not catch you,' she continued, 'we decided to do some research into your background, lest your betrothed would not believe what a wanton you are. We were not one whit surprised to discover you are not a lady, for what lady would behave as you have done?'

Tears of pain and rage rolled down my cheeks. 'Please,' I begged, 'let me go.'

'We are not the only ones who know,' Lady Adel said. 'Others of our party have watched you performing profane acts by the seashore. Believe me, there are many witnesses, Maryse. You have been caught.'

'Why have you waited so long to tell me?' I asked.

'I wanted the lord to see you at it himself. But no matter, I have since thought on another strategy.' She shifted herself off me. 'There will be no wedding in two weeks. You will go to the lord and confess that you are no lady, but only an upstart serving girl. If you agree to tell the lord this — yourself — and recommend *me* as a more suitable wife, then I'll agree not to tell him of your antics with the squire. It is a fair proposition, I think, Maryse, for you would certainly be sent away penniless and disgraced if it was known how you tricked him into thinking you a virgin, while all the time you were enjoying the pleasures of the flesh that he himself abstains from.'

'Yes, yes, it is fair,' I said, bitterly. 'I shall recommend you, but I cannot guarantee he'll want to marry a fat old sow like you. You are welcome to him if he does, for I'm weary of his piety. So what if I enjoy the pleasures of the flesh, why should I not? Who says it is only men who should have appetites? Why give women the instrument of pleasure if it's not meant to be played upon? You're welcome to him,' I said. 'He'd not have satisfied a *real* lady like me.'

I stood up tall, straightened my skirts and marched back to the château.

Alone in my bedchamber, I collapsed into tears. All I'd worked for was as though washed away in one foul flood and I was left with nought but a damaged reputation. It was what I'd always feared would come to pass. It was hard for me to believe I would not be marrying the lord in two weeks and I'd not be wearing my fine dress, nor would I be made a lady.

Maria was astounded when she learnt the wedding was called off. 'But it was all you've ever dreamed of,' she said. 'Why did you not give him a chance to speak his mind before you called it off? Perhaps he would not have minded your lowly birth.'

I said I could not bear to have all the court saying I had tricked him into marriage.

'But,' she said, 'all this time you've spent pursuing him, all this time now wasted.'

My brow furrowed deep with worry.

'Well...' She changed her tune to console me. 'I believe you may have been right to call it off, Maryse. If he had really loved you, he would have fought for you. This proves the lord lacks spirit and is no match for you. It is not our blood which makes us noble, Maryse, it is our spirit, and you have lots of spirit!'

'Yes,' I said, hopefully, 'perhaps he was not the right man for me after all.'

'Believe me, Maryse,' she said, ruefully, 'you do not want to spend a lifetime married to the wrong man.'

'But I never believed I would marry for love,' I said, dismayed. 'I was content to marry for security.'

'Love is everyone's birthright, Maryse,' she said, firmly. 'You'd better start believing it.'

CHAPTER TWENTY-FOUR

With Gui and Gerard both away, Maria and I passed a long and dreary summer at Ventadorn. Maria was still steeped in sorrow and sometimes she'd not utter a word all day. I too was full of woeful trepidation at the prospect of becoming an old maid. We made such a sorry pair, none of the other courtiers sought our company and we were left to ourselves. So much the better, for we had no great friends at Ventadorn.

'Come kneel with me, Maryse, and pray that God will send you a decent husband,' Maria would say.

But God had never listened to *my* prayers. No, indeed, I was out of ideas on how to procure a rich husband. From time to time my thoughts did fly to Gerard. It was rumoured he was caring for a sick relative, and this was what delayed his return to court. I thought on him with tenderness often, but sometimes I was angry, for he had stayed away too long.

The summer was again long and hot, and I had a dreadful itch that was aching to be scratched. Whether it was the devil's business or some more natural urge I could not say, but I reckoned any sturdy fellow would do the job. More than one man looked hotly at my figure and, though I longed to roll about with him, I did not take the risk. I would, rather, take off to the kitchen and find something to eat that would distract my appetite.

One day, towards summer's end, I suggested taking a horseback ride to a cool stream where we could bathe. Maria blushed and mumbled that she did not wish to ride that day. She said I might go alone.

'Come, it is not healthy to be always at prayer,' I said. 'You should get out in the fresh air for a time. God will still be in the heavens on your return!'

'I do not wish to ride today, Maryse,' she repeated.

'Come,' I insisted, 'you should get out, Maria. You never used to coop yourself up so long indoors. Come, you'll thank me for it.'

'Oh, very well,' she said, 'I suppose now is as good a time to tell you as any other. Maryse, I am pregnant!'

'Pregnant?' Envy shot right through me, for I had dearly wanted a child of my own. 'Well, that's good, I suppose. You are the dutiful wife,' I said, airily. 'The viscount will be pleased, I am sure.'

'He *is*,' she said. 'He's overjoyed.'

But *she* did not sound overjoyed.

'I'll go out riding by myself,' I said, quickly, wishing to avoid a heart to heart.

Whenever I saw a pregnant belly now, something deep inside me swelled as though in pain. I longed so for a child of my own and did not think it fair that Maria could again have what I could not.

My uncle had arrived the eve before at Ventadorn and I was soon summoned to him. I'd known I could not hide away forever, so I gathered all my strength to go and face him.

A servant ushered me into the great hall where the more formal, daytime meetings were conducted. Raoul was sitting with Ventadorn and Maria.

'Sit here, Maryse. Take some refreshment.'

I bided my time pouring a cup of ale.

'We are all friends here,' Raoul said, flashing his unsettlingly long, sharp teeth by way of a smile.

'We were just speaking of the troubadour, Gui d'Ussel,' said Ventadorn, turning back to Raoul. 'He promised he would not practise the Albigenses religion and he has kept his word, so there is no problem.'

'It is not so simple, I'm afraid,' said Raoul. 'He has kept his word to you but, though he does not *practise* it, Gui d'Ussel is strongly suspected of penning verse in support of the heresy. Someone of remarkable ability has been writing inflammatory verse and rallying the heretics into further subversion. It is thought this person is none other than the troubadour — Gui d'Ussel — you have under your patronage here at Ventadorn. For he *is* still under your patronage, is he not? You had only suspended him temporarily, I believe?' He did not wait for a reply. 'Well then,' he continued, 'he is your responsibility. You must go seek him out and make him swear to stop this nonsense. He must cease all involvement in the sect at once or … I cannot tell what the consequences will be.'

'You cannot be serious, Raoul,' Ventadorn said. 'Must the writing of verse now be considered dangerous?'

'Absolutely,' Raoul retorted. 'Absurd though it may sound, the verse must be stopped or the hand that penned it will be. By order of the bishop — for whom I am only a messenger — you must stop this wayward troubadour.'

'I cannot go seek him out now,' Ventadorn said, curtly. 'I am needed here for harvest. The business will have to wait until afterwards.'

'The business cannot wait,' said Raoul, 'but must take absolute priority.'

The very air bristled with tension.

'I would be careful, if I were you,' warned Raoul, presently. 'If you do not comply with the bishop's orders…'

'*I'll* go seek out Gui d'Ussel,' Maria interrupted.

We all stared at her.

'I won't allow it,' said Ventadorn, 'not in your condition. It could be dangerous.'

'For heaven's sake!' She threw her hands up. 'Why must you men insist on our weakness when we are perfectly capable of looking after ourselves? I'll take a carriage, and some men can go before us. Maryse will accompany me.'

'As you wish,' said Raoul, flashing his sharp teeth. 'If the women wish to chase after Gui d'Ussel, *I* care not who goes as long as he is found and made to stop.'

After just a few enquiries, it seemed that Gui would not be hard to find; the troubadour had not even left the county.

'Unusual eyes, you say?' one fellow we stopped said. 'More like a wild animal's than a human being's? I surely saw him then...'

When we told him Gui was a renowned troubadour, he nodded, sagely. 'I said to my wife he must be some personage of note, though you wouldn't think it from his clothes. He had an air about him that made me certain he was of noble birth...' The man halted his speech and narrowing his eyes, slyly, strained to see past me into the carriage. 'Who is it who enquires after him? It is a high-born person, surely, to afford so fine a carriage. How much is he willing to pay for news of the fellow?'

I thanked him coldly and we went on our way.

That night we slept at an inn, keeping Maria's identity secret.

'He is about these parts and no mistake,' I said, for almost everyone we had spoken to had seen him. 'Funny, all this time he has kept so close. I thought he might have wandered farther off.'

Maria's hands shook as she poured herself a drink.

'You're trembling,' I remarked.

'I am a little tremulous, yes,' she said. 'I am ill prepared for this meeting. I thought it would take longer to find him and by that time, I'd have thought on what to say to him. Maryse, I cannot sympathise with his involvement with this sect. I do not think less of him for it —' she paused — 'but I confess I do not understand it. Surely he knows that if he persists, it puts us all in jeopardy. I cannot help but be angry when I think on it, for he promised he'd not be involved anymore with it. Why is he not content to write his verse of love? Why is he not content to do what he does best?'

'I cannot say,' I replied, 'though I always said he was as wilful as an untrained pup, and perhaps it is time he learnt his lesson.'

'Thank you, Maryse,' she said. 'I think I'll turn in early.'

I joined the men-at-arms downstairs for a night brew. It was hardly proper, but — since we were travelling — the rules were laxed. I was as quiet as a mouse, listening as they gossiped amongst themselves.

'He has a gift and no mistake,' said one, 'whether he uses it for good or not.'

'He has,' said another. 'When he sings, it's as though angels were strumming on my heartstrings.'

The others muttered their agreement.

'He cannot be bad then, can he?' another said. 'If he has a gift that brings joy to peoples' hearts, it must be a gift from God?'

'Does it come from God or from some darker force?' one voice said. 'I have heard that devils sometimes disguise themselves as angels, and that is how they lure their prey...'

I crept away with a queer, uneasy foreboding of what the future held for Gui d'Ussel.

By morning we'd received definite tidings of Gui's lodgings and discovered we were less than a mile away. I noted Maria took pains with her toilette before we set off.

She wore a burnt-ochre dress of raw silk, with an abundantly adorned round bodice and a hem with little, black, velvet bows. Her matching russet headdress was tied under her chin with dainty, gold cord and her eyelids had been dusted a glistening green-gold, making her eyes look huge. Her lips and cheeks were tinted with rose blush, and all in all she looked like some gorgeous, exotic fruit with divine inward properties.

The men-at-arms gaped as she descended. I was irked, for they had not even noted me.

'Oh my, you've dressed yourself up nicely,' I remarked, sourly.

'You know this old dress, surely,' Maria said, curtly. 'I wore it at your betrothal.' She whispered to me so the men would not hear, 'I painted my cheeks to cover up my paleness. I do not want him to sense my fear. I *am* afraid for him, Maryse.'

It struck me then that I too was afraid for Gui. I did not wish any harm to befall him. Sadness washed over me and I was suddenly tired.

Alone in the carriage, I suggested to Maria she advise Gui to stop writing his heretical verse and stick to what he was good at. 'Tell him he wastes his gift else,' I said. 'A love poet should write words of love, not strife.'

She glanced at me, surprised. 'Thank you, Maryse, that is good advice…'

Maria requested we give her some time alone with Gui. I didn't know what passed between them, but when we joined them, all seemed well.

'So you agree to cease writing for the heretics,' she stated, formally. He nodded. 'Good.'

She glanced furtively at the men. It struck me that the interview was staged for our benefit and they'd made some alternate, secret arrangement. As we were preparing to leave, Gui stared, suddenly, at her pregnant belly.

'You are...' Stunned, hurt, he looked at her.

She turned away, exiting the chamber quickly.

CHAPTER TWENTY-FIVE

Maria's daughter, Angelique, arrived with the first lambs of spring. A bonnier babe never had I seen, with her bright, juniper eyes and heart-shaped face — skin as clear and smooth as marble. She was quieter and gentler than her energetic older brother, and her mother seemed in awe of her. I believe she saw her as a tiny re-incarnation of her beloved, lost sister. So jealous was she of the midwife, she dismissed her after a few days and suckled the child on her own, sculpted breast, to the great scandal of the court! The weather being soft, she stayed long hours out of doors now, rocking her daughter and watching over her robust son. I brought out my embroidery and stayed oftentimes alongside her, for there was little else to do.

Though she poured much energy into them, I noted her smile was sad and her laughter did not ring out as frequently as it had once done.

'Life has not turned out as I expected,' Maria sighed. 'I am so disappointed, Maryse. Why did no one tell us there is so much sorrow ahead of us in life? At least if we were told, we would be better prepared for it. My heart is so bruised it makes me sick and bitter. What is there to look forward to now — only more loss? We live in fearful times. We should love each other, but people are intolerant and so there is only strife...'

Such morbid reflections held no weight with me; they were a waste of time. 'Look to your bairns,' Maria,' I said, curtly. 'That would be happiness enough for me.'

'If only it were so simple,' she said, 'but we pay a price for the people that we love, and that price is our suffering when we lose them. It follows, then, the deeper our love, the higher the price we pay. Maryse!' She gave a little cry as if in pain.

'Maria!' I said, concerned. 'Maria, are you well?'

She caught again her breath. 'I am, Maryse, for now. But my heart is in so much pain I fear it will break and I shall die from it. I cannot continue like this. The pain is more than I can bear sometimes. Yes, we pay a high price for love, in the end...'

I *shall pay no such price*, I thought, *for no one will suffer at* my *expense.*

The days were now growing longer and warmer, and sounds of the courtiers' laughter and flirtations sometimes punctuated our discussions. But the laughter was muted, compared to other years and the usual summer frivolities were dampened by fear.

The Abbot of Citeaux had sent envoys to our court to spy and report back on any subversive or amoral activities, and the château was under surveillance. Hard-faced, impenetrable figures arrived unannounced at our evening banquets, and we were forced to show them hospitality as they watched us from the shadows. The Church was determined to stamp out the heresy which had been gaining ever more powerful support from the nobility, and it had threatened to annex any château discovered to be in sympathy with — or harbouring — heretics.

One evening as I was rising after supper, one of these sinister strangers held me back, slipping a letter into my hands under the table.

'Be sure it is delivered to the viscountess tonight,' he whispered. 'Tell her he waits for a reply. I am stationed here for two more days. You must send it with me and only me; trust no one else... These are dangerous times.'

I did not care for his insistent manner or his rough, unshaven face, but I dared not refuse him.

I did not deliver it to Maria until first light, and by that time I'd read and skilfully re-sealed it and knew its content almost by heart.

Beloved,

I am writing — as promised — to assure you of my love, in spite of the change I perceived in your physiognomy, which I can only guess must be a child. I have thought on it and I am happy — love — to treat it as my own, for any part of you is part of me...

Nothing could have persuaded me to give up my beliefs. I do not give them up so much as sacrifice them to the God of Love, who presides over all great and noble things. For You I have ceased my religious writings — though they were but the verses of a humble poet. I referred only to the hypocrisies of a Church which claims to care for the poor and sick when — in fact — it plunders and ravishes the same and grows fat on their misfortunes. But I do not wish us to quarrel.

Beloved, you spoke of a time when we would be together. I believe that time is approaching fast. Remember when you spoke of a small tower in the forest where we would be together, away from court life? I have found just such a place. It was a mere ruin when I found it, but I have chipped away at it to make it a habitat. There is yet more work to be done, but you can add your delicate touch to it when you are its mistress. We will be as two birds in our woodland nest.

Tell me you will come to me, my bird. I am waiting for you to fly back to my heart.

Your heart is in my heart.

Although it was unsigned, the hand, of course, belonged to Gui d'Ussel. But I was confused. Had Maria then promised, finally, to leave her husband for Gui? Was this the true arrangement that had stopped Gui's hand? Little else would have persuaded the wilful troubadour to stop. Yet I did not think it like Maria to make promises she could not keep. Unless she really intended on leaving the viscount, in which case, we were all doomed. The county would not allow it; they would be followed, Gui would be imprisoned — or worse — Maria would be dragged back to her husband and Lord knew what would happen to me...

When I delivered the letter to Maria, she seemed to guess at once who it was from.

'Did you read it, Maryse?' she asked.

I turned away without reply.

As she read, she muttered, 'I said we would be together in heaven. I meant we would have a tower in the next life. How could he have misunderstood me?'

She penned an impatient reply, which I delivered to the messenger that very day.

Later, Raoul made one of his surprise visits to our court. He rode in an impressive carriage now — as good as the viscount's own — and his team of horses was magnificent. I took off to my chamber, marvelling at how well Raoul had done and — though I knew he was a cruel man — admiring his success. I was not alone for long when a loud rapping began at the door.

'Lady Maryse,' a servant called, 'the viscountess looks for you.'

I followed the fellow out to the lawn where Maria was watching over her children.

She rose hastily. 'Thank heavens you are here, Maryse,' she said. 'I need your advice.' She paused, thanking — and dismissing — the loitering servant. 'It is Gui,' she whispered, urgently. 'He has broken his promise to us. He is writing his heretical verse again. Raoul says if he does not stop it now, the Church may decide to annex the château. I offered to go speak with him again, but Eble forbids it absolutely and Raoul says the county has grown too dangerous for women to travel out alone... I don't know what to do, Maryse. He has grown out of control.'

'Look to your children, Maria,' was my advice, 'and trouble yourself no more over Gui d'Ussel. The matter is out of your hands now. He has always been ... free of spirit. So let him fly from you.'

'You are right, Maryse, thank you,' she said. 'I have no more strength left to help him — or myself — but at least I can guard my children. I don't know how to thank you,' she added. 'You are a true friend.'

'Maryse.'

I nearly jumped out of my skin at the sound of my uncle's voice. Wearing the sumptuous fabric of the wealthy, Raoul looked even more imposing than before.

'A word?' He drew me aside, his black, silk cloak swishing elegantly as he pointed an exquisitely dressed foot my way. 'You have heard, I suppose, that the troubadour Gui d'Ussel refuses to bend to his superiors and must be stopped by force. We are counting on you to act as witness against him, Maryse, if he is tried. Though a trial may not even be necessary,' he added, darkly. 'There may be something in it for you as well, for Gui's home, the château Ussel-sur-Sarzonne, will be annexed and it is one of the richest châteaux in the South. I *know* how much you have your own interests at heart, Maryse; we are not so unalike, you and I.'

He flashed his teeth unpleasantly and was gone.

Gerard returned with the last of the summer blooms. With his locks sun-bleached and lengthened to his shoulders, he appeared to me as a beautiful, blazing angel. Forgetting all my woes, I ran into his arms. He took my hand silently and led me towards the forest.

'I know a place,' I said, 'where we will not be seen.'

Picking our way cautiously through the luxurious undergrowth, we came at last to the same raggedy, uprooted tree where Gui and Maria had held their rendezvous.

Gerard lowered himself in first, then lifted me down into the cool hollow of the tree. Soon we were playing the love sport vigorously until, spent and satisfied, we lay in each other's arms.

'You're crying!' he exclaimed.

'I am not!' I said. 'It is just the morning dew has brushed off on my cheeks.'

'How similar to teardrops these dewdrops are!' he teased, but soon he grew pensive. 'I realised something when I was away, Maryse,' he said. 'I realised that you are my soul's mate. That is why I did not return to Ventadorn sooner. I was trying to find the means to make a better living so I could ask you for your hand.'

He drew a thick, gold band out of his pocket.

'You found the means to make a rich living, then?' I asked.

'I did not,' he admitted, grinning. 'I thought my aunt would leave me something when she died, but she did not.'

I huffed, impatiently. 'You waste my time then, Gerard,' I said. 'You *know* I cannot marry you, if you've not the means to keep me. Come, help me up. We've had our sport and now we must return and carry on like before.'

'Maryse,' he said, 'how can you be so hard?'

'Hard? You dare to call me hard?' I said. 'I must *survive*, Gerard, that is all. I must live; some people have the luxury to live for love, but I live to survive and thrive. I have learnt that a woman must be strong and stand alone, or she grows weak. I shall never be a slave to love. Look elsewhere for your soul's mate, Gerard. I care nothing for such talk. You have not found your soul's mate in me!' I stood to go.

'Maryse, wait! Listen to me further. What if I said I will do everything in my power to prove my worth to you? I'll do everything I can to get rich. Your love will give me the strength I need to do so; if only you would promise to wait for me awhile, I *know* I can do it. I just need time. Would you wait one year for me? I promise if I do not have the means by then, you can turn your sights to another. *Please* accept this ring. Give me a chance to prove my worth.'

It *was* a nice ring... 'To prove your worth?' I repeated, slowly.

'To prove my worth ... as your knight,' he said.

'You speak just as the courtly lovers speak,' I said, bemused. 'You speak as though I were a lady.'

'You are a lady to me,' he said. 'Please accept my ring. Promise you will wait for me.'

I took it from him, trying it on my third finger. 'I'll take your ring, Gerard,' I said, 'on condition that you prove yourself to me by making your fortune before one year is out.'

He hugged me tightly to him.

'Funny ... I never thought on myself as a courtly lady who would make her lover wait for her. I had always thought the practice futile and conceited, but perhaps I grow to understand it better now. One year, that is all,' I added, proudly, 'one year to prove that you are worth my hand.'

As soon as I uttered the last, it was as though a hair-fine crack struck the hard shell about my heart, threatening to shatter it, and I almost relented and accepted his proposal there and then.

I tied up my bodice quickly and hurried back to the château.

CHAPTER TWENTY-SIX

A few months later, I woke with a sinking feeling to the sound of mayhem about the château and its grounds. Such a troubled land had it become I hardly dared to venture from my bedchamber, for who knew what fresh madness the day would bring? I did not follow well the affairs of State, but since the Pope's legate had been murdered, the crusaders of the North wreaked havoc on the peoples of the South — peasants and nobles alike.

All the châteaux hereabouts had been ordered to hand over any vassals suspected of heresy to the crusaders and — if they did not comply — their lands would be seized, the people slaughtered. A huge army had gathered in Lyon and was marching towards the South, burning alive those heretics who refused to renounce their faith. Loyal to their vassals, many Southern nobles were fortifying their town walls, preparing to defend against the invaders to the bitter end.

All was turbulent at Ventadorn, for the viscount had ordered his courtiers to flee to safety, fearing they would be slaughtered else. With their policy of peace, love and tolerance, the viscount and viscountess of Ventadorn were not prepared to fight, but neither would they stand about and watch their people murdered. Ventadorn and Maria had refused to conduct a manhunt of the heretics in their county, and now there would be a price to pay for their disobedience. Still, they attended to the safety of their people first, before making arrangements for themselves.

Maria asked me to go seek out Gui d'Ussel, for we had had no news of him and she was worried.

I arrived at his lodgings on horseback and was surprised to find him there, alone, with no men in attendance.

'They have all left in fear,' he explained. 'Only I am left.'

'Surely you, too, should leave,' I said. 'You know it is not safe... They will surely come for you.'

His verse had made a target of him, and he must have known his life was in grave danger if he did not take flight.

'My lady is concerned for you,' I said. 'She begs that you take off to some safe hiding place until the frenzy has passed. We are all to leave Ventadorn shortly.'

His face was thin and haunted-looking, but his eyes burnt with the same ferocious passion as before. 'Tell Maria,' he replied, 'if she wishes to save me, she should come for me herself.'

He took up his quill and I stole away.

'Did you see him, Maryse?' Maria asked, anxiously. 'How is he — is he safe?'

'I saw him, Maria. He is well,' I lied, to comfort her. 'I think he will take himself off to somewhere safe now.'

'Thank the heavens,' she said, much relieved. 'Eble and I must take the children and go away to some secret place. We cannot tell a soul where we are going — not even you. We must part ways for a time, Maryse.'

A sudden weakness came over me, and I swooned for the first time in my life.

When I came round I was lying on Maria's bed, her anxious face bent closely to mine.

'Thank heavens,' she said. 'I promise I'll come find you as soon as it is safe. We always knew our arrangement would not last forever, though I'd hoped to lose you only to a secure marriage. I hoped to see you well set up, Maryse, for I care for you like a sister. But these are not secure times, I'm afraid.'

Sitting up, I noted her hand was resting on some solid, curiously shaped object covered with fabric. Seeing my eyes on it, she drew the drape off and revealed what was underneath: it was the treasure chest which held her share of the sisters' inheritance.

'You have been as a sister to me, Maryse,' she said. 'Half of this belongs rightfully to you.'

I could hardly believe my eyes and ears. My heart was thumping so fast in my chest I thought that it would burst. The sorrow I had felt just moments ago was transformed into joy.

'You can keep the chest,' she said. 'I cannot easily carry it with all our other belongings. Perhaps now, you will be able to marry a man of *your* choosing. You see, Maryse,' she smiled, 'love *is* everyone's birthright.'

PART FOUR

CHAPTER TWENTY-SEVEN

Abbey of Gellone, 1211

I woke to the alarming sight of steep rock rising up around me on all sides. After a moment's confusion, the motion of the carriage (and stiffness of my muscles) reminded me that I'd been travelling through the night. I knew we must be nearing our destination, for the obstructed view meant that we were passing through the narrow gorge of the Gellone river. I stretched myself out and groaned loudly, hoping Gerard would hear. Soon the cover lifted, and Gerard lowered himself in beside me, leaving the other fellow to man the horses.

'Are you well, Maryse?'

'Oh, my bones are aching all over,' I said with great self-pity. 'For such a fine carriage, you'd think it would be more comfortable.'

'The finest carriage on earth would not roll smoothly over this cobbled pass,' he said. 'It was meant for monks on foot and not for horse-drawn carriages. See that bridge up ahead?' He pointed to a broad stone arch. 'It's known as the Pont du Diable,' he remarked, cheerfully. 'They say the devil has appeared there, tempting weary travellers to hurl themselves into the waters below.'

'Well, that's a pretty tale to tell a lady in my condition,' I sniffed. 'Anyway, I don't believe in such nonsense.' But I looked away again quickly, lest I see something horrible.

It was our first proper journey in our new carriage and I missed the comforts of our home. I'd kept my wealth hidden from Gerard until he had fulfilled his promise to prove his worth to me. It had not been easy, for I had longed to buy rich gowns that would match my splendid jewels. I'd badly wanted, too, to purchase a huge estate with land for horses, pigs and fowl, with a river running through for fish, the likes of which would madden my old enemies with envy. But I'd controlled these urges in the same way I'd learnt to curb my other appetites over the years. For I'd wanted to be sure that Gerard would not just exhaust my riches if I were to make him mine, but would provide for our family himself.

I'd often go down to the basement of the townhouse I was renting, where I'd stowed the chest of jewels. Many hours did I pass there, all alone, staring at the gleaming objects and contemplating all that I would buy. At first I thought the jewels would bring great joy into my heart, but soon I found that they did not.

So I was relieved when Gerard came one day and requested I walk out with him. I said I'd rather stay indoors, for it was the time of year when the evenings were drawing in early, but he took my hand anyway and led me to a fabulous, armoured warhorse in the square. Recognizing its master, the horse strained towards Gerard, who took the reins and invited me to mount up first. We rode then to a nearby town, where he showed me a respectable house he'd saved to buy, equipped with a proper kitchen — the kind a lady could order her servants about in. I said the house would do nicely for now, but perhaps we'd find something better once both our incomes were put together. Gerard knew then that I meant to be his wife, and from that time I kept almost no secrets from him.

When I told him about the riches Maria had bestowed on me, he said it showed that she had appreciated me and had rewarded me for all my years of service and loyalty. But then I confessed to him that I'd not always been loyal to Maria — or kind — and sometimes I'd been jealous of her and even wished her ill. He listened without comment, just squeezing my hand, and so I felt free to continue. I told him how, when I looked on the treasure, instead of making me happy as I had expected, it reminded me of her and made me sad.

'And I've been so very lonely without her,' I confessed. 'Rubies and emeralds, gold and diamonds, though they are beautiful to look upon, do not make very lively company. I wish I'd realised then what I now know; she was my only friend — besides you, Gerard.'

He helped me wipe away my tears.

'But I was not as good to her as I should have been... It is my one regret in this life.'

It was Gerard who suggested we try to locate Maria's whereabouts. I would not have thought it possible, but he pointed out that the nobles of the South were starting to surface again out of their hiding places and the land was not as dangerous as it had been before.

After many months, when we'd almost given up hope, word came to us through some pedlars that the viscount and viscountess of Ventadorn were lodged in the cloister of Gellone. We purchased the carriage specially and set out as soon as the roads became passable after the winter snows. Seeing Maria again had become a matter of great urgency for me, especially since I'd learnt that I was going to have a child of my own.

One crisp spring morning, after a weary three days and nights, the carriage rolled into the village of Saint-Guilhem-le-Désert, at the foot of the abbey of Gellone. Gerard suggested we rest first, but I was too impatient to see Maria, so I told him to wait at the inn and I would go to her alone.

The abbey was spread across a hill like a comfortable guardian angel keeping watch over the village. It was such a sleepy-looking place, I could not imagine the lively Maria housed there. The sun shone pleasantly on my face as I surveyed the richly cultivated land; I noted many vines, as well as olive and fig trees bearing young fruits. Cows and sheep were grazing peacefully in the fields and I paused to admire some newborn lambs, touching my own belly in satisfaction. *The monks must make a pretty penny*, I thought. *Still, I would not like to live in such a rural, backward place, despite the scenery.*

A bell rang out lazily, labouring up to the stroke of ten. I noted a small group walking towards me and I waited where I was for them to pass. Three monks were accompanying some small children, who walked before them in single file. One of these — a boy of six or seven — caught my eye, and in an instant I called out to him.

'Eble? Is that you, dear Eble? It is I, Maryse. Do you know me?'

He stared a moment but then he ran to me. I cuddled the little fellow for some time before turning to face the monks and answer their inquisitive stares. Wasting no time, I told them who I was and what I was doing there. They eyed up my expensive clothing before agreeing to take me to the viscountess. One of them guided me back through a maze of finely pruned hedges until we came to a large entrance. He showed me into the visitors' parlour and asked me to wait awhile.

I smiled at the sumptuousness of the carpet, the crackling fires and the exquisite artwork that adorned the room — Maria's touch. A bowl of fragrant rosewater and linen towels had been placed for visitors to refresh themselves and just as I was splashing my face, Maria rushed in.

'Maryse! I did not think I'd see you again in this life!' she cried. 'We have lived through such terrible times, Maryse... But look at you; you look so radiant and well!'

I returned the compliment, though in fact she was most plainly dressed and her glorious hair was hidden under a stiff headdress and veil, the kind a nun would wear. Still, her face had not aged.

'How have you fared, Maryse? You must tell me all.'

We chatted away for hours, sipping rose and lavender water and nibbling a variety of dainty cakes like two ladies of equal status. I enjoyed the conversation and I talked mainly of myself. I knew that, sooner or later, I'd have to say what I had come to say, but I put it off awhile.

'But I've spoken only of myself,' I said at last. 'I am sure you have spent a tedious time here, away from the entertainments and good society of our court. I'm sure you'll want to leave here as soon as it is safe?'

'No, indeed, Maryse, you are quite wrong. I am happy here and have no desire to return to the life I knew before. I wish to retire permanently from the world, only teaching the children here how to read and write. In this holy place I can at least meditate on my past life and pray that my sins may be forgiven.'

'You have committed no great sins, Maria,' I began, but she shushed me, gently, saying we must each answer to our own conscience. I nodded gravely, saying I knew exactly what she meant. Sighing deeply, I realised the time had come for me to speak the truth. 'I too have been troubled by my conscience of late,' I began, 'and have a heavy feeling brooding about my heart. I was not always truthful with you, Maria, and there is something I must confess.'

She tried to shush me, but this time I knew I must speak.

'It's about the troubadour, Gui d'Ussel,' I said, quickly.

Her eyes flickered in painful remembrance. 'What of him, Maryse? Have you had news of him?'

'I've had no news of him, Maria.'

She looked perplexed. I cast my eyes downwards at the carpet's intricate pattern.

'I lied to you, Maria, at the end. When you sent me to find him and order him to fly to safety, and I said that I had seen him and that he was leaving with the others.'

'You mean you did not go to him, Maryse?'

'Oh yes, I went to him and found him with little difficulty, but he was not going to leave, Maria, he said, unless *you* went to him. I told him he'd be killed for sure, for everyone knew his whereabouts and he was considered a dangerous enemy, but he'd not listen to me... He always was so...'

'But have you had *any* news of him, Maryse?' she interrupted.

'I've had no word of him,' I said, truthfully, 'though Gerard and I searched for him. But, Maria, he is certainly dead along with all the others; they were coming for him and they never would have spared his life.'

Then she asked the question I'd been dreading.

'Why did you not tell me the truth, Maryse? If you'd only told me, I would have gone to him, persuaded him to leave...'

'Exactly,' I said, miserably. 'I knew that you would go to him and get us all in trouble. You would have put yourself in danger, Maria, and you had your children to care for... There's more,' I went on. 'I was not always kind to you, neither was I kind to Gui d'Ussel.'

I told her that it was I who had snitched on Gui d'Ussel when as a boy he'd thrown the toad at Hugh La Marche. I said that later, when Raoul had come to me, I'd spoken about the night we'd met the medicine woman in the woods with

Angelique. Maria winced. 'Then,' I said, my voice breaking, 'you gave me the gift of treasure that was your sister's part and I thought that it would make me happy, but it did not. In fact, it brought sadness into my heart, because every time I looked on it I thought on when we'd parted and you'd told me that I'd been like a sister to you. That is what I'd always wanted, really, not the treasure, but for you to love me like a sister. But I saw it all too late. Now I'm here because I want to give you back the treasure.'

'Maryse,' she interrupted, 'I *do* love you like a sister. We are all haunted by memories and regrets. I am as guilty as you, for it was only after we parted I realised how much I missed you.' Her voice lowered to a whisper. 'You know that Gui asked me to fly away with him and live in a tower he'd built in the woods? I do not regret my decision not to go, for how could I have gone? But I *do* regret that I could not build my life with the only man I have ever truly loved. I regret that I was never able to give myself to him fully or to return his love as he wanted it returned. Who is to say your sins against Gui d'Ussel are greater than mine, Maryse?'

'But do you not love your husband too, Maria?' I asked.

'He is the kindest of men and the father of my children, but I have only ever truly loved one man and that is Gui d'Ussel. I know I'll never be with him again in this life, Maryse, but I will always love him and I hope we will be together in the next life.'

'I cannot say I share your faith, Maria, but now that I am to be a mother, I want to make peace with my conscience.'

'You are with child!' Maria exclaimed. 'I suspected it when I saw you, but I didn't want to say for fear of offending you if I was wrong!'

I flushed — with pleasure — and because I could not help flushing these days. 'Maria, you said you hoped that God

257

would forgive you your sins. Well, I hope that *you* will forgive me mine.'

'Oh, Maryse,' she sighed. 'There is nothing to forgive. It occurred to me only recently that my son is now the age you were when you first came to live with us at Turenne. When I thought on it, I was appalled that any child could be sent from its parents to serve among strangers. I should beg your forgiveness, Maryse, for it was wrong. And for my thoughtlessness every time I overlooked your needs while you took care of mine. So let us agree to forgive each other equally. Who knows,' she added, 'maybe one day my children will meet the child you are carrying and they will be friends. It is all we can hope for, Maryse, that the next generation does not repeat the sins of their parents.'

I liked very much her line of thought and I thanked her by saying, 'If it is a girl, then I will call her Maria. I'll tell her all about you and about your many gifts and your generosity, and I hope she will learn from your example. I'll tell her, as you told me, that love is *everyone's* birthright.'

It was last light of the rose-tinted day as I departed. One of the monks led me downhill, by donkey, so I would not lose my way. As we descended slowly, I cast my eyes about over the dusky landscape. I admired how the sun's last, brilliant rays had flushed the trees deep red. Butterflies were fluttering out of sight to their beds and seeds, lighter than air, were wafting upwards towards the young stars. There was no wind, and all was as still as sleep.

A screech-owl, close and loud, disturbed the peace. My donkey halted abruptly as a swooshing pair of golden wings brushed by, stirring up the air. I found myself staring into a pair of golden orbs, somehow familiar to me. In a moment, the wild bird had flown right over my head towards the cloister. In its wake, it seemed to leave a dazzling trail of gold.

'A golden owl!' exclaimed the monk. 'I did not believe they existed! What can it mean?'

'The owl forebodes death,' said I, 'but the gold signifies alchemy. Years ago, at the château of Turenne, such a bird was sighted. I know not whether it is a good or bad omen.'

'Such beauty must come direct from heaven,' said the monk, 'and must be a good omen.'

'I hope so.'

I thought of Maria gazing out of the window as I'd left her, in her stiff veil, a pensive expression on her face, and I wondered if she'd seen it. I felt sure she must have, for it had flown straight towards her.

For the first time in my life, my heart felt light and free, like a weightless seed drifting upwards to the sky.

A NOTE TO THE READER

Dear Reader,

In the Spring of 2006, I went to the south of France searching for troubadours. It was my MA year and my thesis was looking at the influence of the courtly love tradition on Chaucer's writing. Troubadours (and the female, trobairitz) were nowhere to be found. The closest I came was a café named Le Troubadour. However, evidence of their lyrics was there in the beauty and lushness of Languedoc in spring. This book is a continuation of my quest for the troubadours of Medieval France. I think I'll spend the rest of my life chasing after them!

I hope you enjoy the book. It is a huge privilege for me to have you read it. I would be so grateful if you let us know what you think by leaving a review on **Amazon** or **Goodreads**. You can also contact me directly on my website: **www.coirlemooney.com**. Many, many thanks again.

Coirle

Sapere Books is an exciting new publisher of brilliant fiction and popular history.

To find out more about our latest releases and our monthly bargain books visit our website:
saperebooks.com

Printed in Poland
by Amazon Fulfillment
Poland Sp. z o.o., Wrocław

94552399R00148

the

PAINTER'S
GIRL

BOOKS BY HELEN FRIPP

The French House